beneath this

INK

MEGHAN MARCH

UNAPOLOGETICALLY SEXY ROMANCE

about the book

I've always known she was too good for me, but that never stopped me from wanting her.

And then I finally had her for one night.

A night I don't remember.

I figured I'd blown my one shot.

But now she's walked back into my life, and this time, I have the upper hand, and I want my second chance.

Will she be able to see the man *beneath this ink*?

> *Beneath This Ink can be read as a standalone novel, but is the second book in the Beneath Series. Beneath This Mask is available at Amazon, BN.com, Kobo, iTunes, and Google Play.*

1
con

"Con, can you take this walk-in?" Delilah called from the front of the shop.

I pushed back from the desk and shoved my hair away from my face. It was too damn long. I needed to get it cut, but the girl I'd been going to for the last year had basically fallen onto my cock last week, and I wasn't going to be letting her near my jugular with scissors any time soon. She wasn't enamored of my, 'I don't go there twice unless there's something worth going back for' mentality. I probably could have phrased it a little nicer, but why give the girl false hope when I'd all but forgotten her as soon as I'd slid the condom off my dick? I didn't have time for bullshit, and I didn't like to be misunderstood when I spoke. So I was firmly in the 'tell it how it is' camp. Women didn't seem to appreciate my particular brand of honesty. Mostly because it didn't line up with what they wanted to hear. Not my problem.

I stood and headed for the door of the break room. Time to meet my newest walk-in.

If I had to tattoo one more "YOLO" on some idiot kid, I might hang up my tattoo gun and call it a day. Thoughts like that made me feel older than thirty-one.

I scanned the shop, looking for my next client. If I hadn't learned a hell of a long time ago how to lock down my reactions, I might've missed a step.

It was no kid.

And if she wanted YOLO tattooed on that body, it'd be a crime against nature. Anger flared within me at the sight of her. I might not remember the night we'd spent together, but I sure as hell remembered the morning after when I'd interrupted her escape from my bedroom. We'd thrown words like grenades, and it was a miracle we'd both walked away without bloodshed. Even with that memory vividly replaying in my head, I still had to tell my dick to calm the fuck down.

Vanessa Fucking Frost was still out of my league. Hell, out of my fucking universe. She'd been too good for me in high school, she'd been too good for me two years ago, and as sure as she was standing in my shop today, she was still too damn good for me. And I bet she'd be the first person to say it. I still couldn't figure out how she'd ended up in my bed that night. Not because my bed didn't see action with rich chicks—it saw plenty—but not like her. Classic elegance like Grace Kelly. Joy Leahy used to make me watch *To Catch a Thief* with her, and that's exactly who Vanessa reminded me of.

Her platinum blond hair was twisted up into some fancy-ass bun, and her tan skirt suit clung to her curves in all the right places. One perfectly manicured hand toyed with the gold bracelet on her wrist. My jeans tightened uncomfortably at the peek of a lacy pink bra from beneath her pink silk blouse.

My reaction to her pissed me off.

Do you know what it's like to *finally* get something you've always wanted, but not remember a single fucking detail?

It ate away at me. The not knowing. Part of me wanted to tell her to get the hell out of my shop, but the other part of me wanted to drag her upstairs, strip her naked, and tie her to my bed so this time she couldn't leave until I was damn good and ready. Which might be never. And that thought—that weakness—infuriated me.

"Never thought I'd see you darken my doorway again. What can I do for you, princess?" A mocking edge colored my words.

Her nervous twirling of her bracelet halted, and her blue eyes, several shades lighter and more vibrant than my own, met mine. Her pink tongue darted out over her perfectly plump bottom lip slicked with gloss. This nervous, off-balance look of hers raised all my red flags. I was used to the quiet, sexy-as-all-hell confidence that had always drawn me in. At least until she'd opened her mouth that infamous morning and told me what she'd really thought of me.

"I need a few moments of your time."

I raised an eyebrow. Now that was a new development. She'd never sought me out.

"Is that so?"

"Yes, if you could spare me five minutes."

Some of her words from that morning, which I might as well have tattooed on my skin, came back to me: *Do this again? Are you crazy? I must have been insane to do this the first time. This can never happen again. And no one can ever know. No one.*

And now she wanted a favor?

"In this shop, the only way a woman gets my time is if she's getting a tattoo, or is on her knees or her back." I knew my answer was crude, but that was what she undoubtedly expected from me. And I hated to disappoint.

A flush of color hit her cheekbones, and I wondered for a brief second whether she was remembering what it had been like to be on her knees in front of me. *Fuck. I wish I remembered. Then I could just fucking move on.*

I waited for the clipped *go to hell* and an abrupt exit. But instead of turning and walking out, she surprised me.

"A tattoo it is, then."

My eyebrows hit my hairline.

"Really? Of what?" The disbelief was evident in my tone.

She hesitated a moment before answering, "A fleur de lis." She held up her fingers to indicate the size. "Right here." She pointed to her hipbone.

"No shit?"

"No shit." A grin tugged at the corner of my mouth when she echoed me, but I beat it back. She was here because she wanted something from me. Badly enough that she was willing to let me get her partially naked and under my tattoo gun to accomplish it.

Interesting.

"Then follow me, sweetheart." I led her back to my room and pulled the door shut.

She moved to sit, but I stopped her. I wanted to see just how committed she was to whatever the hell had brought her here. "Drop your skirt first."

Her head jerked up. *Yeah, I figured that'd get your attention, princess.* "Are you serious?"

"You expect me to give you a tat through your clothes? Even I'm not that good."

Those vivid blue eyes turned to ice. "Fine. But you have to listen to what I have to say."

"Fair enough. You lose the skirt, I'll listen." Didn't mean she'd get what she came for, but I could at least listen if it got her clothes off. *Jesus, I'm pathetic.* Bargaining for her to get naked? With most other women, all I had to say was *strip*, and the clothes hit the floor right before the female in question hit her knees. I wasn't vain, but even I knew that being six-four, covered in tats, and built like a brawler had an effect on the ladies.

I forced myself to turn away and grab my gear. The rest of the blood in my head went south with the delicate hiss of her zipper. Fractured images of her naked and bent over my bed, ass blushing red from where I hadn't been able to stop myself from smacking it, rushed through me. I just didn't know if they were memories or fantasies.

Fuck. I'd never be able to give her this tat with a hard-on the size of a goddamn redwood.

I glanced over my shoulder, unable to resist getting a look at what she'd uncovered. But the slice of skin exposed between her skirt and jacket wasn't the nakedness I'd envisioned.

And the words that came next doused my libido.

"I need you to donate a piece of property you own, through your parents' trust, to the L.R. Bennett Foundation."

I crushed my fist closed around the alcohol prep pads to keep them from scattering to the floor. So that's what brought her here. Should've figured. Think Bill Gates' foundation, and then scale it back a few billion, and you had the L.R. Bennett Foundation. The top of the heap of New Orleans do-gooders. And founded and run by Vanessa's mother's people.

My anger, which had already been steadily bubbling since she'd walked through the door, rose hot and fast.

"You came here to ask me for money." I needed to hear her say it again.

She shook her head, and not a single strand of hair moved from her perfect style. That perfection was like fuel to the fire.

"No, not money. Land. Your parents' trust owns a piece of property next to several lots owned by the foundation. But there was some sort of legal mistake in our deed, and it says the foundation owns part of your lot as well. It's never been an issue before, because all the buildings there are empty. But, as you might have heard, the foundation is launching a building project there for our new headquarters and a nonprofit incubator. The architect designed the plans assuming we owned all the property and not just part of it." She stared at her clasped hands as she explained.

"If it's a legal problem, then get a lawyer."

Vanessa looked up at me. "I don't have time to go through the proper channels. That would take months. I already have a demolition scheduled."

"So make me an offer to buy it."

She bit her lip. "I'll blow my budget. Just like I'll blow my budget if the architect has to redraw the plans." Frustration tinged every word when she added, "Trust me, I wouldn't be here asking for your help if I'd been able to come up with an alternative."

At least she's honest, I thought. "And you think I'd help you out... why?"

She stiffened as though readying herself to deliver a rehearsed speech. Which probably wasn't far off the mark.

"Because, despite your reputation, I think you actually care about the wellbeing of this community, and our building project is going to help propel New Orleans. Forget the headquarters part for a minute. The section of the building that extends onto your lot is going to be used to house new nonprofit organizations that are getting off the ground. We're doing this to make a difference. Right now, you've got a run-down building that's going to cost you money to rehab or demolish, and this is a chance for you to donate it, take the tax write-off, lose the headache, and, here's the bonus, you'll know you've helped your community."

Gritting my teeth, I reeled in my temper, which was about to jump its chain. "You've got balls of steel coming in here to ask me this. And not just because I could easily sell it to a developer for six figures."

She broke our stare to look at the ground for a beat. "It's not like this is easy for me, Con." She glanced back up at me. "I need this, or my entire project is screwed."

"And this should make me want to help you because...?"

She pushed off the seat and stood. "This was pointless. I don't know what I was thinking, coming here."

I leaned back against the wall. "Then why did you?"

She slid her zipper up and straightened her suit jacket. Once again, she was prim and proper and too damn far out of my reach.

"This is my one shot to prove I'm capable of running the foundation. So basically, I'd do anything to make this project a success. Including throw myself on your mercy."

She crossed the small room and laid a hand on the door. A perverse part of me didn't want to see her walk away without some promise of seeing her again. I liked this dynamic—the one where she needed something from me and I had the upper hand. It was an unexpected gift I wasn't about to throw away.

"Anything?" I asked.

She paused, slowly turning back toward me. Her expression was guarded.

What? Did she think I was going to demand she drop to her knees and suck my dick to get what she wanted? For a fleeting second, with that image firmly in my mind, I wondered if she would. *No.* I wouldn't let her whore herself out for this, even if she were willing. And she better fucking not be. She was better than that, and surprisingly, so was I.

"You ever get your hands dirty in the projects that your little foundation funds? Or do you just sit up there in your ivory tower and write checks and let other people do everything you take credit for?"

Her shoulders visibly stiffened. "I do a lot more than sit in an ivory tower and write checks."

"Prove it."

"How?"

I grabbed a business card off my counter and scribbled an address on the back before I held it out to her.

"Be at this address tomorrow at three o'clock." I looked at her suit and blouse. "And wear something you ain't afraid to get dirty."

She took the card by the edges, as though scared to handle something I'd touched.

"You think you can manage that, princess?"

She didn't answer, just spun and shoved open the door, as if she couldn't wait to get away from me.

I wondered if she'd show up tomorrow. My gut said she would. But I'd just have to wait and see.

vanessa

The words *a deal with the devil* came to mind as I sat in my car outside the deserted warehouse. I checked the address on the back of the Voodoo Ink business card for the fifth time. Surprisingly, Con's handwriting was completely legible—almost artsy, even. Far better than my own. Which meant there was no mistaking the address. This was where I was supposed to be. No other cars were parked along the road, and I wondered if, in this neighborhood, my Mercedes would still be here when I came back out.

At this point, I was willing to sacrifice just about anything I owned if it would get me what I needed.

This project was my baby. My one shot at proving to the board and the outgoing executive director that I was capable of taking the reins when he retired at the end of the year.

As the last remaining descendant of the Bennett family, I should have been the presumptive choice for the position, but the board was increasingly skeptical that a thirty-year-old woman should take the helm. My great uncle, Archer Bennett, was the current executive director, and was also open to the idea of considering outside candidates for the position. His one concession to the fact that I was family: he'd given me a shot to prove myself by overseeing the fundraising, planning, and construction of the new headquarters.

If I couldn't complete that project on schedule and on budget, I was as good as out of the running. It wouldn't matter that this error on the deed was in no way my fault; it would only matter that I hadn't caught it before the architect drew up the plans. In Archer Bennett's eyes, shit didn't roll downhill. Anything that went wrong on my watch was on me. I didn't disagree with his outlook, but it also meant that if I didn't get Con to donate the property, I was screwed.

God. When he'd asked if I'd do anything for this project, my entire body had frozen, as though waiting for his verdict. What would I have done if he'd told me he wanted a repeat of that night I still couldn't get out of my head? It was easy to tell myself that it'd been a drunken mistake, but that didn't stop the memories from coming back all too frequently. And *dear Lord*, did I remember.

Part of me wanted Con to throw down the challenge so I'd have an excuse to relive it. Because otherwise it would *never* happen. Even if my common sense didn't stop me, my pride would keep me from going back. We were like oil and water. Although that night, to be cliché, we'd been like fire and gasoline. I still blushed at the things he'd done to me. The things I'd let him—no, *begged* him—to do. Forget blushing, my panties were in serious danger of needing a change when I thought about... I shook my head. I was clearly the only one remembering that night with any kind of longing, because from what I'd heard, Con needed a new bed-frame to keep up with the notches he'd accumulated. Yesterday he'd had me in the perfect position to demand whatever he wanted from me. And he'd demanded... what exactly?

I stared at the warehouse again, and this time my imagination went wild. The possibilities were too ridiculous to even allow them space in my head. But seriously, I had no idea what I was walking into. Con had mentioned getting dirty. So I was probably going to be scrubbing floors or painting over graffiti. I was beyond embarrassed to admit I'd never done either.

The clock on my dash clicked over to three o'clock, and I climbed out of the car and locked it. Twenty-seven steps to the steel door. I knocked hesitantly and waited.

And waited.

Finally, a plate in the center slid open.

"What you want?"

Jesus H. Christ. It was like a speakeasy. Was there a password I was supposed to know?

Before I could gather my wits enough to say something, I heard a familiar voice. "It's cool, Reggie. She's with me."

"You had your tail come *here*?"

"She ain't tail; she's here to help," Con countered.

"Whatever, man. I'll believe that when I see it."

I was still processing their conversation about *tail* when the door creaked open to reveal a well-lit hallway with black and white checkered tile. And Con.

He lifted his chin in greeting.

"You came."

"Did I have a choice?" I asked.

"You've always got a choice, princess."

I glanced down at my jersey knit skirt and pink Fleurty Girl NOLA T-shirt. "Then it looks like I made mine."

He examined my attire. "Don't you own jeans?"

I looked pointedly at his basketball shorts. "I think even you can agree that it's too damn hot to wear jeans this time of year. Besides, for all I know, I'll be outside scrubbing sidewalks."

"Fair enough." He tossed a glance toward my car. "You probably want to park around back. That ride might not be here long, otherwise."

I bit my lip. "Can you explain exactly where 'around back' is? Because I was lucky to even find this place."

Con's grim expression fell away, and he grinned. In that moment I was struck by how intensely gorgeous he was. Not that I wasn't already keenly aware of that fact, but his smile brought it to the forefront of my mind. Unruly dark blond hair, dark blue eyes, over six feet of tattooed, muscled man. His jaw was covered in a few days' worth of stubble, but that just made him even more ridiculously attractive. My panties were indeed a lost cause. "I'll do you one better—I'll show you."

What the heck is he talking about? I'd completely checked out from the conversation we were having.

My eyebrows lifted as he plucked the keys from my limp fingers and strode toward my car.

"What are you are doing?"

"Showing you where to park. And since I don't let chicks drive me around, you're going to have to suck it up and get in the passenger seat."

I followed him, my flip-flops making it easier to keep up than my normal pumps would have.

"Is that your version of asking for permission?" I felt like the token protest was necessary to preserve the rapidly deteriorating buffer zone between us.

Con stopped at the passenger door, opening it for me. The courtesy was surprising, but I didn't get a chance to linger on it before he replied "Honey, I'm not sure where you got the impression that I'm the kind of guy who asks for permission. I would've thought I'd made that clear two years ago." He waited until I dragged my eyes up to meet his. "Or have you managed to block that night out?"

And the buffer zone just disintegrated completely.

My mouth went dry, and I tried frantically to come up with some sort of response. I didn't think saying *'no, I remember that night altogether too well for comfort, and those memories have given me more than a few dozen orgasms over the last two years'* was appropriate.

"Umm..."

His grin spread wider and took on a stupidly attractive smug quality. "Girls like you always like it better when I don't ask for permission. When I just take what I want."

I froze as the memories battered me. Heat licked along my insides at the same time goose bumps prickled along my skin. I needed to shut this conversation down. *Now.* Before I sacrificed any more of my dignity at the altar of Con Leahy. So I went with the most obvious lie. "That night barely registered on my radar, and I surely don't remember any details."

I squared my shoulders, tamped down my inconvenient libido, slipped past him, and got in the car.

A few moments later, Con was in the driver's seat, and we were circling the block until we came up to a sketchy alley—the kind of alley you didn't go down in New Orleans if you wanted to come out alive. Any wayward thoughts were eradicated from my mind.

"Are you sure...?"

He didn't bother to answer, just drove down the narrow brick passageway into a small enclosed parking lot, and pulled into a spot next to a wicked-looking black Harley.

"Is that yours?" I asked, nodding toward the motorcycle.

He jerked his chin in what I assumed was a response and hopped out of the car without offering anything further.

I hurried after him, not wanting to look like I was waiting for him to open my door. *Because I wasn't.* I surveyed the back of the warehouse. It didn't look any more reputable than the front. Con tossed me my keys with orders to lock the car.

Con unlocked the heavy steel door before pulling it open and gesturing for me to enter.

"After you, princess."

I stopped on the threshold. "Could you not call me that?"

One side of his mouth quirked up in a smirk. "Why? That's how I've always thought of you. Vanessa Frost, the perfect princess."

I didn't know what stunned me more: Con's confession that he thought about me, or that he thought I was perfect.

I straightened and tried to look confident.

"I'm not perfect. Not by a long shot. And since my tiara seems to have been misplaced, I think princess is out, too."

"I like nicknames. I give 'em to everyone. So if not princess, what the hell am I supposed to call you?"

I thought of several things he'd called me that infamous night. *Sexy. Gorgeous. Tightest fucking pussy I've ever had.* OH MY GOD. I can't believe I just thought that. Even being around Con was a mistake.

I cleared my throat, as though that would clear the smut from my brain. "I can live with Van, if I get to have an opinion."

"Done. But don't bust my balls if I slip and call you princess now and again. Might be hard to break me of that one."

I decided this conversation needed to move on to whatever reason we were really here. "So, you going to show me what's in this warehouse, or are you going to keep me guessing?"

The semi-intimate moment broken, Con led the way inside. "Come on. I'll introduce you to the guys."

I followed behind him, trying valiantly not to focus on the way his basketball shorts hung off his hips and molded to the curve of his ass. And I tried even harder not to study the way his rippling, tattooed biceps extended from the cutoff sleeves of his T-shirt. It was hard to believe I'd had my hands—and mouth—all over that body once upon a time.

Sounds of *thump thwack thump* drew my attention back to the here and now.

We entered a large open room with a boxing ring set up in the middle, punching bags hanging from thick beams, old exercise bikes, weight lifting equipment, coiled jump ropes, and sections of bright blue mats filling the rest of the space.

Every piece of equipment was in use. At least a dozen boys stilled when we walked in. Whistles and catcalls filled the cavernous space.

"Con's got a girlfriend!"

"Holy shit, did you see the curves on that one?"

"I'd tap that."

"I'll take her when he's done with her—tomorrow."

A shrill whistle ripped through the din.

"Pipe down, knuckleheads, and get back to your workouts, unless you want to be running laps from now until Judgment Day," called the man who'd originally answered the door on the front side of the building. The one who'd called me *tail*.

Con spoke up. "This is Ms. Frost. If I hear any of you say anything disrespectful about her, you'll be my cleaning bitch for a month and have zero ring time." Groans and protestations filled the air. "Shut it down, boys, and get back to work."

Con glanced at me. "Sorry 'bout that. They've still got some rough edges, and well... they're teenage boys. I guess that's an explanation all in itself. And no woman has ever set foot inside here, except for Mrs. Girdeau. And she doesn't look anything like you."

I shrugged off his explanation. I was still stinging from the truth the one boy had yelled. Even these kids knew that Con operated on a one-night M.O., and I'd already had mine. *Not that I want another*, I told myself. Sternly. *And don't forget it.* Mental tongue-lashing completed.

"What is this place?" I asked.

A soft smile spread over his face, and I had to harden my heart. "This is the gym. A sort of afterschool, weekend, and summer program Reggie started a while back. He lets me hang out and pretend I'm partially in charge."

"In charge of doing what? Teaching them to fight?"

Con's smile turned mocking. "Yeah, *Van*. Teaching them to fight. To box. It keeps these guys off the streets and away from the gangbangers. They learn discipline and dedication. We've even been able to get a few of them scholarships."

"College scholarships? For boxing?"

Con crossed his arms, his shoulders hiking up. "That ain't good enough for you?"

He'd completely misinterpreted my tone. I laid a hand on one bicep. It was the first time I'd voluntarily touched him in two years, and the heat beneath my palm told me it was a bad idea. But I needed to wipe the defensiveness away. I wasn't judging him. I was... *in awe*. "No, that's not what I meant. I'm... impressed. I just didn't know there were colleges around here that gave out boxing scholarships."

"The two guys who've gotten scholarships are at schools on the East Coast. They got a chance to get out of here, and they took it. We've got two more headed that way in the fall."

"That's... amazing." I was being completely sincere. Because it *was*.

He shrugged, and I desperately wanted to lighten the mood. I told myself it was because a defensive, angry Con wasn't going to help my cause... and if I lied to myself, I wouldn't have to admit that I much preferred seeing him smile.

I decided shock was the best alternative. "So, am I your cleaning bitch today?"

My pointed question did the trick. Con's head swiveled, and his eyes locked on mine. But then he turned it on me. "You wanna be my bitch, princess?"

A hot shot of lust hit me low in the belly, and I dropped my gaze to the floor. "I thought you weren't going to call me that anymore."

He flicked the end of my ponytail as he walked past me.

"Follow me, and I'll show you what I've got planned for you."

What Con had planned for me became evident when we entered a huge, gleaming kitchen. Where the outside of the warehouse looked like it was on the verge of being condemned, most of the inside was immaculate and new.

"You know how to cook?" Con asked, flipping on still more lights.

"Do you?" I asked.

"I gotta eat, so yeah, I can cook."

I wished my relationship with food were so simple.

I ate because it was an evil necessity. It didn't mean I enjoyed it or looked forward to it. Too many years of being the chubby girl with the pretty face and a mother who just wanted me to be thin like the other kids had screwed me up royally in that area.

Vanessa, you have to watch everything you put in your mouth. You could lose this weight if you'd just be more mindful. Vanessa, I just want you to be healthy, that's all.

She'd been gone for years, stolen from my father and me much too soon by ovarian cancer when I was in eighth grade. The doctors had caught it too late, and she was gone within months. One of my biggest regrets: the words of hers I remembered best weren't the 'I loves yous' she'd whisper tucking me in at night.

"And I'm still waiting for your answer," Con said.

"I can handle the basics." To myself I added, *as long as you don't expect me to eat with you.* There was a very select group of people I was able to eat in front of without my stomach twisting into a Gordian knot.

I knew it was a messed up problem, but if you put yourself in the shoes of a younger me, and thought about what it would be like, at a birthday party, to have a friend's mother watch you eat a piece of pizza and say to another mother: *I can't believe she's eating that; you'd think she'd know better by now. If Madeline were that heavy, you'd never see another piece of pizza on her plate ever again.*

After that day, I'd stopped eating anything but fruits and vegetables in front of other people.

Shaking myself out of that *lovely* trip down memory lane, I watched as Con opened the freezer and pulled out giant trays of premade lasagna and set them on the stainless steel prep table in the center of the room.

My stomach tensed just looking at them.

"The hard stuff is already done; you just have to throw it all in the oven, babysit it, and put together PB&Js for them to take home."

I could do that. I could *so* do that.

"What's with the PB&J?"

Con looked up from where he was now turning on the oven. "They're burning a ton of calories here, and they need the fuel. So we feed 'em dinner every night, and lunch if they're here during the day, and then send them home with a snack. It's not like they've got overflowing pantries. Although, between you and me, I would guess that most of them hand off what we give them to a younger sibling."

I was floored. "You really feed them every day?"

His face took on a militant quality. "If we don't, they might not eat. And that's not something I'm gonna let happen." He surveyed me before continuing, "Come on, Van. You fund plenty of soup kitchens and food trucks. The fact that a good chunk of this city is going hungry on a regular basis can't have escaped your notice."

He was right. My psychological problems with food were nothing compared to actual hunger. I'd read the grant applications. I'd made recommendations about different programs we should fund. And I'd felt good about what I was doing. But I was ashamed to admit I'd never done more at a soup kitchen than attend a ribbon-cutting. I'd never handed out meat and bread and fruit to someone waiting in line at a food truck with a laundry basket. And here was Con, bad boy of the first order, combatting childhood hunger from the front lines. My shame multiplied, but I tried to mollify it by telling myself that those food trucks and soup kitchens have to be funded by someone. And if the foundation didn't do it, who would? I *was* making a difference, dammit.

"Have you applied for funding for your program? You could probably get a grant."

Con opened the freezer again and yanked out several loaves of garlic bread.

"You don't get it, do you, princess? This isn't about the money. This is about the kids and making sure they go home tonight with a full stomach and something to stop it from growling later."

"I get that, but if you're shelling out all of your own money on this..."

"I got plenty, if that's what you're worried about. Besides, I don't have time to waste filling out some hundred-page grant application and justifying what we do here for a few bucks. Reggie started this thing on his own, and he and I will make sure it stays going."

He laid the bread on the table in front of me and grabbed several aluminum cookie sheets from the counter. "You think you can handle this?"

I grabbed the bread, and, in an attempt to turn this conversation back to something lighter, I tossed out, "I'm pretty sure anything you want me to handle is way out of my league, Leahy. But I'll give it a shot."

His answering grin was brilliant. "Holy shit, you do have a sense of humor. I would've been willing to bet good money that you didn't know how to crack a joke."

"Well, I guess that means you would've been wrong."

Con slid behind me, and his heavy hands dropped onto my shoulders. His breath was warm against my ear as he whispered, "You're the one who's out of my league, sweetheart, and we both know it."

The bread fell from my shaky grip onto the stainless steel surface. I had no response. But that didn't stop my mouth from opening in preparation to say something completely stupid.

I was saved from myself when Reggie stuck his head into the kitchen. "Con, you gonna help with drills, or you gonna fuck around in here all day?"

Con stepped away, and my traitorous body immediately missed his heat.

"I'll be out in a few, Reg. Just showing Ms. Frost the lay of the land in here."

Reggie guffawed. "Sure, man, whatever you say." He slipped out of the kitchen, leaving an awkward silence behind him.

Con cleared his throat. "So, you think you can handle this? We've got fifteen eating here, and we need a dozen PB&Js to go home."

I nodded, words still escaping me.

"Good deal. Yell if you need help getting the lasagna in or out of the oven. Those things are fucking heavy."

My mumbled *okay* was less than impressive, but it was pretty much all I could get out.

Con paused in the doorway and looked back at me. "Don't go running off after you're done either. We've got some shit to talk about."

I wondered if he was talking about the crazy feelings ripping around inside me. *Good God, can he tell?* I forced myself to remember the reason I was here: the piece of property I needed to keep my shot at running the foundation that had been my mother's passion—a passion that had been imbued in me since childhood. My mother might have been happy to sit on the board in a figurehead position, but I wanted more. I wanted to think bigger, *do bigger*. I wanted to make the final decision on how we changed lives in Louisiana for the better.

Just focus on the goal, Vanessa. Push everything else aside.

I reached for the garlic bread, declaring my mental pep talk successful.

Mostly.

con

We all see what we want to see. And we expect our assumptions to play out accurately in real life. But in this case, the case of Ms. Vanessa Frost, it seemed like my assumptions may have been off—if only just a little. She was still gorgeous and eminently fuckable, but she wasn't the stone-cold bitch I'd thought she was since she'd walked out and left me with the taste of her still on my tongue. It could have been a show to soften me up to get what she wanted, but she'd actually seemed to care about making sure these kids had food to eat. The way to most men's hearts might be through their stomachs, but the quickest way to mine was through the stomachs of my boys.

The flirty banter had also thrown me for a minute. She'd sounded serious when she'd said that anything I wanted her to handle was out of her league. I'd been equally serious when I'd reminded her that she was the one out of *my* league.

A pair of gloves and headgear smacked me across the chest. *Reggie.*

"Need you in the ring. I can't watch all of them at once."

"We need to get another guy on board, to cover when Lord or I can't be here." Lord was the third in our motley crew of role models. Not that I was a good role model for any kid, but I did my best. And since I wasn't a gangbanger, it made me more of an example to follow than most of these kids had.

"Agreed, but it's got to be someone who can handle these kids. They don't respect just anyone. Though they seem to like that girl of yours just fine."

"She ain't my girl. She's just here doing some work in exchange for a favor." *And don't forget it, Leahy,* I chastised myself. Vanessa wouldn't have set foot in this neighborhood if not for the prize on the line.

"Whatever you say, boss. I saw the way you were lookin' at her."

"Drop it, Reg."

"Touchy."

"Seriously, fuck off." I stopped at the bench and grabbed a roll of tape. "Make yourself useful and tape me up."

"Yes, sir. Yes, sir."

Helping the guys in the ring was the cure for any lingering thoughts about Vanessa. Trey and Jojo were both so fucking quick that if I wasn't on my game, I'd get beat down. And I had my rep to protect.

Ninety minutes and buckets of sweat later, the boys tromped toward the showers, and I ducked into the kitchen. The heavenly scent of lasagna and garlic bread wafted through the air, and the gorgeous girl standing in the center of it all, oven mitts on both hands, a smear of what looked like strawberry jam across one cheek, had me freezing at the doorway.

When she looked up and smiled, I felt something weird in my chest. What exactly, I wasn't sure. But that shit wasn't normal.

"I can take those out to the table." I jerked my chin toward the steaming pans of lasagna on the center prep surface. "If I can borrow the oven mitts."

She looked down at her hands. "Oh, yeah. Sure." She pulled them off, and I stepped closer to take them from her.

I glanced at the dozens of brown paper lunch sacks on the counter and raised an eyebrow. Her cheeks flamed crimson. "I made a few extras. Okay, a lot of extras. But I'll pay for the supplies. I thought if maybe they had brothers and sisters... and once I started making them, I just couldn't stop. So, yeah. That."

Her self-conscious rambling had my heart doing that funny thing again.

"It's okay. And you don't need to pay for any supplies. I've got it covered. I'm sure they'll appreciate the extras. There are always more mouths to feed."

Her frown didn't detract from her traffic-stopping beauty, but it made me want to...comfort her. *What the hell?* I didn't have time to question my weird ass reaction when Vanessa started wringing her oven mitt-less hands.

"I just want you to know that regardless of whether you decide to donate the property or not, I'm going to do whatever I can to help fund more programs to feed these kids. I mean, we already do a lot, but clearly we're not making a big enough impact. And that's not right. The foundation can do more. Change more. No kid should be going to bed hungry in this city. We have the resources, we just need to deploy them better." She looked up at me for a split second, before spinning around toward the fridge. And in that tiny glimpse I got of her face, I could swear her eyes were glossy with unshed tears.

"Then join us for supper. Meet some of the kids you want to help change things for. They'll be on... better...behavior."

She froze, half-in and half-out of the fridge.

Her voice was small when she said, "I can't."

After her impassioned speech, it wasn't the answer I expected.

"Busy?"

"Ummm...I just...well..." She took a breath and looked at me straight on. "I just can't."

My hands clenched into fists. "You want to help feed these kids, but you're too good to sit down and actually eat with them?"

"No! That's not it."

"Then what?"

She squeezed her eyes shut. "I just can't. Okay?" She turned. "I should go."

I wasn't satisfied. For a split second, I'd seen a glimpse of a different woman beneath the layers of polish and ice—one who had a heart that might rival the size of her bank account. *She* was the woman I wanted sitting down at a table with these boys and me. But apparently what I'd seen was a figment of my imagination—and that pissed me off.

"You ain't got a hot date with your boy toy, Simon Duchesne. Because I heard that's over. And that it never really was what it seemed." I hadn't been able to stop thinking about it since Duchesne had spilled the beans to my receptionist, Charlie, that his relationship with Vanessa had been a cover. Because, according to Duchesne, she might be digging someone her dad didn't find acceptable. That mystery was one that had kept me up more nights than I'd admit.

Her look of surprise was priceless. That sinful mouth dropped open just far enough to give a guy ideas. I wondered if I pushed hard enough, would she spill who this unsuitable mystery guy was? *You want it to be you*, my subconscious taunted. I flipped it the mental bird. There was no way in hell it was me.

When she stayed silent, I continued, "You think I don't have my ear to the ground when it comes to you, Vanessa? I know all about your thing with Duchesne. Using him to keep your daddy off your back while you sample men with less-than-perfect pedigrees. So who was it? Some blue-collar guy you're sneaking around with so your old man doesn't find out?"

Her features hardened into the same expression she'd worn as she walked out of my bedroom.

"You don't know anything about me, so don't pretend you do. Except you're right—I'm not seeing

Simon. I think that's pretty common knowledge. So if you were going for shock value to get a reaction out of me, you missed."

Frustration mounted. She was like one of the puzzle boxes I'd gotten from Joy for my sixteenth birthday. I knew there was something cool as hell waiting inside, but I'd never figured out how to solve it. In the end, I'd found a hammer and smashed it—and almost destroyed the St. Christopher medal waiting inside. "Then why? Why won't you sit down and share a simple goddamn meal with me and some kids?"

She inhaled sharply and looked away. "I just...I just can't, Con."

My expression hardened into a mask to rival hers as my temper slipped its chain. "You're not too good to make them dinner—because that's your daily act of fucking charity—but you're too good to actually sit down and eat it with them."

Her spine stiffened visibly. "If that's what you think of me, then I'm sure you were never going to donate the property anyway."

"Yeah, because let's not lose sight for a second why you're actually here: you need something from me."

"Why else would I be here?" she asked quietly.

I just shook my head. "I think it's time for you to go. Probably just in time, too, because for a second I thought you might actually be more than a stuck-up bitch."

She snatched her purse off the counter. "Then I'll just get out of your way."

"You're kissing that property goodbye."

"Like I said, we both know you were never going to give it to me anyway."

Her skirt flared as she turned on her flip-flops and headed for the door. It was an exit to rival the last notable one she'd made out of my life.

And just like the chump I'd been then, I once again followed at a discreet distance behind her and made sure she got home all right.

vanessa 4

I sorted papers and filed until my desk was spotless. That much easier for packing up my stuff when I resigned my position. I hadn't taken my diplomas off the wall, and my heart sank when I realized that if I followed through with my plan, that was exactly how I'd be ending my day.

I'd always regretted that my mother didn't live long enough to see me become the skinny girl she'd always wanted me to be. The full effects of my late growth spurt hadn't been readily apparent before she'd passed. In my grief, it had been hard to appreciate the extra five inches bestowed on me in less than a year. That vertical magic, combined with months of barely eating, had taken me from a chunky five-foot-three eighth grader to a willowy five-foot-eight high school freshman.

Well, now I suppose I ought to be grateful that she hadn't lived long enough to see me leave the L.R.

Bennett Foundation with my tail between my legs. A failure. It was especially hard to stomach because even when I'd been the chubby girl, I'd always been the smart girl. The straight A student. The one with the answers. And in this, I was admitting defeat. My melancholy attitude would require copious amounts of wine. And I already wanted to kick myself for being grateful that my mother wasn't alive to see this. Who thought stuff like that? Me, apparently.

Elle interrupted my pathetic moment of self-reflection.

"You've been avoiding me all day. That shit has to stop."

There were a lot of good things about working with your childhood best friend, but there were also some bad things. Like not being able to hide anything—personally or professionally—*ever*. She'd been the mastermind behind the plan of me begging Con. She'd also advocated the on-bended-knee-and-in-the-dirtiest-way-possible method, but I'd demurred.

Elle dropped into the chair across from my empty desk.

"I was going to stop by as soon as I delivered this to Archer." I plucked a single sheet of paper from my credenza, and Elle snatched it out of my hand.

"Oh, fuck me. You did not write your letter of resignation."

"What else am I supposed to do?"

"You're supposed to fight for this. Leave no stone unturned until we figure out a solution. And if we can't figure something out, then you go to Archer, and you tell him that it was a legal problem. You explain that it wasn't your fault, and you still deserve to run this place."

"You know it won't work like that. You *know* he'll expect me to admit that running this project was more than I could handle, which means running the foundation is clearly too much for me to handle, which is just as good as tendering my resignation."

Elle shook her head.

"I'm disappointed in you, Vanessa."

Her words crushed my already battered self-confidence. "Thanks. I'm disappointed in me too."

"Not because of the project, you idiot, but because you're ready to walk away from your dream without even fighting for it."

"I fought, Elle. I went to Con, and he said—"

"I don't care what he said. You have to go back. I will not let you walk away from this. Besides, what do you really have to lose now, if you're so sure you've already lost it all?"

I closed my eyes for a beat. "My pride."

"I think you left that at the door when you did your walk of shame two years ago."

"Thank you for the reminder," I clipped out. As if I really needed one.

She stared me down. "Seriously, Vanessa. You've wanted to run this place for as long as I've known you. I don't understand how you could give up so easily."

My shoulders stiffened. "This isn't easy. I'm trying to put the foundation first."

Elle's snapping brown eyes bored into me. "And *you* are what's best for it. So go fix this shit and prove it."

I exhaled a long breath before replying, "Okay. I'll do it."

"Good girl." She slapped a small piece of paper on the desk in front of me. "And this is where it's going to go down."

My swirling emotions slowed in confusion. I looked down at the cream-colored embossed invitation. "The Boys and Girls Club Banquet?"

She produced several more sheets paper. "Here's the guest list. And guess who's on it."

I grabbed it from her and stared at the highlighted name. "No way. Why would Con be going?"

Elle shook her head. "That's a question you're going to have to answer for yourself, because I think I've hit my limit of solutions for the day. I've earned a bottle of wine. Or two."

I scanned the invitation. There were awards being handed out to several of the kids who participated in the program. Good money said one of them trained at Con's gym.

And he'd RSVP'd to a $5,000-a-plate fundraiser to be there in support of the kid.

I looked back to Elle. "Do I have a date for this?"

She laughed, a cackle if I'd ever heard one.

"I love that you have to ask me if you have a date. Do I look like your assistant? I'm surely not."

"Sorry. I just..."

"I know...I'm the keeper of your social calendar by default. No, you don't have a date. Simon was originally going to go with you, but..."

"Right. Okay. So I'm going alone." Which meant it would be easier to corner Con and make my last ditch effort at begging without an audience.

"But you're seated at the VIP table. With the keynote speaker," Elle added.

"That's fine."

I mentally flipped through the contents of my wardrobe. My confidence was going to need a serious boost to do this. There was one dress I hadn't yet worn. It wasn't scandalous, just more body-conscious than I was usually willing to wear. When I'd tried it on in the dressing room, I'd felt...strong. Capable. Like a woman who knew what the hell she was doing and what she wanted.

I looked at the clock. I had three hours until the fundraiser. Three hours to apply my war paint and armor and come up with a strategy. I had to find some way to get Con Leahy alone and convince him to donate that damn property.

Elle was right. I'd had a moment of temporary insanity. I was *not* walking away from my dream— my heritage—without a fight.

con

I stood in the shadows of the bar, nursing my Jack and Coke, as I watched her flit around the crowd. A perfect social fucking butterfly. She moved from one group to the next, making conversation and smiling her polite company smile. That smile was nothing like the one I'd seen on her face when her cheek was smudged with strawberry jam—before we'd both lost our tempers, and she'd walked out on me. Again. I didn't know when I started making a study of her different smiles, but I could tell this one was practiced. It was the one that graced the society pages. While she always looked fucking gorgeous, this smile wasn't going to launch a million ships or whatever the hell the saying was. There was something missing from it. It didn't reach her eyes.

She turned and visibly stiffened. Apparently my subtle observation of her was actually several notches less than subtle. But it wasn't shock I saw on her face. Whatever that emotion was, it was wiped away so quickly I wondered if I'd really seen it. Her perfect façade was in place again—except for the pointed look in my direction and one raised eyebrow.

Yeah, princess, you caught me. I'm watching you. I'd watched her from the sidelines more times over the past two years than I would care to admit. Hell, even longer than that. I wondered if I'd ever get out of the high school mindset where I was the charity case and she was the perfect princess I'd accused her of being. God I hoped so. It was time to grow up. I shifted and adjusted the collar of my tux.

And yeah, you heard me right. *My tux.* I would've worn jeans and a T-shirt if I hadn't given a shit, but I did. Not because I'd expected Vanessa to be here—which I had—but because I was here to support Trey. I couldn't very well force him to wear a tux and not wear one myself. Even though I'd rented his, you couldn't help but see the pride in his eyes when he'd walked out to my car tonight. He looked good, and he deserved his moment to shine.

He was the poster boy for success of an organization like this one. The only son of a single mother working three jobs, raised in the projects, and completely at risk for joining a gang. But he was smart, and his mama wanted more for him than a short life that would end with a drive-by bullet. So she started sending him to the Boys and Girls Club when he was young. They kept him out of trouble and up to his eyeballs in activities. He'd moved up to be part of the afterschool staff and a mentor. He'd started training with my guys over a year ago and dropped down to two days a week at the Club. The program director had been downright suspicious and had hauled his ass over to the gym to talk to me himself to make sure Trey was staying out of trouble. We came to an understanding: Any of the boys who wanted to box or had anger issues that required a little more... physical activity...to keep them in line, he'd send my way, and I'd vowed on my mother's grave to keep them on the straight and narrow the best I could.

So tonight, Trey was receiving the Boy's Award for Excellence. His mom had been excited to come, but at the last minute, she'd been called in to work. Too afraid to say no and lose a vital piece of their income, she'd consented. So I was the only one here for him. I turned to watch Trey being paraded around by the director to meet all of the big wigs. He hadn't yet been introduced to Vanessa, and in this town, she certainly qualified as a big wig. I wondered if he'd recognize her in a designer dress, since he'd last seen her in a T-shirt and simple cotton skirt. My guess was probably not.

I looked over to where she stood, that dress clinging to her every curve. *Goddamn*. For the thousandth time, I wished I'd been fucking sober that night. But then I probably would have said or done something to fuck it up. I needed another shot—a do-over. But after the way we left things yesterday, that wasn't likely.

Except...I had something she wanted. Desperately, considering she'd voluntarily sought me out. If nothing else, that should at least give me another opening.

That deed was leverage. A better guy wouldn't dream of using it to his benefit. A better guy might do the charitable thing and donate the property and hope he'd win the girl over through his generosity and kindness.

I wasn't a better guy.

Did I really want to get her back into my bed that way? Knowing she was only with me to get something from me?

Who was I kidding? I didn't fucking care how I got her back there. Now that she'd walked her fine ass back into my life, I refused to let her walk out again without getting my second chance. With Simon Duchesne out of the picture, and me holding all the cards, there was nothing standing in my way.

Well, except for Vanessa herself. I allowed myself another long, lingering look. I cataloged her every dip and curve as I dragged my gaze from her red-soled stilettos to her slick, red lips.

I barely stifled a groan. *Jesus*, but I wanted that mouth.

My visual enjoyment died a quick death when a man approached her from the side. Vanessa smiled, head tilting toward him. I pushed off the wall, my fist clenching so hard it tested the strength of the glass clutched in my hand. I needed to see the guy's face. I edged around the room, nodding at several people in attendance until I could get a closer look.

I got my look—and kept fucking walking.

Mother. Fucker. I tossed back my drink and headed straight to the bar. If I had to watch her with that prick, I needed my good friend, Jack.

She was a magnet for his type. Not that I knew him. I only recognized him from the papers, and they'd dubbed him "Louisiana's Hottest Titan of Industry." Relatively new in town, he hadn't wasted any time before making a splash and pissing off the old guard. It seemed that every move he made was analyzed and copied. Old money loved to hate him because, as the story went, he came from nothing, but everything he touched turned to gold. If big business had a rebel, it would be Lucas Fucking Titan.

My lips curled in disgust when he slipped an arm around her and led her toward the bar on the opposite side of the room. Fury raged hot and fast. First, at the realization that he had the right to approach her in this crowd, and second, because she'd followed him willingly.

I grabbed my drink off the bar, and my attention snagged on my wrist. Even my tux couldn't hide the ink that spilled out from beneath my cuffs and collar.

The ink was a brand. And in this case, it branded me unsuitable for public acknowledgment by Vanessa Frost. I'd bet good money that if she even spoke to me in front of these society types, it'd get back to her daddy so damn fast, her head would still be spinning when he came and dragged her away from me.

I sipped the straight whiskey and reveled in the burn. I needed to slow it down, because I was here for Trey, not to dwell on the fact that I'd never belong in the upper class I'd been adopted into. Changing your last name didn't change how people saw you—how they judged you.

Even fifteen years didn't change the fact that I'd been the kid who showed up in the Garden District, garbage bag in tow, because Joy and Andre Leahy had decided they wanted to give being foster parents a shot. Their friends and neighbors had been horrified. And when Joy and Andre had decided to adopt me? You better believe their sanity had been questioned.

I laughed humorlessly to myself. Because those judgmental pricks had been right—bringing me into their lives had ultimately gotten them killed. Joy and Andre deserved better than being gunned down in a home invasion—a home invasion that had happened because me and my Army buddies had been on leave and gotten into a fight with some gangbangers at a club off Bourbon. We'd just gotten into town, hadn't even changed out of our uniforms. Better for picking up pussy anyway. But they'd seen our names. Given that the Leahy name was fairly well known in this town, it wasn't too hard to figure out that they'd tagged me as a local and tracked down my family in retaliation. Three nights later, when I was already back on base, someone had broken into Joy and Andre's house.

Two bullets. Execution style.

They should've been rocking on the back porch on a night like tonight, sharing a bottle of wine. Instead, they were resting in a burial vault. Because of me.

I swigged the rest of my drink. All the booze in the world couldn't wash away the blood on my hands.

Only justice would wipe away some of the guilt I felt—and even that would be a far cry from absolution. The memory gave way to the need to pound my frustration out on a bag. I hated the restrictions of this fucking monkey suit. I hated the polite conversations humming around me. This wasn't my world. I didn't want it to be my world. If it weren't for Trey, I'd get the hell out of here right now.

My thoughts turned even darker as I watched Titan press his hand to the small of Vanessa's back and guide her closer to the bar. I wanted to rip that fucking hand off.

"Hey, man. You having fun back here?" Trey's voice pulled me back to reality. He nudged my shoulder conspiratorially.

I forced a smile for his benefit. "Don't I always? Just waiting to see you get that award and give your speech."

Trey's eyes widened. "I have to give a speech? No one fucking told me that."

I grinned, and this time it was sincere. "I'm kidding, man. You just have to smile and look pretty for the camera. And watch your language. You shouldn't be dropping the F-bomb around these kinds of people."

Trey rolled his eyes. "That stop you?"

"Don't worry about me. But you better clean it up before you get to the Point, or they'll clean it up for you."

He breathed a heavy sigh. "Okay, okay. I get it. You and my mama both. Seriously." He jostled my shoulder again. "You'd think with all this ink you wouldn't be such a drag."

"Don't make me teach you some manners, boy."

Although it was likely that Trey's mama had already beaten manners into him. She was a tough woman. And probably the major reason why he'd been accepted to West Point. The day he'd gotten his congressional nomination...I'd shed a tear, though I'd never admit it. It was a hell of an honor, and there wasn't another kid who deserved it more. It had started with him asking me about some of my tats. What they meant—especially the military ones. I'd given him bits and pieces about my history in the service. Honestly, there was plenty I couldn't tell, but I could give him the basics. He'd latched on to it like an infant on a teat. I could understand the appeal. There was something about honor and serving your country that reached into your gut and made you want to be part of something bigger than yourself. At least that was what it had done for me. The military had taken my punk ass and turned it into a hell of a soldier. I'd taken bullets for my brothers. Had watched one throw himself on a grenade to save another. The brotherhood was something civilians would never understand. I was glad that Trey would get to be a part of that.

"Con, you good, man?" Trey asked, as I realized I'd let myself drift.

"Yeah, just thinking about some shit."

A tall, thin man took the stage and spoke into the microphone. "Ladies and gentlemen, dinner service will begin shortly. If you would, please begin to make your way to your seats."

"That's your cue. Better go find the head table, man." Trey smiled again and took off toward the front of the room.

I looked toward my table, but a blonde heading in the opposite direction caught my attention. It didn't take a genius to figure out which way I went.

vanessa

I saw him watching me. But even if I hadn't seen him, I would have *felt* him. Con was... potent. A heck of a lot more potent than the wine swirling in my glass as I stepped away from a group of society matrons. My one glass. Because that was all I ever allowed myself at events like these. Why? Because a lady was never tipsy in public. I broke that rule at my own peril. Like the anniversary of my mother's death two years ago. I remember drinking three glasses of wine at dinner that night. Obviously that day wasn't one my father handled well, and he handled it even more poorly when we stayed home. Something about sitting around the dining room table my mother had loved so dearly would set him off every single time. So, instead, we went out, and our quiet family dinner had deteriorated into my father asking me why I hadn't brought a man up to snuff yet, and pointing out that my mother would have wanted me settled and having babies of my own by now.

Three glasses of wine had loosened my tongue and glazed over my good sense. I'd said something about Mother probably being too worried that my finally-skinny figure would be ruined by pregnancy and would have probably suggested I hire a surrogate. To this day, I could feel the sting of the back of my father's hand as it connected with my cheek.

He'd never struck me before or since.

We'd both sat in stunned silence in our private dining room at his favorite restaurant and, face throbbing, I'd quietly excused myself from the table.

I'd never looked at my father quite the same after that night. Did any girl look at her daddy the same way after he backhanded her?

An hour later I'd found myself wandering the French Quarter. I'd lost myself in the revelry, and while, at first, it had been comforting, I'd started to panic as the crush had become overwhelming. Con had been a lone familiar face in a crowd of strangers. I'd tripped over a curb and crashed into him. Instead of being the too-good looking punk with a chip on his shoulder I'd remembered from high school, he'd been drunk and charming. His arms had been strong and steady when they'd wrapped around me and kept me from face-planting onto the dirty sidewalk.

His teasing had made me smile, when all I'd wanted to do moments before was cry. I'd needed more of that—more levity and lightness to smother the horrible darkness that had stalked me all night. I'd needed to forget.

So I'd taken an insane leap and let him lead me back to Voodoo and up the stairs to his apartment. Being laid out across Con's bed and catching an eyeful of what he was packing in those ripped up jeans had sobered me up pretty damn quick. *Good God.* Even intoxicated, Con was... an experience. My cheeks burned just thinking about him.

The unforgettable night had given way to my hangover and the harsh light of morning: *If my father ever found out... that backhand would seem like a love tap.* My father's judgment of Con had come down early— just after he'd arrived at the Leahy's as a foster and decided to test their boundaries. My father had found Con passed out drunk, lying against our fence, and their interaction hadn't gone... smoothly. My father had thought he was trouble then and had never missed an opportunity to comment over the years about what a disgrace Con was to his adoptive parents.

"Vanessa, it's a pleasure to see you again," a smooth, deep voice said from a few feet away.

I jerked my gaze away from Con's direction and looked up into the face of Lucas Titan.

Several inches over six feet, with thick, inky black hair cropped close to his head, Lucas Titan was an attractive man, especially when you added in his mossy green eyes, wide shoulders, and narrow hips. A diagonal scar slashing upward through his left eyebrow into his hairline gave his face character and kicked it from being classically handsome to dangerously gorgeous. His billions and philanthropic nature had made him a darling of the New Orleans charity scene, even if the old money crowd almost universally hated him. He didn't play by their rules, or anyone else's.

It was one of the things I admired most about the man.

He'd also bought himself a seat on the board of directors of the L.R. Bennett Foundation about six months ago.

"Mr. Titan, I didn't realize you'd be here tonight."

After all, the only name on the guest list Elle had bothered to mention had been Con's.

"Then I'm guessing you didn't read your invite beyond the plate price."

I laughed politely. "You're probably right about that."

His smile revealed perfectly straight, white teeth. "I'm the keynote. I'll be talking about the importance of getting technology into the hands of underprivileged youth at early ages to help level the playing field, and how organizations like this one are perfectly suited to accomplish that goal—if only it had the funding."

"Well, hopefully between your speech and the open bar, people will give generously. It makes sense to have the tech guru sell it."

His smile broadened. "I've yet to leave my nerd days behind."

My face must have shown my surprise at his admission. "I would've never guessed. The nerds from my youth weren't quite so suave, nor did they wear black tie quite as well as you do."

A dimple I hadn't previously been aware of winked. Damn, the man really was attractive.

"My growth spurt and tuxes came late in the game, Ms. Frost. It's much easier to know who your friends are when you're the least popular kid in school than when you're sitting on billions."

I nodded. I knew all about people befriending you for reasons other than your sparkling personality.

"I understand completely." Wanting to move off that uncomfortable subject, I added, "I'm sure your keynote will be interesting."

"Well, I'll try to keep from putting you to sleep anyway. And it's short, which is probably the best quality any keynote can have."

I lifted my wine. "Cheers to that, Mr. Titan."

He clinked his highball with my glass, and his eyes dropped to my shoes and made a lazy perusal up my body. "You look stunning tonight, Vanessa."

I waited for the flash of heat I'd felt when Con's gaze took the same path. And I got... a warm breeze. It was pretty much the same reaction my body gave when Simon complimented me. Here was a gorgeous man, richer than Croesus, and my body decided it wasn't interested.

It was probably for the best. Despite his money and business prowess, my father was firmly in the *Lucas Titan is the spawn of the devil* camp. It had something to do with Lucas's sustainable energy agenda and the lobbyists who were pushing it in the state legislature. As a steel man, my father didn't want anyone telling him how he needed to power his mills.

"Thank you," I replied.

He looked down at my drink. "And you need a refill. Would you like me to get you another?"

My polite smile smoothed across my face. I didn't like to explain my one glass limit, so it was easier if I just got my drinks myself. I'd be switching to club soda with lime after this one.

"How about we head that way together?"

His hand somehow found its way to the small of my back, and I wasn't sure how to graciously remove it. After a long wait and small talk in line, I had my club soda, and our impending dinner service was announced.

"I'm assuming you're also at the head table?" I asked Lucas.

"Indeed."

"Would you mind taking my drink? I need to excuse myself for a moment."

Lucas accepted my glass. "Of course. I'll be waiting."

❦

I pushed open the door to the powder room and stepped into the lobby. A large hand wrapped around my upper arm.

I turned and opened my mouth to protest, but was silenced when I saw the tattoos peeking out from beneath the shirt cuff.

"What are you doing?" I hissed, shocked that Con would manhandle me in public, although maybe I shouldn't have been.

He tugged me toward an unused coatroom, and shut and blocked the door.

"Are you crazy?" I'd wanted to get him alone, but not like this. This was dangerous.

Con stalked toward me. I backed away, feeling very much like a rabbit facing off against a wolf.

"I decided I'm not done with you yet."

The words were so low and quiet; I felt them more than I heard them. I tried to keep my breathing steady as I asked, "So you accost me outside the ladies' room and drag me into a coat closet?"

"Would you rather I'd approached you while Lucas Titan was cye-fucking the shit out of you?"

So that was what this was about. "First, that kind of language is unnecessary. And second, Lucas is an acquaintance. He's on my board of directors. And... I don't even know why I'm explaining myself to you. It's none of your business."

"Always good to know where I stand."

Con trapped me in the corner between the empty coat rack and the wall.

I needed to get out of here before I did something stupid.

"What do you want? I have to get back." I hoped my tone sounded unaffected.

"Same thing I've wanted for two damn years: another taste of you."

I sucked in a breath and fought the shivers of anticipation coursing through me. *No. Absolutely not. Can't happen.*

"Why would you want another taste of the stuck up bitch you threw out of your gym?" I crossed my arms, ready to block any verbal blows that might be coming. Turns out, I didn't need to.

Con looked up to the ceiling and cleared his throat before speaking. "Life doesn't give us many second chances. If this is mine, then I'm not going to waste it."

My mind reeled as my heart kicked into a gallop. "I don't even know what that means."

He dropped his eyes back down to meet mine. The intensity of his stare pressed me into the wall. "It means this is how it's going to go down: You want that property. I want a shot with you. I get what I want, then you get what you want."

My entire body stilled. Well, everything except for my mouth dropping open. Was he *seriously* expecting me to whore myself out for the deed? My temper flared, but I held back the imminent explosion. I wanted confirmation before I shoved him away and slapped him across the face.

"What *exactly* are you proposing?"

His chin lifted, and his dark blue eyes sparked with heat. "What do you think I'm proposing, princess?"

My hands shot out, palms connecting with the solid muscles of his chest. I shoved, but Con didn't budge. Instead, he brought his hands up to cover mine, trapping them against the fabric of his tux. I yanked my hands back, but Con's grip didn't break.

He leaned down and spoke quietly just above my ear. "That wasn't very ladylike, Vanessa. You didn't even let me finish."

I struggled against his hold as he added, "I didn't say I expected you to fuck me for it. Your dirty mind went there all by itself."

The sound that crawled out of my throat was *also* not ladylike. "Let. Me. Go."

His fingers slid along the backs of my hands and curled around my wrists. I fought as he raised my arms and pinned them to the wood paneled wall above my head.

"Not until I'm good and ready. And I can't be sure I'll ever be ready."

My nipples hardened in response to his cocky declaration. I squeezed my eyes shut for a moment, hoping naively that the move would block out the effects of his words and touch. It didn't.

"So what do you say, Vanessa? You willing to give me a shot?"

I swallowed, and my heart hammered a staccato rhythm in my chest. Pressed so tightly against me, there was no way Con could miss it.

Fixing my eyes on his, I decided that being on the defensive wasn't going to gain me any ground. So I asked the question burning on my tongue.

"Why?" I asked. "Why would you want a chance with me? You don't even like me."

His lips quirked up into a sardonic smile. "I don't really remember if I like you or not."

I glared at him. "You're a pig, you know that?"

The smile faded, and a hard look settled over his features. My attention cut to the door. Con didn't miss it.

"Oh, no, princess. I told you—you ain't going anywhere until I'm ready to let you go." He leaned in until I could feel his breath against my temple as he added, "And I wasn't joking when I said I might never be ready."

I refused to look up, knowing that his expression would be smoldering, promising me things I couldn't have.

"No." My tone was implacable.

"Look at me."

"No," I repeated.

"Then you're screwed. And not in the way that ends with you coming all over my dick."

His crude taunt worked. I ripped my gaze away from the studs of his tuxedo shirt and up to his face.

"Like I said before, you're a pig."

"And it turns out that you're not a whore." He shifted his grip on my wrists to one hand and lowered the other to brush a lock of hair away from my face. "Good to know."

"Then if you don't want me to whore myself out, what do you want from me?"

"Like I said, a shot."

I huffed out a frustrated breath. "But what does that mean?"

"What would you do if I told you I wanted to pick you up at your front door and take you out on the town?"

My blood froze. If that was his requirement, then it was out of the question.

A perfectly executed project wouldn't matter if my reputation were in tatters. When I didn't answer right away, Con released my wrists and pushed away from the wall. He crossed to the other side of the coatroom as though wanting to get as far away from me as possible.

"That's what I thought," he said, spinning back around to face me.

"I didn't say anything."

"That look of horror on your face said it all." He punctuated his words with a humorless laugh, and I felt my chance slipping away. But the strange part was, I didn't know if it was the chance at the property or the elusive second chance with Con that I was going to be more devastated to lose.

That can't matter. But I could be honest with him.

"It's not personal. I couldn't publicly date any guy with the kind of reputation you've carved out for yourself. Right now, I'm an asset to the foundation. Even if I were to get the property, if at any time my reputation were to become... a liability, I'd kiss my chance at running the place goodbye."

Con's eyes lit with something I couldn't identify. But I was pretty sure it wasn't defeat. It looked a lot more like... victory.

"So the flip side of your statement means that you wouldn't have a problem dating someone like me under the radar."

When had a *shot with me* moved to dating? Was that really what he wanted? Con didn't even *like* me. None of this made sense.

"Why would you even want that? I mean, if I were you, I wouldn't bother with someone who wasn't willing to stand beside me in public." I knew I was damning my own cause with that statement, but it had to be said.

He leaned back against the paneled wall and watched me. With the licks of ink escaping from beneath the crisp, white collar and cuffs of his shirt, his unruly hair, and relaxed stance, he looked like he should be posing for the *Toss Me Your Panties* calendar. *Stop thinking about him like that, dammit.*

"I'm not a regular guy, Van. I've spent years in the shadows, and I have no problem with staying there."

"And what exactly does that mean?" I asked.

"You don't need to know. Suffice it to say, whatever happens between us, for now, I don't want it to be any more public than you do."

My mouth fell open into a little O, and a small, vain part of me burned to know why Con Leahy wouldn't want the world to know he was dating me.

Con pushed off the wall and strode toward me. Three steps and he was once again too close for comfort.

"So what do ya say, princess? Ready to make a deal?"

A deal. I could make a deal. *Holy crap, am I really considering this?* Yes. Yes, I was.

"Give me your terms, then."

Con grinned. "You agree to be where I say, when I say, for the next... let's say... six weeks."

"Six weeks?" My voice pitched higher with surprise.

"You think I can melt the ice queen faster than that?"

I glared at his use of my least favorite nickname. "I can't do six weeks. I need the deed before the demolition."

"One month," he offered.

"Three weeks," I countered.

"Done." The word was a decree, but I wasn't satisfied yet.

"What if you don't feel like you got your 'fair shot' with me? Would you back out and leave me hanging?"

"Guess you'll just have to trust me. And actually give me that shot."

I arched a brow. "Trust you? You want me to put my entire career on the line, and your only reassurance is 'trust me'?"

"It's called a leap of faith, princess. Besides, you got any better alternatives?"

I didn't—and he knew it.

I inhaled a shallow breath and asked, "What about sex? Because if you think that's a given, you've got another thing coming."

His lazy grin was pure sin. "Sweetheart, if I can't get you in my bed in three weeks, I don't deserve to call myself a man. And when I get you there, it won't have jack shit to do with that deed."

Heat streaked up my body, licking at my chest and neck. I was getting in way over my head. He was too confident. But what other choice did I really have?

I held out my hand, pleased to see it wasn't shaking. "It's a deal."

Con came toward me slowly, and took my hand but didn't shake it like I'd anticipated. Instead, he backed me into the corner one more time.

"This ain't the kind of deal you seal with a handshake."

Shock prevented my protest from forming, because the only thing I could focus on was Con's mouth descending on mine. His big hands cradled my jaw and angled my head. His lips were hot as they took mine, his tongue delving inside. It wasn't a polite kiss. It was a show of dominance. Memories of that night rushed back, and goose bumps prickled along my skin. By the time Con lifted his head, we'd *sealed the deal* so well I was going to need to change my panties.

I made my way back to the table, legs shaking and mind racing with what I'd just done. With what I'd just agreed to do. I was *dating* Con Leahy in secret... Sweet baby Jesus.

Before I'd left the coatroom, hopefully a discreet few minutes before he did, Con had programmed his number into my phone and texted himself. Given that our schedules were both relatively flexible, he'd said he would text me the time and location of our first rendezvous.

Oh God. *Our rendezvous.* The forbidden thrill that shot through me almost had me stumbling on the carpet in front of five hundred people.

When I reached the table, I'd completely missed the first course and was arriving just in time for the main course. Waving off the server with his plate of chicken and keeping the salad that had been laid at my place, I offered up some lame excuse about getting stuck on a call and apologizing for my tardiness. I purposefully did not look for Con, but a fanciful part of me thought I could feel his eyes on me.

I went to pull out my chair, but Lucas beat me to it.

"Let me." I smiled up at him as he pushed it in while I sat. He had pretty manners, even though I had a feeling he didn't grow up in circumstances where they would have been emphasized.

I reached for my napkin and jumped when the woman to my left asked me to pass the salt and pepper.

"Is everything okay, Ms. Frost?" Lucas's voice was smooth and concerned.

"Yes, just fine. A little distracted from my... phone call. A million things to worry about with this... building project."

"Yes, I often have... calls... that are distracting. And you're very diligent if you're continuing to work well into the evening while you're here representing your family as well as the foundation."

"We all do what we have to do, I suppose. I'm sure you are no less diligent than I am." I turned to face him. He really was almost too handsome for words. Smooth, put together, a sheen of polish over his ambition-honed sharp edges.

"Indeed. I'm diligent in a great many things, Ms. Frost. One of which has been trying to get your attention since I joined the board, but I've failed miserably at it."

Well, that's awkward. And polite manners would dictate it not be discussed in this venue. "I'm sorry, I hadn't realized..."

"It's fine. If I'm going to be overlooked by a woman, I prefer it be by one as stunning as you. At least now I'm starting to understand why."

His tone had become less than complimentary at the end. I decided to ignore it, but Titan didn't take the hint.

"I had a call of my own take me away for a few minutes during our first course."

A feeling of dread pooled in my belly. *He couldn't have seen...* Heat burned at the back of my neck, and the field greens on my fork fluttered back to my plate.

"We both have the habit of working too much, then," I replied lightly.

Turning away, I intended to join the conversation of the woman seated on the other side of me in hopes Titan would just drop whatever point he was trying to make.

My attempt was fruitless. He placed a hand on my arm and leaned closer.

"So was it your relationship with Leahy that ended yours with Duchesne? Or was it your relationship ending with Duchesne that allowed Leahy to move in?"

I gave him my best *sugar wouldn't melt in my mouth* smile. "I'm sure I don't have the faintest idea what you're talking about."

His expression twisted into something predatory. "And I'm sure you do. Although I have to say I'm surprised; I wouldn't have thought you'd put your entire career on the line for a quick fuck in a coatroom."

All of the blood drained from my face. I straightened my shoulders, unwilling to show any other outward signs of distress.

"Does this conversation have a point? Or are you just trying to ruin my appetite."

"Oh, rest assured, I always have a point."

"Then I'll thank you to make it and move on, Mr. Titan. I'm finding your company is growing tedious."

His green eyes flashed, and he lowered his voice. "Would you find it less tedious if I took you into the coatroom for a second round?"

I embraced the burn of anger. I turned my head so I spoke directly into his ear. "You can go fuck yourself, Mr. Titan, and I don't give one good goddamn where you do it."

His grin stretched across his face as he leaned back. "I knew I liked you, Vanessa."

Stunned by the rapid change in his behavior, which only moments before had been downright crude, I refolded the napkin on my lap.

"The feeling isn't mutual," I clipped.

He chuckled and draped his arm over the back of my chair. "I wondered if you were truly the ice queen they call you behind your back."

I rolled my eyes. "It's not behind your back when you're well aware of the nickname."

"I think they've got it all wrong. I think you're more fire than ice. And I think that's why Leahy can't keep his eyes off of you... even now. He probably wants to break my arm."

My only response was to stab the field greens and dried cranberries on my plate.

"I've heard the rumors about your relationship with Duchesne and how it wasn't really a relationship at all."

At his abrupt change in subject, I lowered my fork and reached for my water glass, wishing it were wine. "This really isn't the proper time or the place for this conversation, Mr. Titan. In fact, I'm fairly certain there is no proper time or place for this conversation."

He eyed the remaining guests at our table. The dinner conversation around us was vibrant and loud, with the award recipients telling fascinating stories of life growing up on the other side of the proverbial tracks. As one of them was a boy from Con's gym, I would have much preferred to spend my meal hearing what he had to say, but Titan wasn't backing down. As a member of the board of directors, he had all of the leverage he needed to torpedo the future of my career. But he wanted something—that was clear. I just had no idea what it was, or whether I'd be able to deliver it in a way that extricated myself from this situation.

"Call me Lucas, please, Vanessa."

I took another sip of water. "I think I'll pass on that delightful invitation, Mr. Titan."

His smile faded, and I got a glimpse of the man who wasn't afraid to go toe-to-toe with Louisiana's toughest negotiators on unpopular positions. "I don't think so, Vanessa. In fact, I think you're going to be accompanying me when we leave so we can discuss exactly what I want from you."

"And I think you're crazy if you believe I'm going anywhere with you."

In an almost inaudible tone he said, "If you want to keep your fling with Leahy under wraps, you'll do exactly what I say."

"Why are you doing this?" I turned to stare him straight in the eye.

"Because I find that I need a service you can offer, and knowing what I know now, I doubt you'll do it willingly. But because of what I know now, you'll probably do it anyway."

I was fairly certain flames shot from my eyes.

Titan rolled his. "Not that, Vanessa. Spending too much time in the gutter has rubbed off on you already."

We sat in silence as those around us finished their meals and our plates were cleared. When Titan's name was called for his keynote address, he turned to me.

"Don't go running off. We have a date when I'm finished."

I gritted my teeth and stared longingly at the exits. Well, all but the one in Con's direction. I deliberately avoided looking that way. I didn't need to give Titan any more ammunition. Although it seemed he already had plenty.

As Titan gave his speech, I couldn't stop myself from trying to figure out what the hell he could possibly want from me. He made it clear it wasn't sex. But he also made it clear that it wasn't something I'd do willingly. True to his word, he kept it short, and ten minutes later he was rejoining me at the head table. The award-winners received their recognition from the executive director, and the event was officially over. I stood, desperate to get the hell out of the room, but Titan grabbed my elbow.

"This way, my dear." He led me toward the door, directly past where Con was speaking with the boy from his gym.

Con's expression darkened when he saw Titan's hand wrapped around my elbow, but I just smiled and placed my hand over it. I didn't want Con to think I was being manhandled, which I was, out the door. There was no telling what he'd do. I'd have to explain it later.

I stood next to Titan at the valet stand and waited while they brought around both of our cars.

He helped me into mine and told me to follow him to Emeril's Delmonico. Given the public nature of the location, I wasn't as uneasy as I would otherwise have been. But still, I really had no idea what I was walking into.

I caught a glimpse of Con striding toward the valet as I pulled away. His eyes were hot and hard.

I had a feeling my explanation had better be good, or this deal of ours would be over before it started.

Ten minutes later, I pulled up in front of another valet stand and handed off my keys. Titan once again took my arm, but didn't speak as he led me to the maître'd. A few words exchanged and we were ensconced in a private dining room. So much for thinking a public location would be safer. But I supposed this might be better if we were going to argue, and he was going fling around accusations about Con and me.

I declined when he offered me a glass of wine, but he filled it anyway, saying, "You're probably going to need it." I was finding his high-handed nature incredibly annoying.

I purposely didn't speak. I waited in sullen silence while he sat back and eyed me.

"Oh come on, Vanessa. That's a thousand dollar bottle of wine you're shunning."

"And you think that impresses me?"

His boyish grin was *almost* infectious. "I guess that's a no. I'll be taking notes, in case you're wondering."

"The only thing I'm wondering is what the hell you want."

He nodded and sipped his wine. "I think that's pretty simple. I want you."

"Well that's a problem, because I'm not interested."

"Right, because you're fucking the one guy who shouldn't have been allowed in that room tonight."

"You have no idea what you're talking about." Nor would I be filling him in.

"Maybe not, but I watched him haul you into that coat closet. If you didn't have something to hide, you wouldn't be sitting here right now."

"If you'd be so kind as to cut to the chase, I'd like to get home and get my beauty sleep."

"I kind of like it when you pull out that bitch tone on me."

"I don't give a damn what you like."

As though I'd flipped a switch, Lucas Titan's joking mood evaporated.

"All right, then. This is the deal: essentially, I need you to do for me what you were doing with Duchesne."

"I don't understand."

"I need access to the upper circles of New Orleans's society. For instance, the one your father orbits."

The reason I was sitting here became much clearer. "And you've managed to burn the bridges that would have let you get there on your own."

He lifted his wine glass as though toasting me. "You're not only beautiful, but smart."

"And you need this badly enough to blackmail me into helping you?"

He tsked at me. "Blackmail is such an ugly word, Vanessa. I prefer mutual assistance with repercussions for failure to deliver."

I narrowed my eyes. "You sound like a lawyer."

"Rest assured, I'm nothing but a simple engineer."

"I get the feeling there's nothing simple about you, Titan."

"And I already said you are as smart as you are beautiful."

"And if I agree? You'll, what? Forget you saw anything—even though I maintain you didn't see what you thought you did—and you won't intentionally destroy my chances at the executive director position?"

"Exactly."

Two deals in one night with two very different men. It was exhausting. I wanted to curl up in my bed and forget this night had ever happened.

"Then you better lay out exactly what you want from me, because if I don't agree to it up front, I'm not agreeing to it at all."

His lips curled into a mocking smile. "I really do like you, Vanessa."

"And like I said before, the feeling isn't mutual."

"Then you better be a hell of an actress, sweetheart. Because to hold up your end of the deal, you've gotta sell it."

"Wait, you want me to pretend to be your *girlfriend*?"

"Fiancée would probably be more effective, but girlfriend should do the trick. Like I said: what you did with Duchesne."

"I never pretended to be Simon's girlfriend. I just didn't correct assumptions."

"Fine. That'll work. For now. As long as you don't correct *anyone's* assumptions."

"You mean anyone we're introduced to at an event."

"No, Vanessa, I mean absolutely anyone. Including Con Leahy."

My heart knocked against my chest. "Why? What purpose could that possibly serve?"

"Because the minute you tell Leahy I'm blackmailing you, I'll never be seen or heard from again. And no one will ever find my body."

"You're not serious."

"Oh, honey, I don't joke about my own death. And if you think he wouldn't do it... well, then I suggest you might not know the man you're sleeping with all that well."

I almost screeched, "I'm not sleeping with him!" But suddenly I didn't want Titan to know a damn thing about my relationship with Con. He'd already assumed what he was going to assume, and my protestations would be met with deaf ears or outright disbelief.

"I really, really don't like you."

"Well, then that's just too damn bad, sugar."

"Don't call me sugar. Or honey. Or sweetheart. Or anything else."

He ignored me and pulled out his phone. "What's your email address? I'll send you the list of events I want to attend but haven't received invites to. I'm assuming you've already been invited to most, but if you haven't, I'm sure you can figure out a way to get invited. Just make certain you RSVP for a plus one. Don't list me by name on the RSVP unless you absolutely can't avoid it."

I studied him, wondering what his master plan was. "Why? Want to approach them on a sneak attack?"

"Something like that. Don't worry your pretty head about it."

"You have to know I'd never actually date a man who said things like that to me."

I wanted to smack the smirk right off his face. "I'm just trying to perfect my condescending Southern masculine attitude."

"Where the hell did you come from anyway?"

"That discussion is not on the agenda for this evening."

"I really, really dislike you."

"You're becoming repetitive, my dear. And you're excused. Watch for my email. And please keep me informed as you've confirmed our attendance for each event."

"Yes, sir, Mr. Titan, sir."

"Now, that I can live with."

I grabbed my clutch and rose.

"And don't forget to come up with a story for Mr. Leahy. I'd hate to have to explain what I saw to Archer."

"Thank you for the reminder. I assure you, it's unnecessary. And if you out me to Archer, you better believe I'll be accusing you of blackmail."

"Yes, my dear, but the difference is I'll still have a job regardless of any accusations you make."

I turned toward the door. "Asshole."

"That's Mr. Asshole to you, Vanessa."

vanessa

I got a text from Con at nine on Monday morning. It was terse. As I read it, my palms began to sweat.

C: This thing still on?

V: Yes.

C: Back door of Voodoo at noon. Park in the alley.

Three hours. I had no idea what I'd find when I got there. If the look on Con's face Saturday night was anything to go by, he was not impressed that I'd left with Lucas Titan's hand on my arm. Thank God I'd had my own car. Because how the hell would I have explained getting into a car with Titan?

I should have stipulated to Lucas that we'd be arriving separately at any and all events we attended together.

I'd gotten his email at approximately two o'clock on Sunday morning. It would appear the man didn't sleep much. I'd expected a huge list of events, and was surprised—and relieved—to see only a few. Two I'd already planned on attending, one I'd been invited to but had declined, and one other I had no idea how I was going to wrangle an invite, especially with a plus one. Titan better plan on paying our way, because that particular one cost thirty grand to attend as a couple.

I'd spent several hours lying in bed thinking about the various ways I could tell him to go to hell. And then several more playing out those scenarios. None of them ended well for me.

So I'd do what Titan asked. For now. Keep your enemies close and all. Once I had enough dirt on him, I'd use it to negotiate a way out of this mess.

I'd yet to figure out how to explain to my father why I was about to be seen all over town with Lucas Titan. Even if my father weren't at the events, he wouldn't be able to miss the pictures that were sure to show up in the society pages. Which meant that Con might see them too. I needed to come up with a believable story. Four coincidental meetings wouldn't fly. For the moment, my only plan was to hope that Con didn't read the society pages, and maybe I could put it off. The first event wasn't until Thursday evening, which meant I had less than four full days to come up with something else.

It was a bad plan, but it was the only one I had for the moment.

I was also a little concerned about how I was going to manage to do my job, secretly date Con, not-so-secretly 'date' Titan, and sleep. It appeared that sleep was certainly going to be the losing factor in this one. Which just made me more pissed at Titan. That man better get ready to use his checkbook, because several of the events he wanted to attend included silent auctions. You'd better believe that I was going to make sure those charities got their dollars for my pound of flesh.

This morning I'd gone out on a limb and contacted the demolition contractor. I'd told him that the misunderstanding about the deed had been cleared up, the demolition could go on as planned, and he'd have access to the buildings whenever he needed it. I still needed to discuss that part with Con. I'd made a similar 'oops we got confused about the deed thing, so no worries' call to the architect. I really, really hoped those calls weren't premature. But regardless, I couldn't put them off.

A sharp rap on the door pulled me out of my thoughts. Archer stood on the threshold.

I rose, pushing aside my to do list for the day.

"Archer, it's a pleasure to see you. What can I do for you?"

Archer was seventy-four years old, and he looked every day of it. His twenty-year-old suit hung from a frame so painfully frail it looked as though he might break if you touched him. He'd been that way as long as I could remember, and my mother had had the same Bennett build. It was one more reason why she'd despaired of my weight as a kid. She'd never understood how I'd managed to draw the Frost card out of that portion of the genetic lottery.

Archer's hair was a distant memory, but his grayed toupee was actually one of the better ones I'd seen. Regardless of his age or fashion sense, he was an amazing mentor and role model. I still remembered the first time he let me sit behind his desk when I was six years old. I think I'd known even then that this foundation was my future.

"Vanessa, how are you this morning?"

"Very well, sir."

"Good, good. I just wanted to check in and make sure everything was still on schedule for the project."

"Of course. And once the debris is hauled away after demolition, the groundbreaking will move forward, and we can kick off construction. We're still targeting an early completion, God-willing."

"Good, good. I had heard an offhand remark from someone that there might have been a hold up over some property concerns."

Where the hell had he heard that? Only the demolition guy and the architect had known. But then, Archer always knew more than one would think. Which meant that if I were going to keep whatever I was doing with Con a secret, I'd have to be vigilant.

"No, sir. No hold up," I replied.

"Excellent. Well, I'll let you get back to work. I'm in meetings with Herzog all week going over financials."

From the board meetings I was invited to attend, it was apparent that the foundation was on the cusp of hitting its budgeted numbers, but stress levels were always climbing this time of year. Extraordinary fundraising results would be required to keep us on pace. If we didn't hit our numbers, we could lose our prestigious position on the Top Fifty Most Influential Foundations list. It might sound like a silly ranking, but in the nonprofit world, it was a little bit like the U.S. News & World Report's rankings for grad schools. The higher your rank, the more likely you were to get donations and bequests and continue to grow. More donations and bequests meant we were able to fund more programs and help more people. The fact that the L.R. Bennett Foundation had been on that list since its inception was a point of pride for Archer, and I couldn't imagine him retiring without maintaining that status. Actually, if we slipped off the list, Archer would probably have a cardiac event and drop dead on the spot.

"Of course. If there's anything else I can take off your plate to clear your schedule, sir, please feel free to let me know."

"I appreciate that you're always willing to lend a hand. Thank you, Vanessa. You're a good girl. Your mother would be proud of you. We need to have lunch one of these days. There are some things we need to discuss as we get closer to December."

Unexpected tears pricked my eyes at the mention of my mother. I nodded in response, and cleared my throat. "You name the day, and I'll be there."

"Good, good. Well, off to deal with the numbers. We've got a big target to hit, and I know we can do it."

Archer tapped the doorframe twice before he left. It was the same move he'd made every time he'd left my office since I'd begun working there. It was a strange little comfort knowing that I could always count on those two taps as a period at the end of our conversation.

The next knock on my door was equally welcome—and a heck of a lot less stressful: Elle.

"Hey, hey, hey, girly. You got news for me or what?"

I jerked my head toward the door. "Close it, and I'll fill you in."

Elle pressed the door shut and strutted to my guest chair. "You did it, didn't you?"

"Why would you say that?"

"Because your shit isn't in a box, and Archer just bounced out of here like he'd discovered his hair had grown back. I know you, and if you hadn't figured this out yet, you would've caved and told him. So?"

"I did it."

"Hells yeah, baby. I knew you could." She planted her elbows on the desk and leaned forward. "Did you have to get on your knees and beg, if you know what I mean?"

I covered my face, the heat of a blush burning my cheeks. "No. No, I did not."

"Then how...?"

I looked at the clock. It was closing in on eleven, and it would take me fifteen or twenty minutes to get to Con's. Could I explain all of the craziness that had gone on last night in less than forty minutes? I guess I'd find out.

Elle's mouth was hanging open when I finished my rushed explanation.

"Holy mother of all things unholy. Are you flippin' kidding me?"

"Not even a little bit."

She blew out a breath. "I don't even know where to start. Except, wait. Yes I do. Let's turn Lucas Titan's dick into a weenie roast."

The visual flared to life in my mind. "Gross. Can you please not say things like that?"

Elle smirked and looked down at her watch. "You better get going, and I'll handle changing your plus one on the two invitations, change your RSVP on the other, and see what I can do to hunt down an invite to the last one. I'll just say I'm your social secretary, which is mostly true anyway. But you have to swear to fill me in on every little detail."

"I'm meeting him at noon; I doubt there are going to be any details worth hearing about."

"Sweetheart, you've clearly never had a *nooner* then."

I pushed away from my desk and stood. "True story. I better go."

She hugged me hard. "Give 'em hell, girl."

"Done."

"And don't let him bully you about Titan. You do exactly what we talked about."

"What did we talk about again?" Our conversation had been so rapid and filled with Elle asking about Con's dick size that I lost track of whether we actually came up with a solution for how to handle the Titan situation.

"You lie. That's what you gotta do."

"Glad we have a viable plan."

con

I checked my watch. 11:56. I had a feeling she'd be punctual, so I waited by the door like a chump and watched the seconds tick by.

Frustrated with myself, I ducked back into the break room and headed toward my desk. I forced myself to sit and study the new tat I was drawing. It wasn't for me—and not just because I didn't have much dermal real estate left to cover. It was a little too feminine. Charlie would probably love it, but I was reluctant to offer it to her. It wasn't really her style. Although maybe her style was changing now that she was getting more serious with Duchesne. I really hoped that girl knew what she was doing.

A knock on the back door of Voodoo interrupted my thoughts. Which was probably for the best, because Charlie's personal life was no longer any of my business except as a friend. Bittersweet maybe, but again, *for the best*. She'd never quite fascinated me like the woman knocking on my door—the woman I wanted to demand explanations from about why that slick son of a bitch had touched her like he'd had a right to. But I wouldn't. Instead, I beat back the urge to grab my tattoo gun and brand her with my name.

She wasn't mine.

And let's face it; she'd *never* be mine. I might get a few stolen hours here and there, but it could never be anything more. My choices had ensured that. So I'd live with them and jack off to the memories of Vanessa in my bed. First, I had to make those memories.

Last night I'd had to watch her on the arm of another preppy douchebag. I wasn't sure I'd be able to handle that again without drawing blood or breaking bones. I knew dozens of ways to kill a man with my bare hands, and I'd be happy to demonstrate on Lucas Titan if I ever saw him touch her again.

I pulled open the door, and the orangey-peach colored dress she was wearing cast my dark mood into the gutter. She reminded me of a Flintstone's push-pop I'd had as a kid, and I wanted to lick her from neck to knees.

"Can I come in?" Her question and hesitant smile almost had me stepping aside to let her in. But that wasn't the plan. And with this woman, if I didn't have a plan, everything would fall to shit in a hurry.

"No. We're going out. For lunch."

She froze. "I don't... I can't..."

Her stomach rumbled, breaking the awkward silence that followed her trailing words.

"You don't what?" I prompted. "Because it sounds to me like you're hungry."

Her hands clenched the fabric of her skirt before smoothing it, and her stomach growled again.

I crossed my arms and leaned one shoulder against the doorframe, daring her to refute the fact.

"Is this part of the 'be where I say, when I say,' stipulation?" she asked.

"Yes. And it's just fucking lunch. It's not like I'm telling you to strip and climb into my bed. Although, if you'd prefer..."

Her eyes flicked to the door just beyond me—the door that led up the stairs to my apartment above the shop.

I shoved off the doorframe, hot anger spreading through my veins. "You'd rather go upstairs and fuck than go out to lunch with me?"

She bit her lip and looked at the floor. "It's complicated."

"It's just lunch. How fucking complicated can it be?" And then it dawned on me. "If you're worried I'm going to take you somewhere we'll be recognized, don't be."

"It's not that."

"Then what?"

Her silence fueled my annoyance. Picking her up by the waist, I kicked the door shut, carried her over to my bike, and dropped her onto the seat. I ignored her sputtered protests and the skirt hiking up around her thighs as I strapped a helmet on her head.

"Wait—"

"Done waiting, princess."

I secured my own helmet and climbed on the bike.

"Just hold on."

vanessa

The man was a brute. Apparently no one had informed him that picking up a woman and moving her where he wanted her was passé. As in, men haven't done that since they stopped painting on cave walls.

Constantine Leahy had missed the memo.

When he tossed out the command to 'just hold on,' I'd stubbornly refused. For about three seconds.

As soon as he fired up the bike and revved the engine, my self-preservation instincts had overridden my pique. I wrapped my arms around Con's middle, and he rocketed away from Voodoo, the brick walls of the alley flying by. I buried my face against his back, certain I was going to die before we even made it onto an actual road.

With my eyes squeezed shut, I yelled over his shoulder, "What if someone sees me?"

The wind carried Con's laugh back to me. We slowed at a stoplight, and he turned his head to reply,

"Princess, *no one* would ever think *you* would get on the back of my bike. If anyone sees us, they'll just assume you're my newest piece of high class ass."

I opened my mouth to deliver some sort of scathing reply, but the light turned green, Con gunned the engine, and we were off again.

"Where are you taking me?" I yelled. The wind whipping the ends of my hair drowned out my words. Con ignored me, changing lanes and heading into an area of town where I'd be more than hesitant to venture alone.

He didn't stop again until we pulled up in front of a crumbling brick building. There was no sign, no awning, not even a flashing neon light announcing 'topless women' in sight. He booted down the kickstand, hopped off the bike, and unhooked his helmet.

He reached for me, and I flinched, unsure of what he was trying to do.

"Easy, princess. Just want to get your helmet off."

I relaxed as he unbuckled the strap and sat it on the seat.

He held out a hand, and I stared at it, eyes caught on the name tattooed on the inside of his wrist. *Joy.* His adoptive mother. She'd been a happy, vibrant woman. I'd heard that she and Andre had died holding hands. I glanced at Con's other wrist. Sure enough, *Andre* was written in black script. It seemed overly sentimental for the tough exterior Con exuded.

Which just highlighted how much I didn't know about this man.

The question was, did I want to know him?

I looked up at the brick building. I supposed the question I should really be asking myself right now was whether I trusted him enough to take his hand and follow him inside?

The heavy, humid June air pressed down on me as I sat, showing *way* too much leg, on the seat of his matte black Harley. The fact that I was sitting on the motorcycle told me that I trusted him. When he'd picked me up and sat me on it, he'd ignored my protests...but they'd been half-hearted at best. Because a part of me—the part that had made the decision to go home with him that night two years ago—already trusted him far more than I should.

I took his hand and swung my leg over the bike.

Instead of going through the front door, Con tugged me along around the side. He reached over a section of the wooden stockade fence and flicked a latch.

I glanced around nervously, looking for some indication that we were allowed to be here. The lack of "Beware of Dog" signs was heartening at least.

"Are we breaking and entering? Because I'm on my lunch hour. I don't really have time for jail at the moment."

"It'd be the parish prison, sweetheart." He pushed open the fence, and the mouthwatering aroma of barbeque connected with my olfactory receptors. "But either way, the only thing you need to worry about right now is whether you prefer ribs or chicken."

And then that mouthwatering aroma made me want to vomit. I grabbed his arm and squeezed my eyes shut. "I can't."

Con stopped, swung the gate back shut, and turned on me. "You need to quit telling me 'you can't' without any other kind of explanation. It really fucking pisses me off."

I wrapped my arms around my middle, and my mind raced for a good excuse. Something...anything but the truth.

Con's callused fingers tilted my chin up, and I was forced to meet his stare.

"Just fucking tell me what your deal is. Are you trying to be difficult? I know you can be a righteous bitch, but over ribs and chicken? Or is it me? Are you really so much better than me that you can't sit at the same table and share a meal?"

At that, something flashed in his eyes. I remembered the angry boy sitting alone at a lunch table in our prep school. The foster kid. The boy who solved every problem with his fists. The chip on his shoulder may have shrunk slightly, but the habit of lashing out at anyone who thought they were better than him hadn't completely disappeared.

"It's not you. I swear."

His eyes narrowed on me.

"Then what?"

I tugged my chin out of his grip and looked away. I couldn't look him in the eye when I confessed.

God. Why was I going to tell him? *Because I hate having him look at me and assume I'm a stuck up bitch who thinks she's better than him.*

The words came out in a big mumble.

"What? Was that Cajun? Because I didn't catch a word of it."

Once again his big hand lifted my chin. "I have issues with eating in front of people."

Confusion washed over his features, and his eyes turned hard. "That's a damn lie. And a stupid one."

My mouth would have dropped open if Con's hand wasn't holding it up. *Seriously? I finally share something incredibly personal and embarrassing with him, and I get...that?*

I shook my head and spun, stalking back toward the bike. I'd grab my purse out of the saddlebags and call a damn cab.

I didn't make it more than two steps before Con grabbed me by the arm and backed me up against the house.

"Now wait just a minute."

I struggled against his hold. "Let me go."

Con didn't loosen his grip. "I watched you eat while sitting next to that slick fucker, Titan. So don't lie to me."

"But that was a salad!"

The angry edge faded, and once again confusion reigned over his features. "What the fuck does salad have to do with anything?"

"Fat girls can eat salad in public without being judged. It's like a rule!"

"What?" Con reared his head back before staring down at me. "Princess, I don't know if you've looked in the mirror, but you ain't fat. You've got the kind of body a man wants to grab hold of and never let go."

I exhaled and dropped my head back. Before it could connect with the brick wall, Con's hand was there, protectively cupping it, bringing our bodies flush.

"Careful."

Our proximity made it nearly impossible to explain what I needed to, but I did it anyway. "Look, I was big as a kid, and my mother never let me forget it. She was a Nazi about everything I was allowed to eat. Other kids had moms who baked cookies; mine made sure I had seaweed crisps. Sure, it was all under the guise of being 'healthy,' but she was as much of a perfectionist as anyone you've ever met ... and I wasn't perfect. It didn't matter how many laps I ran, or how many 'healthy' diets she put me on, I was the chubby kid. Food became the enemy." I shuddered. "You don't understand what it's like to have someone judge you for what you put on your plate. Knowing that they're thinking *should she really be eating that at her size?* Hell, you know they're thinking it because you've *heard* them say it behind your back." I thought about the pizza incident at Madeline's birthday party, and...I took a deep breath and shared it with Con.

By the time I was finished, my heart slammed against my chest so hard, I was sure Con could feel it too. His brow was scrunched in confusion. "I've known you since you were, what? Sixteen? I don't remember any of this."

"Because I'd already hit my growth spurt by the time you came. By then, I'd become one of the 'popular' girls because my size was finally 'acceptable.' And if you think those girls didn't watch everything I put in my mouth, wondering if I'd get big again, you'd be dead wrong. Teenage girls are *mean*. I lived on Diet Coke and salad for all four years of high school."

Con tilted his head to the side, considering everything I'd just admitted. "It's been like fifteen years since then, and this stuff really still bothers you." It wasn't a question.

I dropped my eyes, staring at his chest as I tried to explain. "Those kinds of feelings don't just go away overnight because you grew five inches and magically all of the weight you were carrying was right for your frame. Hell, if they were burned into you the way they were burned into me, they might *never* go away." I looked up and met his eyes again. "Trust me, even after years of therapy, I'm still just coping. I'll never have an easy relationship with food, and when I'm around people I don't know or trust, it's pretty hard not to wonder if they're watching me—judging me—when I eat."

He lowered his head toward mine, and I could feel his breath on my skin. "Woman, the only things they're watching when they see you are those delicious tits and that luscious ass. If you think anyone's judging you, you're crazy."

"I'm not crazy," I whispered. "And don't call me woman."

His full lips stretched into a lazy smile. The awkwardness I expected to linger after my confession faded when Con said, "You're bossy. You know that?"

I was staring at the dimple in his cheek when I replied, "I'm not bossy; I'm just not a doormat."

His dimple deepened, "I didn't say bossy was a bad thing." He lowered his lips another fraction toward mine. "It's pretty fucking hot."

Holy shit. Con's going to kiss me. Sober. My eyes drifted closed.

A jingle of metal and the sound of wood slapping against wood caused us both to jerk backward, and I smacked my head against the wall.

I cringed, and Con swore. "Shit! Are you okay?"

Eyes firmly shut this time, I nodded. "I'm fine. Hard head."

A quiet chuckle washed over me, and Con's hand cradled the back of my head once more, massaging the bump. "Not surprising that you've got a hard head."

"You gonna kiss that girl, Constantine? 'Cuz if you ain't, you better get yourself to the table. My barbeque don't wait for no man. No woman, neither." My eyes darted toward the voice. A stout woman in a red 'Kiss the Cook' apron stood with her arms crossed. Her dark gaze didn't miss a thing.

Con glanced her way. "Give us a second, Mama Vee."

"Mmmhmmm. And a second'll be all you're gettin', boy, if you plannin' on eatin'." She retreated back inside the fence line.

"Who is...Mama Vee?" I whispered.

"*That* was Mama Vee. She's Jojo's gran—he's one of my boys. She invites me, and I come." He stepped back. "This eating thing...I get that it's a big deal for you. But I have to ask—are you going to be able to sit at her table and not insult her? Because if you can't eat in front of her, she's going to take it personally."

I opened my mouth to respond, but shut it again. I didn't know what to say to that.

"The only greens on that table are going to be drowned in butter."

Shit.

Rock, meet hard place. Also known as my insecurities versus my Southern manners. In my circles, it wasn't hard to eat only socially acceptable foods if I absolutely had to eat in public. Salads were on the menu at every event, restaurant, and dinner party. Mama Vee's menu...not so much. But Con hadn't made me feel self-conscious when I'd explained; he'd just listened and accepted what I'd said. It seemed that he wasn't going to judge me. I straightened. I could do this.

"I won't insult her."

Con reached down and grabbed my hand. "Thank you. Now come on, before she throws us out for being late."

con

I hadn't known what to expect when I'd brought Vanessa to Mama Vee's. I wouldn't lie and say it hadn't been a test. Because it had been. But by the end of lunch, I wasn't sure who was being tested.

Vanessa hadn't insulted Mama Vee. Not in the least. She'd been gracious. Charming. Engaging. There was no doubt that Vanessa would have an open invitation to return—with or without me.

Vanessa had opted for the rotisserie chicken, and the smear of BBQ sauce across her cheek reminded me of the strawberry jam I'd wanted to lick off her face in the kitchen of the gym.

And while I didn't pretend to completely understand her hang up with food, at least I had some sort of explanation for her behavior.

It was startling to learn that Vanessa's life hadn't always been as easy as I'd assumed. It was even harder to believe the perfect princess hadn't always been quite so perfect. I wondered how I'd never known. Probably because I'd kept to myself in school and had paid no mind to gossip of any kind.

Then Mama Vee surprised us both.

"Your mama would have loved seeing you all grown up like this," she said as I collected the plates and shoved them in the trashcan, and Vanessa gathered the condiments on a tray.

My attention fixed on Vanessa, who was flicking the edge of the ketchup label with her fingernail. Her eyes came up and met Mama Vee's.

"You knew my mother?"

Mama Vee nodded. "Before I had my own catering business, I spent a lot of years prepping in kitchens for other people. Your mama was a very particular woman."

Vanessa blinked and reached for the salt and pepper. "Yes, particular was a good word for her."

Mama Vee wiped her hands off on her apron and laid one over Vanessa's. "That little girl you were? She was a beautiful child. And the woman you are now? Is a credit to you. Not even your mama could find fault with that."

Vanessa squeezed her eyes shut, and I was afraid that tears would start spilling. Crying women were not something I knew how to deal with effectively. Man down and bleeding from shrapnel? That I could handle. Flying bullets and incoming mortar rounds? Bring 'em on. But a crying woman? Not so much.

But Vanessa didn't let the tears fall. She straightened her shoulders and looked Mama Vee in the eye. "Thank you."

"You look like you need a hug, child," Mama Vee whispered in her gravelly smoker's voice.

I figured Vanessa would just shrug it off, but she did something that surprised me even more than Mama Vee bringing up Vanessa's mother: she rounded the table and wrapped her arms around Mama Vee's neck.

Mama Vee hugged her right back, and I just stood and watched. Amazed.

It seemed that I'd judged Vanessa wrongly when I'd decided to label her a stuck up bitch without a heart. Because she very much had a heart, and I didn't know many stuck up bitches who would lower themselves to hug a woman clearly their social inferior. But I was seeing it.

I owed her an apology.

That feeling didn't last long.

I helped Vanessa off the bike in the small garage tucked behind Voodoo. I felt like I was looking at a completely different person than the one I'd helped climb on only an hour and a half ago. Taking her to Mama Vee's had peeled away a few layers and revealed things I hadn't expected. Vanessa Frost was more than met the eye. I wanted to keep peeling back those layers.

And her clothes.

I retrieved her purse from the saddlebag, and we stood beside her car in the alley. I wasn't ready to let her go back to her world quite yet. I liked having her in mine. A little too much. "You busy tomorrow night? I've got appointments until late, but I want to take you somewhere."

"I'd have to check my calendar. It's gotten really busy with everything going on these days."

I gritted my teeth. "Blowing me off already? I wouldn't recommend it." My words carried an edge I didn't even try to hide.

She blinked. "What are you talking about?"

"*I'd have to check my calendar* isn't giving me a shot, princess."

Hitching her purse higher on her shoulder, she stared me down. "Would you rather I agree and then blow you off later? I'm trying to be honest. If I'm supposed to trust you, then I guess you're going to have to trust me, too."

I crossed my arms and huffed out a laugh. "Guess you're right. But it's a little hard to trust someone who tried to sneak out of my bed so she wouldn't have to look me in the eye and admit we'd slept together."

As soon as the words were out, I wanted to snatch them back. Fuck. I hadn't meant to bring that up.

Instead of turning on her heel and climbing in her car, she followed my lead and crossed her arms over her chest. I tried not to notice the way her tits plumped up under that orange dress. Tried—and failed.

"You're the king of the one-night *hit it and quit it* program. It's rich that you're giving me hell about something you've probably done dozens of times." On a roll, she uncrossed her arms, stepped forward, and poked a finger into my chest. "The only reason it pisses you off—"

I didn't let her finish. I grabbed her hand and dragged her closer. "The only reason it pisses me off is because I wasn't done with you."

That shut her up. For about five seconds.

"That's not how I remember it, Constantine." The way she spat my name heated my blood.

I wrapped my other arm around her and pulled her flush against my body. I stared into those arctic blue eyes when I said, "I don't fucking care how you remember it, *Vanessa*. This time, we're not done until I say we're done."

Her delicate nostrils flared, and I smiled.

"You like it when I tell you how it's going to be. Don't you, princess?"

It was the kind of line I'd throw at a girl I'd just met if I wanted her to drop her panties at my feet. It was the wrong thing to say to Vanessa.

She struggled against my hold, shoving me away. "Let. Me. Go."

I squeezed her tighter until she stilled. "That's the problem. *I can't.* I've got nothing but blanks when I try to remember that night. It eats at me. Do you have any idea what it's like to know I've touched you and tasted you—and I don't remember any of it? It's fucking torture."

The sucker in me thought I could feel her heart hammering against my chest. For several minutes, she said nothing. I said nothing. The silence that stretched between us was heavy, but I didn't care because I had my arms wrapped around her, and she wasn't trying to pull away.

But she would.

A few more seconds passed before she said, "I have to get back to work."

I had to force myself to release her. She stepped back, looking a little unsteady on her heels. *Good.* I wanted her as affected as I was.

"I'll let you know—about tomorrow night. But then, we need to set some ground rules for...whatever this is." She gestured between us.

I didn't like the sound of that.

"I don't like rules."

"Too bad. I do."

"Clear your schedule for tomorrow night, and maybe we'll discuss your rules."

"Like I said, I'll let you know."

"Fine."

She turned away, and a thought occurred to me. I wrapped my hand around her elbow.

"If you're blowing me off tomorrow night, it better not be for Lucas Titan."

Her head jerked up. "Why would you say that?"

My eyes narrowed on her. "You got something going with him, too? He'd be right up your alley after Duchesne."

She tugged her arm out of my grip and dug into her purse. Keys in hand, she looked back up at me. "That part of my life is none of your business."

I closed the space between us, pinning her against the Mercedes before she could yank the door open.

"If you're planning on fucking him, then I consider it my business."

Her gasp was pure outrage, but I didn't care. She needed to understand something about me. My voice was low and harsh when I said, "I don't share. You better know that up front. You fuck Titan, and our deal is off."

She didn't turn, and she didn't reply.

"Look at me, Vanessa. Know that I'm goddamn serious right now. Don't you let him fucking touch you."

She spun, and her blue eyes could have frozen the Mississippi.

"I'm looking at you, Con, but you better hear me. I might have agreed to give you a shot, but I didn't agree to anything more. And if you *ever* speak to me like that again, you can live the rest of your life with the torture of not knowing, because you won't be touching me again."

"Then you'll be kissing your deed goodbye."

"If the only other option is sacrificing my self-respect, then so be it."

"Your self-respect isn't going to get your precious foundation's building built."

Her knee shot up and caught me unaware. I stumbled back a step, grunting, and bent over as the sick feeling in my gut twisted. "Fuck, woman. Did you have to crush my balls?"

She must have lowered her head because I could feel her breath on my ear when she spoke. "One, don't ever talk to me like that again. I'm a fucking lady. And two, don't make fun of my *precious* foundation. Oh, and three, I don't have any intention of fucking Lucas Titan, or you, for that matter."

I straightened halfway, in time to see her climb into the Mercedes.

If I hadn't been in so much pain, I might have smiled.

She's a fucking lady.

I might have gotten more than I'd bargained for with this deal.

vanessa

My sweaty hands clutched the wheel as I drove back to the office. I had no idea where that woman came from. You know, the one who kneed Con in the balls and then drove away while he was bent over and gasping.

Holy hell.

He was already rubbing off on me.

I lifted a hand to my mouth and smothered my laugh.

Had I really said, *"I'm a fucking lady?"*

Oh. My. God.

There was something seriously wrong with me. Because that... whatever that had been... was more excitement than I'd had in a *long, long* time. Yes. There was something seriously wrong with me.

When my heart finally calmed down, I thought about what had set off the whole reaction. Lucas Titan. Con was already wondering what the hell was going on, and there was nothing I could tell him that would make him back off. Elle's answer to lie wasn't sitting well with me. So I'd try Plan B: I'd evade.

Yeah. Like that will work for long.

I had a feeling Con was like a damn bloodhound.

My phone buzzed, and I glanced down. *Lucas.* Shit. I picked up on my hands-free system.

"This is Vanessa."

"Good afternoon, Ms. Frost."

"Mr. Titan. What can I do for you?"

"I'm calling to inquire whether you've been able to secure the invitations I emailed you about."

"I'm working on it."

"Excellent. In the meantime, I wanted to make sure you didn't run into any trouble with Mr. Leahy concerning our arrangement."

My blood froze, and for a split second, I wondered if Lucas Titan was having me followed because his question was eerie as hell.

"No. No trouble. And please don't concern yourself with my life, Mr. Titan. It's really not relevant to you or the... favor... you've asked of me."

"I'll concern myself with whatever I please, Vanessa. I wouldn't have gotten this far in life if I let people dictate to me."

Arrogant son of a bitch.

"Is there another point you'd like to make, Mr. Titan? Because I'm about to hang up."

"I do wish we had clicked on a more basic level. You and I could've had a hell of a lot more fun finding better uses for that sharp tongue of yours."

More like he'd find out how good I am with my knee.
Like Con had.

"Hanging up now."

"Wait—" he started. But I didn't. I'd had enough of men telling me what to do today and attempting to meddle in business that wasn't their concern. Screw them all.

A horn blared and dragged my attention back to where it needed to be: the road. A man in a white delivery van cut off the car in front of me, and I slammed on the brakes.

Men. Assholes. Every last one of them.

Elle had left a folder on my desk with confirmations for Lucas Titan's selected events.

She was a miracle worker.

I pulled up my calendar and saw it had been updated as well. My eyes immediately went to tomorrow night. It was empty.

I pulled out my phone before I lost my nerve or rediscovered my sanity and good sense. I had to retype the message three times before I got it right.

V: I'll see you tomorrow night. Name the time and place.

For any thirty-year-old woman, living with your father would likely be a less than ideal situation. But when your father was Royce Frost, it made things even more difficult. I didn't *want* to live at home. I'd planned to move in with friends after I'd finished grad school, which I could have *mostly* afforded on my meager salary, but my father had been diagnosed with prostate cancer. His oncologist had been the one to tell me that his living alone wasn't the best idea. My father had flatly refused a live-in nurse, and I'd caved under the guilt. So it'd been over five years, two scares of recurrence with the cancer, and I was still living at home, worried that if I moved out, he'd quit taking care of himself, and I'd lose the only parent I had left. He could be an asshole, to be sure, but having one parent was better than having none. At least in my opinion.

Royce Frost was a third generation steel baron, born into money and power. After my mother had passed, his entire focus had narrowed to increasing that money and power. Even derailed momentarily by cancer, it hadn't wavered.

I was just leaving the house to meet Con when my father was coming home from whatever event he'd attended that evening. As the CEO of one of the country's largest steel manufacturers, his social calendar was more complicated than mine.

"You better be headed out to meet up with Simon Duchesne at this hour of the night. Preferably to spend the night in his bed."

Oh, and did I mention that although he was part of the upper circles of society, he could be just as crude as the men who worked in the mill? And he also had to know by now that Simon and I weren't happening. But I guess if holding on to that hope kept him from finding a new man to foist off on me, then I'd let him keep hoping.

"Please tell me you did not just say that."

My father eyed my summer dress and cardigan.

"Where *are* you headed?"

I didn't answer. There was one rule I insisted on since the day I'd moved home: I didn't have to justify my comings and goings to him. We were both adults, and while he might be my father, he didn't get to meddle in my life. He might ignore the rule frequently, but I followed it religiously.

He shook his head. "Fine. Don't tell me." He pointed at me accusingly. "But no decent man is ever going to want to marry you if you're flouncing around town all hours of the night like some kind of tramp."

Still, I said nothing. He turned away and crossed to the center staircase. Pausing on the bottom step, he looked back at me.

"Just promise me you'll be careful. You're still my little girl." My heart panged in my chest. When he said things like that he sounded like an honest-to-God doting father. And what's more, I still felt the ridiculous need for his approval on some level.

"I promise."

⚜

I punched the address Con had given me into my GPS. Less than five miles away, but I didn't recognize it.

I followed the directions until I pulled up outside yet another warehouse type building. This one was rehabbed, and the lights and people all around made it feel safe—trendy, even.

I parked in the lot across the street in between a black Range Rover and a shiny red Corvette. It was certainly a higher-class place than I would have expected. What if I saw someone I knew while I was with Con?

What was he thinking?

He'd agreed this all had to be under the radar, so what was I doing here?

I crossed the street and followed a crowd up the stairs to the main entrance. Once inside the giant foyer, I was sucked into the crush of people. I pushed my way to the corner and pulled out my cell.

Another text from Con had appeared.

C: Take the elevator to the 7ᵗʰ floor.

Going on a date with Con was like going on a scavenger hunt. He doled out the clues one at a time, leaving me to guess at what the heck was going to happen next. For a woman with a carefully ordered, routine life, this was strangely... appealing.

I navigated the crowd to reach the elevator and took it up to the seventh floor. I exited into a lobby, and I could feel the music thumping from the club through the frosted glass doors to my right. My phone buzzed again.

C: Take the door to the roof.

Say what now?

I looked up and glanced around. Sure enough, there was a door marked 'Roof Access—No Admittance' in the left hand corner of the lobby.

I stood, unmoving for a moment, weighing my options. I jumped when my phone vibrated in my hand.

C: Trust me.

And I did.

I sucked in a deep breath as I pushed open the door of no return and saw a flight of stairs ahead of me. I climbed them and pushed through the next door with the same 'No Admittance' sign as the one below. I stepped out onto the roof and could see the lights of the city twinkling in every direction as I turned, surveying the view. The music from the club below pulsed all around me, as though someone had left the windows open.

"You came."

I spun, spying Con sitting on a ledge that surrounded the rooftop.

"I said I would."

"Thought you'd changed your mind when I told you to come up to the roof."

"I considered it."

"But you decided to go ahead and break the rules anyway?"

"Something like that."

Con pushed off the ledge and came toward me. The music from the club shifted into a slower, lazier beat, and I wondered what Con's plan was for tonight.

"So now that I'm here?" I twisted and looked out at the view. "What next?"

When I turned back toward Con, he was standing less than a foot away from me.

"What do you want next?"

That's a loaded question. My good manners dictated that I tackle the elephant in the room—or on the roof—first.

"I apologize for yesterday. I shouldn't have—"

Con held up a hand. "Don't. I deserved it."

"But—"

"It's water under the bridge."

I dropped my eyes to the tarred surface beneath my feet. "I can't believe I did that. I've never..." I let my words trail off because I wasn't sure what exactly I'd planned to say.

"Forget about it."

I looked up at Con, and the easy sincerity in his expression was diametrically opposed to the anger and frustration that I'd seen there yesterday. I couldn't help but tease him a little.

"I hope I didn't do any permanent damage. When I... ummm... crushed them."

His even, white teeth flashed with his smile. "You can say 'balls,' Van. It's not going to kill you."

I straightened. "Fine, how are your balls, Con?"

His grin widened. "How about you check for yourself?"

The laugh that escaped from my throat seemed to surprise us both. "I walked right into that one."

"Sure did, sweetheart." He shifted and thankfully dropped the subject. "Want a drink?"

"Wouldn't be unwelcome."

The giant neon sign perched on the edge of the roof glowed just brightly enough to illuminate the rooftop. "Beer okay? Or you need some Dom?"

I frowned. Every time, it was like one step forward, two steps back. "Are you ever going to lose that chip you're carrying around? It must be getting heavy after all of these years."

Con's grin faded, and I mentally kicked myself for being the cause.

Instead of getting pissed, he just asked me, "You ever not going to be a rich girl, Vanessa?"

It was an odd question. "I suppose it's possible that I could lose everything. But the likelihood of that is probably not very high."

"And am I ever going to be anyone but the foster kid Joy and Andre Leahy adopted?"

"I don't follow."

"We can't change who we've been and how it impacted who we became. So the short answer: that chip on my shoulder is probably there to stay, princess."

"So you're saying because I grew up rich and you didn't, at least initially, you're always going to resent that part of my life and the person I became because of it?"

He shrugged. "Guess we'll see."

"It'd be kind of disappointing if you did."

"That's life."

"On that note, I think I'll take that drink now."

Con laughed, and we both relaxed again. He crossed back to where he'd been sitting when I'd first come up and produced two bottles of Abita from a bucket of ice. He popped off the tops and offered me one.

I grabbed it and lifted it in his direction. "Cheers."

"Likewise."

I took a sip and absorbed the cool, malty flavor before breaking the silence that had settled.

"I know we said we were moving on, but I'm still shocked you wanted to see me again after yesterday," I said.

"Not as surprised as I was when you texted me."

I covered my face with my hand, peeking out between my spread fingers. "I'm clearly insane."

"Insane enough to agree to a favor?"

Dropping my hand, I raised an eyebrow. *This should be good.*

"I need you to go shopping with me."

I almost choked on my beer. "Shopping? With you?"

My belly flipped at his crooked grin. "Trust me, it's not something I want to do alone. I have four boys competing in a big boxing tournament in a couple weeks, and in order to make them feel professional, and to take this all more seriously, I want them dressed up on the way to the tourney. Like the pro athletes do. Wearing a suit on game day. You know what I mean?"

I pictured the boy from the dinner and the others I'd seen training in the gym. These kids were important to him. Now it was my heart that fluttered. He might have more baggage than a cargo hold, and that chip on his shoulder might never go away, but Con Leahy was a good man, with a good heart. "I think it's a great idea." I stared up at him. "I'd be happy to help."

"Cool. I'll let you know when and where," he said, taking a swig from his beer.

"Is that all? Because this seems pretty elaborate just to ask me a favor."

Con laughed and scrubbed a hand through his shaggy hair. "Figured it was a place you'd probably never been before."

"You'd be right about that."

I lifted my beer for another drink, but Con plucked it from my hand. "Wait."

My empty hand hung in mid-air. "Uh. What?"

Con set both of our bottles down, and asked, "Do you trust me?"

I thought about our last encounter. "Should I?"

"Probably not."

He reached out, brushing my hair over my shoulder. "What are you—?"

"I want to kiss you while we're both sober."

My mouth dropped open, and Con wasted no time lowering his head and capturing my lips.

His lips were firm but smooth, and they worked over my own, daring me to open to him. His tongue teased, and I couldn't help but let him inside. He tasted of the same beer I'd been drinking, but when mixed with Con, it took on a completely new kaleidoscope of flavors. I never really thought I'd have another chance to feel his mouth on me, and now that I did, I knew it was the worst idea I'd ever had.

I pulled back, stepping away from him. "I can't. I'm sorry."

I turned and headed for the door. I reached it, my shaky hands tugging at the handle. It didn't budge. *Dammit.* Locked.

From a few feet away, Con asked, "You want to know if I'm always going to be carrying that goddamn chip on my shoulder? Doesn't help that you're always running away from me like you can't believe you got caught with your pants down with the lawn boy."

"It's not you—"

"You've said that. *It's not me*. Well, I'm the only other person up here, so if it's not me, then who the hell is it you're running from?"

"Me! Don't you get it? It's not always about you! This is all too much."

"So that's it?" Con's harsh breaths became louder as he inched closer. "Then why did you even agree to give me a shot?"

I rested my palms and my forehead against the cool metal of the door. My next words were so quiet that if Con hadn't positioned himself beside me, there was no way he would've caught them.

"That night was... a huge deal for me. It was one of the first times I'd ever just... *jumped*. I didn't look first. I didn't think about all of the potential outcomes. I just went for it. I mean, the booze helped, but there was something pushing me to follow you anywhere you wanted to take me."

I craned my head to look at him. His rugged features were dimly lit by the glow, but it was impossible to miss his eyes drilling into me.

I continued, "There's something about you that makes me do things without thinking them through. It's like you're this crazy catalyst that gives me the courage to just... jump. That's why I'm here. That's why I agreed to give you a shot. But when you kiss me, instead of all my thoughts flying away, they come rushing back. That's when I remember all of the reasons this is a bad idea that's going to blow up in my face."

Con leaned against the door beside me. "Damn. That hurts, Van."

I blinked in confusion. "What? What hurts?"

"That you can still think when I kiss you. Means I'm not doing a very good job." He reached out and trailed a finger along the strap of my dress that had been revealed by the cardigan falling off my shoulder.

"Of everything I said, that's the part you care about the most?" I would have been lying if I'd said I wasn't disappointed.

"No." He shook his head, tugging on the strap. "I care about every damn word that comes out of that mouth of yours. I'm still digesting the rest. Might take me a while to figure out how to respond to those. But the part about thinking while I kiss you—that I can do something about right now."

Con released the strap. I twisted so my back was against the door, and Con followed my movements until we were toe-to-toe. He pressed a hand to the door on either side of my head and leaned closer before adding, "Unless you want to go."

With the cool metal against my back, Con's heat at my front, and the heavy summer air all around us, I considered my options. Despite my above-average height, Con still topped me by a good five inches. I felt small standing in front of him. Feminine. Delicate.

"So?" He dropped one hand, dug in his pocket, and produced a key. The shiny silver metal caught and reflected the light. "Stay or go?"

Did I want his lips on mine again? If he could silence the racing thoughts, and allow me to simply enjoy the moment and not worry about the consequences? God help me, but I knew the answer to that.

"Stay," I whispered.

His eyes flashed, and the key disappeared from sight.

"Then stop," he said.

"Stop what?"

"Thinking."

If only it were that easy. "You can't just order me to and expect it to happen."

With the same hand that had produced the key, he flicked at the edge of my cardigan. It slipped down my arm and caught on my hand.

Con's mouth dipped and followed the path from my shoulder, his lips and tongue tracing my collarbone, stopping to tilt my head up and kiss a line up my neck to my chin. He ghosted past my lips and followed my jawline up to my ear. He paused and whispered, "Did you stop?"

"What?" I breathed, dying for him to continue his lazy journey.

"Good girl."

I coughed out a small laugh when I realized that I had indeed stopped thinking. At least stopped thinking beyond where Con's lips and tongue would touch me next.

I smiled, and that was when he finally *kissed* me.

His lips took mine. One hand held my jaw, tilting my head back, and the other hand dropped from the door to grip my hip, holding me against him. I moaned as he angled my head to fit his mouth against mine, tongue diving inside, dueling with mine. My hands couldn't be still, they needed to touch, to participate. I shook off the other shoulder of my cardigan and let it drop before I reached up and buried my fingers in his shaggy blond hair. Con groaned and his hand moved to my ass, gripping it, kneading it, and pulling me in against him.

The hard ridge of his erection pressed against my stomach, and I shifted closer, wanting to feel more. Wanting to feel everything.

Con released my lips, before skimming along my jaw, to my ear, and then down my neck. Almost an inverse of the path he'd taken before—and this one didn't allow for thinking either. When he nipped along my collarbone, the strap of my dress slipped down my arm. I expected him to seize the advantage and brush the other strap away, but instead he pulled it back into place and stepped away.

His chest heaved, and my breathing was just as unsteady. I sagged back against the door.

"Why'd you stop?"

"I gotta know you want this too. Need to hear you say it. I don't want to watch you run from me again because you decide this is more than you can handle." His tone was edged with raw honesty.

My brain had finally kick-started back into reality. All the thinking was back.

"What if I say no? Then where do we stand?" I asked.

He jammed his hands in his pockets. "I guess we go our separate ways."

"What about our deal?" I pressed.

Con hung his head, and his chuckle was humorless. "Guess that would mean I got my shot and blew it."

"You'd still give me the deed?"

He jerked his head up, his eyes pinning me in place. He opened his mouth to respond, but I reached out and pressed three fingers to his lips. "Don't answer that. I don't want to know. I don't need to know." I took a deep breath. "Because I'm not saying no. I'm saying yes. I want this."

Con released a long breath, and the giddiness I felt at his relief quelled the feeling that I'd just made a decision that would impact the rest of my life.

I dropped my fingers from his lips, and he caught my hand and pressed a kiss to the center of my palm. It wasn't the kind of gesture you'd expect from Con, but having seen him at his smoothest once before, it didn't throw me.

"So you're willing to jump without looking again?"

Staring up into his fallen angel face, I knew I didn't have a choice.

"Yes."

con

The back booth of Tassel was supposed to be my information trafficking hot spot, and most nights when I left Voodoo and dragged my ass over here, it was. But tonight it had turned into something else completely—a place for too goddamn much introspection. After Vanessa and I had left the rooftop—separately—I hadn't wanted to go home to my empty bed. So here I was.

What the fuck am I doing?

She wasn't for me. I'd drag her into the gutter and dirty her pristine, lily-white reputation—and her life.

I stared down at my hands. One flat on the table and the other wrapped around a double shot of Wild Turkey.

Those hands had no business touching a woman like Vanessa.

I lifted the glass and sucked down the bourbon.

Not even liquor could burn away my need to bury my hands in her hair, slide them up and down her silky-smooth legs while I spread them wide and feasted on what my imagination had decided was the sweetest pussy I'd ever tasted.

I smacked the glass back down on the table. Drinking surely wasn't going to help. If I hadn't been so wasted that night, I wouldn't have spent the last two years wondering if my imagination was right.

Those kinds of thoughts could wreck a man.

A dancer—a new girl—with dark skin, golden brown eyes, and velvety black curls sat down in the booth across from me. Normally, if a girl was going to attempt to get my attention, she made herself right at home on my lap. Not that it'd do any good lately, because unless you were a smoking hot society princess, my dick wasn't having it. But still, this chick wasn't even trying, which had my radar pinging.

If the girls were allowed to drink on shift, I would've offered to share, but given that I'd already ordered a half dozen or so to be fired for the offense, it didn't seem quite fair.

"Can I help you?" I asked.

It was late, and I was ready to head home and escape from thoughts of Vanessa.

"Heard you're looking for information."

Her long eyelashes were fake and tipped with gold glitter, and she fixed her gaze on the table.

"I might be," I replied.

The gold tassels hanging off her tits barely covered her wide nipples. She looked to be all of about twenty years old. I felt like an old man sitting across from her.

"What's your name?"

She looked up, clearly surprised by my question. "Gold Dust."

I shook my head. "Your real name."

She sat up straighter, eyes darting up to mine and then back down again. "Gina. Gina Mulvado."

"How long you been stripping, Gina?"

"Just had my three year anniversary last week."

"So you're...what? Twenty-one? Twenty-two?"

"Twenty-one. Last week."

The numbers lined up. "Started stripping when you were eighteen?"

One side of her mouth quirked up in a mocking smile. "As soon as they'd let me in the door."

"Why?"

She finally met my eyes. "Why not? I got bills to pay. Ain't like I got any other skills that'll make me this much money, at least not without fucking and sucking my way across town."

"That shit don't fly here." That was my policy, but it wasn't like I had time to personally police it. My manager was on the up and up, and that was the best I could do. But I didn't want girls using my place as a hook up for picking up Johns. It left a bad taste in my mouth.

"I know, and that's why I like it here." She tucked a dark lock of hair behind her ear. "So I heard you pay for information."

"True." And paying for information drew all sorts of attention my way. And some of that attention—especially from the gang bangers, ex-cons, garden-variety lowlifes—I'd never want spilling over onto Vanessa. Which is why keeping our relationship on the down-low was advisable on several fronts.

"Pay good?" she asked.

I surveyed her. "More than you'll earn tonight otherwise."

She nodded. "I used to work at a club on the other side of town, and there used to be this guy who'd come in for a dance once a week. He was always broke. We joked about having to dodge the quarters he tossed on stage because he could barely scrounge together a damn dollar."

I rolled my shot glass back and forth between my thumb and forefinger, wondering where this was going.

"Well, one night he came in flush with cash. He went from digging in the cushions for loose change to tossing twenties on the stage and tipping fifty for a dance. He was drunk as hell, and rambling on and on about it being blood money for the little blood-sucking whores."

I reached for the bottle of Wild Turkey and sloshed another three fingers into my glass as she continued.

"The girls started getting nervous, with all the cash flying around and his crazy ass comments, so we did some checking after he left."

I swallowed a gulp, savoring the burn.

"When was this?"

"The night some rich white folks were murdered. I didn't know...didn't realize they were your folks until I started working here."

I squeezed my eyes shut and gripped the glass so hard it'd shatter if I didn't relax.

I felt a soft hand on my arm, and I forced myself to calm. "You get a name?"

Her voice was whisper soft when she said, "He gave me a hundred dollar tip after my dance. Told me it was a Benjamin from Black Ben himself. He also said that if more white folks wanted to off white folks, the world might be a better place. I thought that was real weird. Never forgot that part."

Black Ben. A name to run down. But it was the last part that threw me.

She started to slide out of the booth, but I grabbed her wrist. "You're telling me he said he was working on the orders of a white guy?"

She stilled, eyes dark and full of sadness. "He didn't say anything for sure. Just ramblings of a drunk guy looking to rub up against a tight ass and fake tits."

"You ever see that guy again? Black Ben?"

She shook her head. "Nah."

I released my hold and reached for my wallet. Peeling off a stack of hundreds, I slid them across the table.

I needed to process the information. It didn't make sense. I was missing something.

Gina scooted out of the booth, folded the bills, and shoved them in the waistband of her thong.

"Wish I knew more."

"Thank you. This is...helpful."

As I watched her strut away, I knew a call to my boy was in order. I didn't understand how this fit with the gangbangers my buddies and I had tangled with when we were on leave. But it had to be connected somehow. Nothing else made sense.

Updating the cop on the cold case wouldn't help. They'd listened to my theory early on, and they'd found "no connection between the two incidents." Those empty words hadn't smothered the guilt rising up from my gut to suffocate me.

It'd been over three years and still the guilt hadn't abated. Which is why I sat in this back booth and paid girls like Gina for information. And anyone else who had a lead I could follow.

After Joy and Andre's funeral, I'd gone back to service and finished out the remainder of my commitment. Instead of doing my twenty like I'd planned, I'd separated and made my way home. I'd bought Voodoo first, then Chains, my pawnshop, and most recently, Tassel.

Lord, the manager of Chains, helped Reggie and me out with the boys. But more than that, he ran a tight ship and kept his ear to the ground. I rarely had to set foot in the store, but I got the benefit of the information he gleaned off customers and the cash flow.

I'd chased down more leads and had my Army intelligence buddies misappropriate more government resources than I could count. Every damn time we ended up in the same place: a dead end.

And now I had a name from Gina "Gold Dust" Mulvado. *Black Ben.*

The hairs on the back of my neck rose like a dog sensing trouble. There was a whole hell of a lot more going on here than I thought.

I palmed my phone and found the contact I wanted. It only rang once.

"Lord."

"I got another lead."

vanessa

I'd replayed those moments on the rooftop over and over. And Con's words.

Sitting at my desk, at work, was not the appropriate place to be remembering. The stack of bids in front of me needed my attention. But reading about interior finishes for the new building paled in comparison to remembering what it had felt like to kiss Constantine Leahy while we were both sober. The few sips of beer didn't count in my book—except for how good it'd tasted on Con's tongue.

"If the scenery in my office was this good, I'd probably never leave."

Those words were more effective than a bucket of cold water. All thoughts of Con were dashed away as Lucas Titan smiled broadly and stepped inside, shutting the door behind him.

"Surprised you ever leave your office at all to begin with, Mr. Titan."

"Board meeting for my favorite foundation qualifies as a good reason."

Crap. How could I forget the meeting—one I was scheduled to attend—this afternoon?

He crossed the room to one of my guest chairs, unbuttoned the jacket of his three-piece suit, and took a seat without being invited.

"Make yourself comfortable," I mumbled.

"Don't mind if I do."

For a moment I was surprised he didn't just kick his heels up on the edge of my desk. Instead, he rested his elbows on his knees and leaned forward.

"I expected a progress report."

"And I expected to leave the banquet without being blackmailed. Guess we both have to live with disappointment."

"I like your style, Frost."

"Don't bother trying to charm me, *Titan*. I'm not interested."

"You know saying something like that is just going to make me want to try harder."

I surveyed him. Pale gray suit, crisp white shirt, orange and navy plaid tie. "I think you're smart enough to know when investing your time in something is going to give you a dismal return."

His grin flashed white and boyish. There was no denying it; the man was attractive. And I *should* have been attracted to him. He was arguably my type, but he just didn't... do it for me. My senses should have been revving, but all I could think was that I wanted him out of my office *now*.

I considered all the ways I could tell him to go to hell, but bit my tongue because I didn't want to antagonize a man who could let one little thing slip and call my judgment and ability to lead into question.

"Can I help you, Mr. Titan?"

"I thought I told you to call me Lucas."

"I'd prefer not to."

He sat up and grabbed the house-shaped stress ball on my desk. He threw it in the air, not looking away from me as he caught it.

"Stressed, Vanessa?"

"What do you want?" I bit out.

He switched to tossing the house back and forth between his spread hands.

"So you got all the invites?"

"Yes."

"And you didn't feel the need to inform me?" he asked.

"Apparently not."

Silence stretched between us as the stare down continued.

I broke first. I looked down at my desk, shuffled some papers, and lined up the pens in a neat row.

He didn't speak—just kept flinging the house back and forth until I wanted to bat it out of the air like a pissed off cat.

He was baiting me, but I wasn't sure why.

I smoothed on my most businesslike *don't screw with me* frown. "Is there anything else, Mr. Titan? If not, I'd like to refresh my coffee and get to the board room."

"You've still got at least fourteen minutes before the first board member, excluding me, will arrive." He didn't even look at his watch.

"How in the world do you know that?"

"I study things. People. Habits. Reactions."

"That's not creepy at all," I mumbled.

His lips quirked to the left. "But I'll admit: I don't quite get you." He leaned back in the chair, lifting the front legs off the ground and balancing, the way the nuns scolded us for at school. "I would've bet good money that a guy like Con Leahy was a no-go zone for the perfect Ms. Frost."

I pushed down on my desk, bolting to my feet.

"I'm not having this conversation with you."

"Sit your ass down, Vanessa."

My mouth dropped open. "What did you—?"

The green of his eyes seemed to freeze. "You heard me. This conversation isn't over until *I* say it's over."

"Fuck you, Titan."

This time his smile bared teeth. "If you talked like that more often, I'd have been a hell of a lot less surprised when he dragged you into that coat room." He shifted forward and the chair landed on its front legs with a *thud*. I glared, hoping my eyes were just as frosty as his.

"I'd think you'd be happy about it, considering it played right into your plans."

Titan pushed out of the chair and loomed over my desk—and me.

"Honestly, it really didn't. Kind of fucked up my plans, if you want to know the truth, Vanessa."

I didn't understand, and my confusion must have shown in my drawn brows because Titan continued, "You see, he stole my play. Although I hadn't planned on dragging you into a coat room, but if I'd known you liked that sort of thing... I could have worked it in."

His meaning crystallized in an instant.

"You were going to try to seduce me? To help you?"

He laughed, and as much as I hated to admit it, his chuckle was a good one—although it should have sounded evil given the conversation we were having. "Sweetheart, I don't have to *try* to seduce women."

I shook my head and grabbed my note pad and a pen. "Whatever you say, Mr. Titan. I'm leaving. Please feel free to stay and enjoy the comforts of my office until the meeting begins. Although I'd prefer you didn't."

He stood, dropping the stress ball on my desk, and followed me toward the door. "So polite. You think those manners are going to be able to keep Leahy in line? Because there's still time to toss him aside and fall in line with my original plan."

Somehow his hand had found its way to the doorframe, and he was close enough to me that I could feel the heat of him on my back.

And once again, that was all I felt. No flare of attraction. No rush of excitement.

The logical side of my brain said that my life would probably be easier if I wanted someone like Titan. He might raise eyebrows in certain circles, but he wasn't *persona non grata* without any hope of reversing that status.

But logic wasn't ruling whatever I was getting into with Con—and that fact was scary as hell.

I wobbled on my heels, and Titan steadied me.

"Whoa. You okay?"

Am I okay? Do I want to be okay? Or do I want to be off balance and recklessly, foolishly not okay?

Clearing my throat, I grasped the door handle. "I think we're done here, Mr. Titan. I'll see you in the board room."

This time he didn't protest. Rather, he stepped back and allowed me to pull open the door and make my escape.

But for the first time in a long time, I didn't feel like I was running from something. I was finally running *to* something.

con

I was officially too old for this shit.

After finishing my last tat, I'd been ready to head up to my place and call it a night. *Alone.*

But instead, my manager had called in with a family emergency, and now I was sitting in the office at Tassel, wondering why in the hell I'd thought buying a strip club would be worth the trouble. I reminded myself that the best lead I'd had in over a year had come out of this place. But that didn't mean it wasn't turning into a giant fucking pain in my ass.

"That was my shit, and she wore it on stage without asking! I want half her tips from that set, because we all know her skanky ass wouldn't have brought in nearly as much if it hadn't been for *my* glitter G-string!"

What. The. Fuck.

"Bitch! Don't you dare—"

"Both of you, shut it down," I barked. Five minutes of this bickering was giving me a fucking headache. "Get the fuck out my office and back on the goddamn stage for your sets."

I looked at Ginger, or whatever the fuck the redhead's name was. "Keep your mitts off the other girls' shit. And if I have to deal with this crap again, you're both out on your asses."

"That's not fair—" Glitter G-string started.

"Out. Now."

They both turned and marched their mostly-naked asses toward the door. My dick didn't even perk up and take notice.

I rested my elbows on my desk and dropped my pounding head into my hands. I had to find an assistant manager and quick. I did not want to be handling bullshit like this—ever again.

I dug my thumbs into my temples and rubbed. The pressure receded slightly, and a cold, hard fact slid into place: The reason my dick hadn't perked up at the ass-tastic display I'd just witnessed was because there was only one ass I wanted to see.

Totally pussy whipped, and I don't even remember tasting that pussy.

I cringed at the knock on the door. This interruption had better not involve glitter G-strings.

I pushed up from the desk, and one of my bouncers popped his head in.

"Need you out front, boss. Got a brawl."

Other than the furniture that might get busted up, and the tips the girls were losing, the idea of a fight didn't piss me off too bad.

I would *never* be too old for cracking skulls together. A little bloodshed never hurt anyone.

Until I stepped into the main room and caught a flash of a blond head ducking behind the bar.

No way. She wouldn't be stupid enough to come here.

A chair swung toward my head. Any answers would have to wait.

I bobbed and weaved, letting the chair fly over my shoulder and coming up to land two solid jabs and an uppercut that put the asshole on the ground and the chair skidding across the carpet. I stepped toward the bar, but halted when a huge motherfucker downed Nick, the biggest of my bouncers, and rushed toward the two girls cowering on the edge of the stage.

"Watch out!" The words and the voice grabbed my attention, and I glanced over my shoulder. A skinny fuck with a broken beer bottle swung it at me and missed. He blanched when I charged him. Grabbing him by the upper arms, I tossed him aside. The crunch as he hit the floor would have been satisfying, except I didn't have any time to enjoy it. Another jackass was heading toward the bar—where my little society princess was hiding. I dodged fists and elbows as I crossed the room.

I reached the jackass before he could zero in on his target. All it took was a single hit to the jaw, and he crumpled to the ground. I jumped over the edge of the bar, uncertain of what I would find behind it.

vanessa

"What the fuck are you doing here?" Con landed on his feet in a crouch. His voice was hoarse, and his chest heaved with exertion. From what I'd seen, he'd taken on about a half dozen really unfriendly looking guys, all by himself.

My eyes must have been the size of dinner plates. What I'd just witnessed was so far out of the realm of my experience I didn't even know how to begin to process it.

It hadn't even been a bar fight. I'd witnessed a *strip club fight.*

When I didn't answer, Con gripped my arm and shook it.

"Vanessa, what the fuck are you doing here?"

The adrenaline that had been pumping through my veins began to dissipate. Con's hold relaxed, and his equally horrified and pissed off expression faded.

"Jesus Christ, you're shaking," he said.

I blinked several times before staring down at my arm. Con's wide fingers were wrapped around it, his thumb skimming back and forth over the vein at my wrist.

I didn't know what to say, but I opened my mouth anyway, and words tumbled out. "Are you okay? Are you hurt?" My voice trembled and had never sounded quite so small. I cleared my throat and tried again, "Are—"

Con's head lifted as the sound of sirens filled the air.

"Shit. Time to go."

He twined an arm around my shoulders and under my knees, lifting me off the ground as if I weighed nothing—which was certainly not the case.

"I can walk. Put me down." I struggled in his arms, but he didn't slow his stride as he crossed the room.

He jerked his head to one of the bouncers and paused at the threshold to a hallway. "You got this?"

"Yeah. No worries, boss."

"Make sure Hennessy gets the report. I'll catch up with him later." Con looked down at me. "I got more important things to worry about right now."

The bouncer may have smiled, or frowned, or burst into flames for all I knew. Because I didn't want to break Con's stare to check.

"Sure thing, boss."

Con finally looked away and headed into the dimly lit passage.

"Where's your car?"

"I took a cab."

"So you did at least one smart thing tonight."

He shouldered open a door, and the humid night air hit my skin. A single bulb was mounted on the brick wall next to the exit, and the yellow glow glinted off the chrome of Con's Harley. He settled me on the bike and strapped a helmet to my head. It didn't occur to me to ask where we were going—because I'd already made my choice tonight when I'd walked out of the house and hopped into a cab waiting at the corner.

Con took his place in front of me and started the bike.

I wrapped my arms around his waist even before he tossed the words "hold on" over his shoulder.

Pressing my cheek against the soft cotton stretched over the hard muscles of his back, I let the vibrations of the bike calm my still-racing heart and focused on the lights rushing past me. When we didn't head toward Voodoo and Con's apartment, but away from downtown, I should have been worried. I should have smacked his arm and demanded he tell me where we were going. But I didn't. I just held on tighter, closed my eyes, and enjoyed the ride.

Because that was exactly what I'd decided to do with Con. Grab hold of this craziness and let myself enjoy life for once without worrying about every which way it could go wrong.

With the exception of following Con home that night two years ago, I'd never stepped off the carefully planned path that was my life. I'd never thrown caution to the wind. Thirty years old, and I'd never done anything else remotely spontaneous and wild. I felt like the clock was ticking—the proverbial sand trickling through the hourglass—and I was letting my life pass me by without doing anything memorable. My greatest fear was waking up, ninety years old, swathed in my lace nightgown, waiting to die and regretting that I hadn't lived every moment of this life to its fullest.

So right now, when it was the absolute worst time for me to even consider straying from my regimented life—when I had the most to lose—I felt this insane compulsion to take a risk. *To jump.*

My arms were wrapped around the sole reason for that irresistible insanity.

I did the math in my head. *Yep, there's a strong chance that this is a mid-third life crisis.*

When I finally opened my eyes again, my confusion levels hit the red zone. *Why would we be here?*

Con turned down the driveway of a house that wouldn't have been amiss in the duPont Registry.

Solar lights highlighted six square columns fronting a wide covered porch that split into two giant curving staircases.

Con pulled the bike between two of the many stilts holding the massive house aloft and killed the engine. Settling it on the kickstand, he climbed off and removed his helmet. I got caught up in watching him and forgot that I should've been attending to my own. Not bothering to wait for me to get with the program, once again, Con undid the chinstrap and set it on the seat.

He held out a hand. I didn't hesitate to take it. I expected him to pull me along behind him, up the stairs and into the house. But he didn't. He swung me back up into his arms and walked farther under the house until we came out the other side, facing Lake Pontchartrain. He didn't slow as he walked down the dock to a pavilion and settled me on a wooden Adirondack chair. He hit a switch and tiny twinkle lights came to life.

"Shit. Should've taken you inside where we had more light. Need to make sure you're not hurt."

"I'm not hurt. I'm fine. Just...a little shaken up, I guess."

Con's posture changed immediately. "Good, then I don't need to hold back when I ask you just *what the fuck* you think you were doing coming to my club?" He jammed his fingers into his hair and tugged outward, giving him a wild and crazed...and incredibly sexy look.

"Well? Because it better be good. So fucking good that I can't even fathom a reason good enough that you'd walk your ass into a place like that." He turned and paced toward the other end of the pavilion. "Jesus. You could have been recognized. Didn't you even think about that?"

Con's pacing continued as I debated how to answer his question.

I went with the truth.

"I don't know. I guess I wasn't really thinking."

He spun and faced me. "That's your answer? You weren't thinking? You're always fucking thinking."

I pushed off the chair so I didn't feel quite so much at a disadvantage. Hands fisted on my hips, I said, "Maybe I don't want to think anymore. I said I was ready to jump. I haven't been able to stop thinking about it. So I guess that's what I was doing. I just wanted to *live* for once in my life without considering every potential outcome."

Con stepped toward me, arms crossed over his chest. "And so you decided to live a little by coming to my strip club. How in the fuck did you even know about it?"

I looked down at the planks of weathered wood beneath our feet. Lucas Titan's taunt as I'd left the board meeting echoed in my head. "Bet you wouldn't be so eager to fuck a guy like Leahy if you knew he spent most of his time staring at tits and ass at his club."

Stunned, I'd gone home, my newly formed plan to grab life with both hands already floundering. A glass of wine later, I'd decided that this development would *not* slow me down. New plan: go see what all the fuss was about. After all, I'd never been to a strip club before.

"I heard about the club from...an acquaintance. When I didn't see your bike at Voodoo, I decided to see if you were there."

His expression hardened for a beat before one side of his mouth quirked up. "You stalking me now, princess?"

I shrugged. "Maybe?"

The half smile fell when he said, "Don't do it again. Tracking me down is a bad idea. Besides, that's not how this deal works." He stepped closer. "You're supposed to be where I say, when I say."

Arrogant bastard. "What if I don't like how that works?"

"That's the deal."

The tension between us was rising, and Con took another step toward me. Was I really ready for this? I looked around, gauging our surroundings.

"Where are we?"

The smoldering intent flaring in Con's eyes died out.

"Joy and Andre's lake house. They'd been in the middle of construction when they were killed."

My mouth fell open into a little O. "I'm sorry. I didn't know."

"Don't think many people do. Or if they did, they've probably forgotten about it by now."

I glanced back toward the house. "You said it was mid-construction. It looks finished to me."

"Because I arranged for it to be finished."

"And you kept it?"

He shrugged. "Didn't seem right to sell it. They were so damn excited about it. This was going to be where they played with all the grandkids they'd hoped they'd have someday."

The mention of grandchildren surprised me. "Grandkids? From you?"

Con's expression twisted at the surprise in my voice. "So hard to believe that I might want kids someday?"

"Do you?" I didn't know why I asked. It was none of my business. But I couldn't restrain myself.

His eyes flicked up and down my body, and I had the urge to wrap my arms around my middle. I always felt like he was looking inside me and seeing all my flaws.

"Maybe. But not until..."

He trailed off, fist clenching.

"Not until what?"

His dark blue gaze, flashing with the blinking twinkle lights, caught and held mine. "You don't want to know."

"Why not?"

"Because you might end up on the witness stand at my trial."

The statement was so raw and ominous—not to mention completely unexpected—that I stumbled back to the railing behind me.

"I don't...understand."

"Let's just say that I can't move forward with my life until whoever ended theirs pays for it."

My hands gripped the railing to hold me upright, but his words cut me off at the knees. It didn't take a genius to figure out that Con planned to extract the payment himself. I was reminded that he was a veteran. A man who had probably killed before. Who might feel compelled to kill again.

How the hell was I supposed to feel about that? In awe of his conviction or terrified that he could so easily end someone's life? Even if it was justified to his way of thinking—which was completely foreign to me—it was still criminal.

"Are you serious?"

Con ignored the question, which was probably appropriate, because it was a stupid one. Instead he jerked his chin toward the house.

"The booze is inside. And I'm not having this conversation without it."

With that, he stalked off down the dock, leaving me stunned and silent on the pavilion.

con

Fuck. Shit. Goddammit.

I don't know why I said what I said. It was a fucking mistake. I didn't need to go shooting off my mouth in front of Vanessa. I'd all but straight up told her I was planning to kill someone and just when she was showing initiative for the first time since I'd thrown down my ultimatum.

Of course I'd fucking ruin it. Watching her cringe as I'd admitted that I planned to take my own justice was not how I wanted this night to go.

I blamed it on the house. I didn't know why I'd brought her here. But when I'd climbed on my bike, wanting to get her as far away from Tassel as I could before the cops showed up, and she'd have to give a statement as a witness, this was the only place I could think to bring her.

My apartment above Voodoo would have been more convenient, and a hell of a lot smarter, but I didn't want to bring her back there. She deserved... better.

Which was ironic considering I hadn't had a problem bringing her there before. Or maybe I had had a problem with it. I didn't know, because *I didn't fucking remember.*

I strode up the stairs at the back of the house and dug the keys out of my pocket. I didn't turn to see if she followed. If she wasn't following now, she would eventually. Or she'd call the cops and have me dragged away in cuffs for planning a murder. I left the door open and made my way to the liquor cabinet.

Spying Andre's favorite Irish whiskey, I poured three fingers into a glass. Tossing it back in one long swig, I lowered the glass and filled it again.

Shit. I'm driving. I can't get hammered.

Normally I'd just crash here for the night, but I couldn't imagine Vanessa would be cool with a sleepover. Besides, spending the night in a house empty of people except for her and me? No way I'd be able to keep myself from climbing into her bed.

A hand on my arm ripped me out of my ricocheting thoughts. "Con, I'm not going to say anything. I can only imagine that if someone had murdered my parents, I wouldn't stop until I'd gotten justice either."

I glanced down at the manicured fingernails resting on the ink-covered skin of my forearm.

"You say that now."

"I mean it. Your business is your business. I won't pry, and I won't try to track you down again." She gestured to the full glass on the bar. "Can I have one? Or are you the only one drinking tonight?"

Wanting to lock away all of the bad shit for just one night, which was damn near impossible while sitting in Joy and Andre's dream house, I forced a smile. Her fingers curled around my glass, and when she held it to her lips, I wanted to snatch it away. I wanted to keep her stone cold sober, because I promised myself that we both would be the next time we were together. I watched as she tipped it back and the amber liquid disappeared.

It was for the best. I was too raw tonight. In this kind of mood, I just wanted to fuck and fuck hard. And I still wondered if Vanessa was just getting this out of her system. Her little field trip to the strip club might've just been a rich girl's walk on the wild side.

I was saved from coming up with a new topic when she asked, "How long has it been since your last one-night stand? Although I guess I shouldn't assume it was a one-night stand. But you know what I mean." The words tumbled out, as if she was unable to stop them.

Her cheeks flared bright red, telegraphing her embarrassment. "I don't know why I just asked that. It's none of my business."

As a rule, I didn't talk about my conquests with anyone. *Ever.* But I think I got what she was getting at. "Before you walked into Voodoo that first night."

"So, if we... take this further, are you going to be... seeing other women at the same time?"

I arched a brow. I'd give just about anything to know what was going through her head right now. Suffice it to say that all the heavy shit going through mine had faded away once she'd started on the topic of sex. Don't look so surprised. I'm a guy, and my dick is in full working order.

"You want to know if we fuck, whether I'm still going to be fucking other women?"

She dropped her gaze to the floor. "Yeah."

"What makes you think I'd want to?" I was truly interested in her response—although, let's not kid ourselves, I was pretty much interested in anything that came out of this woman's mouth.

"You're used to... variety, and I'm only one person."

I reached a hand up to cup her cheek. Her skin was porcelain smooth. "Why would I need variety if I had you?"

"I'm just asking the question. I'd like to know where I stand before..." As if losing her nerve to finish the sentence, she turned away. I thought I heard her whisper, "Jesus. I don't know if I can do this."

I snagged the whiskey and poured another glass as though I wasn't affected by the conversation. Years of training kept my movements steady and my expression neutral.

I recapped the bottle and set it on the shelf. Before I could take a drink, Vanessa snatched up the glass and downed it.

My laugh was strangled and harsh. "It ain't too late to back out, princess. I'm not forcing you into shit."

She replaced the empty glass on the granite bar with a *clunk* and reached up, wrapping both hands around my neck and dragging my face down to hers. Our lips connected, and her hot little tongue slipped inside my mouth.

What the hell?

Breaking out of my momentary paralysis, I buried one hand in her hair and slid the other around her back. I slanted my mouth along hers and took control of the kiss. She tasted of whiskey spiked with something sweet.

Whiskey she'd had to drink to find the courage to kiss me.

If I were a better man, I'd have stopped the kiss. But I wasn't. And I didn't.

I slid my hand lower, cupping her ass and lifting her off her feet. Her legs twined around my waist as she pulled her head back. "You need to stop carrying me everywhere. I'm too heavy."

"Shut up. You're fucking perfect."

I crossed the room and lowered us to the couch. Vanessa unwrapped her legs and knelt above me.

"Are we really doing this?" Her tone was underscored by something that sounded strangely like... amazement.

I needed to set the ground rules for tonight.

"Making out on the couch like fucking teenagers? Yeah. We're doing that. Straight up fucking? No."

Vanessa pulled back, her forehead scrunching in confusion. "But I thought..."

"Told you the next time I fucked you we'd both be stone cold sober."

Realization dawned. "You're seriously worried you're not going to remember tonight? Neither of us is drunk."

"Don't care. I'm not changing my mind."

Her eyes flashed, as though I'd thrown a challenge down. If the woman wanted to try to change my mind, she was more than welcome. But it wouldn't happen.

"Why?"

"I'm not taking the chance that you're doing this only because of the liquid courage."

"But—"

I gripped her around the waist and gave her a little tug forward. "No."

She rested her hands on the couch on either side of my head. "I don't get you."

"I've waited a hell of a long time for this, and I guess I can wait a little longer." She pushed against the cushions and shifted her legs, preparing to climb off my lap. I tightened my grip. "Where do you think you're going?"

"I thought you just said we weren't doing this?"

"Did you miss the first half of what I said? We're totally fucking making out like teenagers. And I might even try to round third base." Her cheeks flushed a deeper red. "Don't worry that you're going to get bored, princess."

"Oh."

"So give me that mouth again." I waited, wondering if she'd take the initiative, or if I'd have to help her along.

She leaned in, her lips an inch from mine. "You're kind of bossy. You know that, right?"

"You like it."

"You sure about that?"

"As sure as you're straddling my lap right now."

"Cocky bastard." She didn't speak the words so much as breathe them, the final syllables lost as our lips collided. My cock, already hard, pulsed against the zipper of my jeans.

Sorry, bud. Not tonight.

vanessa

I was too old and too heavy to be straddling a man's lap. But whiskey was an amazing thing. It wiped away inhibitions and made otherwise questionable actions seem perfectly reasonable. Advisable, even.

Now I understood why Con insisted on no sex until we were sober. Because he didn't trust that I would actually follow through if I wasn't. I was going to prove him wrong.

Even as we devoured each other and heat gathered between my legs, I was firmly aware of what I was doing. I hadn't had *that* much to drink. I was also firmly aware that part of Con's appeal was an edge of danger. It was so cliché, but something inside me had lit and burned brightly when he'd said he wouldn't rest until he'd gotten justice for his parents. That kind of devotion—that kind of gut-wrenching emotion—wasn't something I'd witnessed very often in my life. I wondered what it would be like to be the focus of that kind of ferocity.

Con's hands drifted from my waist to my ass, and I couldn't help but grind down on his erection. *Jeez. I'm such a hussy.* I hadn't done something like this since... well, never. My skirt was hiked up my thighs, and my thong barely qualified as an undergarment. I was surely going to leave a wet spot on his pants, which would be incredibly embarrassing, but I wasn't going to worry about that just now. His hand slipped down to the back of my thigh and then up under my skirt. I froze, waiting for him to comment about the thong, and then realized for everyone else in the world, this wasn't a novelty. Just for sexually repressed thirty year olds who still live with their fathers and wear full butt-covering underwear.

His callused hand skimmed my ass cheek, and he pulled away from my mouth and groaned. "Fucking A, Van. I put you on my bike in a skirt with you wearing practically nothing beneath it. You could have flashed the entire town."

"To be fair, I didn't know I was going to be on your bike, so that's not really my fault."

Con's fingers curled, gripping my ass tighter, and pulling me closer. "I want to feel you on my dick. Jesus, why in the hell did I say I didn't want to do this tonight? A little whiskey, and I decide to take the moral fucking high ground."

I leaned back and looked Con in the eye. "You're not changing your mind now. Not because I don't want to, but because you're right. It matters. And when we do have sex again, I don't want you to wonder if it's whiskey giving me the courage. I want you to know I'm with you because it's what I want. Nothing more. Nothing less."

Even as I spoke the words, I knew they weren't completely true. Because Con would probably always wonder—would have to wonder—if I was only sleeping with him for the deed. Because if not for that deed, who knew if I would've ever set foot back into his world and given him the shot he'd asked for?

His lips landed on my collarbone... then his teeth. Shards of pleasure shot through me, and I moaned his name. His hand, still clutching my ass, squeezed and released, and I rocked against his erection. The rough denim of his jeans rubbed against the flimsy lace of my panties, ratcheting up my arousal. If we kept this up, I was going to come. My head dropped back, and I whispered, "Don't stop. Please, don't stop."

Con didn't listen. He twisted sideways and lowered me at an angle. Pressing my body into the sofa, he covered me completely. My skirt was shoved up to my waist, and my legs were spread, accommodating his narrow hips. If I thought I could feel his hard-on before, that was nothing compared to the thick, solid heat that branded me now.

He was relentless.

Lips skimmed along my jaw, to my ear, to my throat. Teeth scraped against the tendons of my neck, sending shivers through my entire body. My hips bucked, and I relished the friction his body offered.

I cursed us both for putting sex off limits tonight. I hadn't been beneath a man like this since... I didn't even want to admit how long it'd been.

"Con. I lied. Tonight. Now. Please."

My words made no sense as they fell from my lips. But I was certain that the intensity of my need was obvious.

Con pushed up, and I cursed the lack of contact. "Don't stop."

This time he didn't stop. *Thank God.*

He tugged down the neck of my camisole, exposing my lacy bra. It matched the thong and was much more daringly cut than I would normally wear. I could picture myself through his eyes. Face flushed. Breasts spilling out from the tiny demi cups barely large enough to cover my nipples. For the first time in my life, I wanted him to look. I wanted him to want. I didn't think about my boobs being too big or the spidery stretch marks left over from my adolescence. All I thought about was how amazing it was to see the reverent look on his face when he supported himself on one arm and reached out to cup my left breast before freeing it from the bra. His eyes darted up to mine before dropping once again.

"Fucking Christ. You're so goddamn gorgeous." His thumb brushed my nipple and it pebbled under this touch. I released a pent up breath, arching toward him, wanting more.

And he gave me more.

Sliding down and propping himself up on both elbows, Con's big hands squeezed and kneaded my breasts, flicking at my nipples until I was writhing against him. My legs wrapped around his waist, and I desperately sought the friction that would send me over the edge. I didn't care that this was ridiculous. I didn't care that this was insane. I just wanted Con to make me come.

It'd been so damn long since anyone other than me had gotten me off. But when Con pulled away and untangled himself from my legs, disappointment filled me. I was *so close*.

"Please. Don't stop. I just want to—"

"You want to come?"

I nodded helplessly.

"Don't worry, babe. I got you." On his knees, Con stared down at me. "I want to taste you first."

I blinked as his words crystallized in my brain. "Wh—"

"You going to let me get you off my way? Or are you going to make me leave you wanting more?"

My mouth dropped open. "You would seriously—"

Con's grin was wicked, and at that moment, I wanted to slap it right off his face, the arrogant son of a bitch.

"You want to try me? Or do you want to come?" He raised an eyebrow, and his hand trailed up my thigh, teasing me with the promise of an orgasm.

The same stretch marks were there, but in the mostly dark room, he wouldn't see them.

"Yes."

"Yes, what?"

"Make me come."

"Good girl."

His eyes stayed on mine as he lowered his face between my legs. My muscles clenched as his hot breath ghosted over the tiny scrap of lace separating his mouth from my pussy.

Con didn't know it, but he was the only man who'd ever gone down on me. The memory sent quivers racing through me. I'd never known I was capable of multiple orgasms until that night. The things he'd done... the things I'd begged him to do again...

One blunt finger skimmed along the crease at the top of my thigh, lifting the edge of my panties away from my skin. Con's eyes darted up to mine for a split second before he tugged at the delicate fabric and it gave way.

My mouth dropped open, but no words came out because he was already leaning closer to trace the seam of my pussy with his tongue. My nipples puckered, and my hands grew a mind of their own and tangled in his hair. His eyes lifted to mine again, and his grin damn near stopped my heart. The devilish mischief was almost an even bigger turn on than his tongue. Wrapping one huge hand around my hip, Con's thumb followed the neat landing strip of hair left after my last wax.

"I like this." He paused just above my clit, pressing only slightly. Not enough to send me over the edge. The glint in his eyes said he knew exactly what he was doing, and he was enjoying the hell out of teasing me. "And I like that you kept your lips bare."

I squirmed under his close inspection, and his grin faded as his thumb slipped into my heat. "Jesus fucking Christ, Van. You're soaked, baby." When he lifted his hand and brought it to his mouth, I thought I might lose my mind before he finally gave me the orgasm I desperately wanted.

Sucking his thumb between his lips, he groaned. "Just as sweet as I imagined."

A memory of him saying the same thing once before slammed into me, and I had to wonder if that night had been a fluke. If he hadn't been drunk, would he have still brought me home?

I forgot to care about the answer to that question when he finally lowered his mouth to me and *feasted*.

All the pent up tension twisted tighter and tighter until it just... snapped. My fingernails dug into his scalp, and if I'd been capable of coherent thought at that moment, I might have been embarrassed. But I wasn't. I could only focus on the orgasm ripping through me in muscle clenching waves.

⚜

I woke up on the couch with a thick arm wrapped around me, just under my breasts. The heat and hardness of the chest at my back clued me in to the fact that I'd spent the entire night with Con.

Oh crap.

I struggled to free myself, but the arm tightened, one hand slipping to cover my left boob. "You trying to run out on me again, princess?"

I tugged at his arm. "No. I have to go. I have meetings. Appointments. A schedule."

Con released me, and I stumbled to my feet. My destroyed panties lay draped across one of my sandals. Lost cause.

My head pounded, and I realized the whiskey from last night must have been a lot more potent than I'd thought. I usually only drank wine, so my tolerance for hard liquor had been mostly unexplored. Note to self: *take it a little slower next time.* And then I remembered that if I wanted the *next time* to end with actual sex and not just oral, there would be no alcohol involved. Con's decree was more than a little intimidating.

I snatched up my panties, balling them in my fist, as I slipped on my sandals. I did a quick pat down, straightening my skirt and camisole, and then I looked to Con. He was watching me intently through shuttered eyes. Considering I wasn't very good at reading him, even when his expression was more transparent, I was at a loss for how to gauge his mood.

He seemed to be waiting for something.

"Do you mind giving me a ride, or would you prefer I call a cab?" I asked.

He didn't answer. Just kept watching me.

I waited.

And waited.

"Con?"

"You regret it?"

It dawned on me that he was wondering if this morning was going to be a repeat of *that morning*.

"Do you think I regret it?" I waited to hear his answer, hoping it would give me some insight into this complicated man.

He leaned back, one arm resting along the top of the couch. His expression morphed into a more familiar, arrogant smirk.

"No," he replied with a shake of his head. "I think the only thing you regret is that I didn't fuck you."

My inner muscles clenched at his words. "Pretty sure of yourself, aren't you?"

His smirk softened into a lopsided grin, and he reached up with his other hand and scratched the back of his head. I tried not to focus on the way his bicep bulged when he bent his arm. Or on how sexy his shaggy blond bedhead looked.

"Not sure enough, Van. Can't say I've ever worked this hard for a woman."

His words unleashed a rush of insecurity within me. He'd had dozens, maybe hundreds, of women. Was the mystery of not remembering that night the only real appeal I held for him? "What if it's not worth it? What if *I'm* not worth it?"

"I think we both know that ain't the case."

I squeezed the balled up panties in my hand. They were an excellent reminder that I needed to get moving. "As much as I'd love to discuss this further, I really do need to go."

Con dropped his arm from the back of the couch and checked his watch. "It's five thirty. You gonna be able to sneak into Daddy's house without raising the alarm?"

Shit. Given that it was still nearly pitch black outside, I'd hoped it was earlier. My father would already be up. Although, if I were lucky, he might already be gone.

"Let me worry about that." I thought about pulling up in front of our house in the Garden District on the back of Con's bike. Yeah. Nope. "Although, I guess I should probably take a cab..." I let my words trail off.

Con's arrogant smirk snapped back into place as he crossed his arms over his chest. "Don't worry, princess. I get it. I can drop you off around the corner. Your walk of shame will be short, at least."

The bitter tone that had crept into his voice sliced away a little of the pleasure of last night. It seemed like our differences loomed larger than ever. But did they really? I was standing in a multi-million dollar mansion on Lake Pontchartrain. The difference between Con and me wasn't the money we had in the bank, because I had a sneaking suspicion that Con might have more than I did. The difference was wrapped up in how we felt about that money. Con seemed to hate it. Distrust it. Resent it. Whereas I accepted it. Appreciated it. Wanted to use it to change lives. Although Con was doing more than his part with respect to changing lives—his gym and his boys were proof of that. I wasn't sure if we could get beyond this divide. It was ingrained, possibly unchangeable. But then again, maybe not.

I met Con's dark blue eyes. "I'd love a ride. Thank you."

18
con

Vanessa on the back of my Harley should have been all sorts of wrong. But it wasn't. It felt too damn right. Just like it had felt too damn right falling asleep last night with my arms wrapped around her. But that wasn't something I would let myself get used to. I'd trained myself early on not to get attached to things. Like the foster families of my early years who'd had no problem tossing me back into the system over some stupid kid prank I'd pulled. Or even something as simple as a stuffed animal. If it wasn't mine to keep, I didn't let myself get used to it.

So I ignored the feel of Vanessa's arms wrapped around my stomach as I changed lanes and eventually glided into the parking lot of a bookstore a few blocks from her house. Taking my Harley any further into the quiet streets of the Garden District would alert the neighborhood to the presence of a guy who didn't belong. Didn't matter that I still owned a damn house on those streets. Just like the lake house, I hadn't been able to let it go after Joy and Andre were gone. It seemed wrong to sell something they'd loved so much. But it was a house for a family, and I was pretty fucking sure I'd never have one of my own. I couldn't go through losing another one.

I cut the engine and climbed off the bike, once again helping Vanessa with her helmet. I hoped she never got the hang of it because it gave me an excuse to touch her.

Fucking pathetic.

I needed to kick my own ass.

She scooted off the bike, careful to keep from flashing the world with her goods. I knew because I watched closely.

"You good?" I asked.

She nodded, smoothing her clothing into place.

"Thank you. For the ride. For last night. For everything."

"Don't mention it."

I sat on the bike sideways, watching as she turned and took one step away from me. But I wasn't ready to let her go. I grabbed her hand and hauled her back into my arms. I crushed my mouth to hers and stole whatever words might have spilled from her lips.

She'd never know it, but that kiss was to brand her as mine.

I released her, and she stumbled back on her heels, eyes wide. She lifted a hand to that luscious mouth I'd just devoured.

I couldn't stop the grin from forming on my lips. "Have a good one, princess. I'll be in touch."

Hennessy was waiting in the alley at Voodoo when I killed the engine and walked my bike into my garage.

"Heard you had some trouble last night," he called from where he leaned against the brick wall.

I dropped my helmet on the seat. "Yeah."

"And you were conveniently unavailable even though witnesses put you at the scene."

Fucking assholes. Apparently my staff needed to learn they were supposed to be helpful in their statements to the cops—but only to a point.

"Well, detective, I'm conveniently available now. And flattered that you're waiting on me at," I looked down to check my watch, "just shy of six o'clock. Slow morning?"

"Slower than yours, it seems."

He flipped open his little cop book and clicked his pen. "Who was the blonde, Con?"

I surveyed Hennessy and wondered if anyone would miss him if he disappeared. He was about six foot, two hundred pounds, with a buzzed head and a don't-fuck-with-me attitude. He was actually my favorite cop on the NOLA police force. I put his age at a few years younger than mine. Probably twenty-seven or eight. Still young enough to think he was making a difference. Yeah, someone would probably miss him if I fed him to the gators for asking about Vanessa.

I'd taken too long to answer, because he looked up at me, dark eyes narrowed. "The blonde?"

"Didn't catch her name."

One eyebrow lifted. "And yet you were carrying her out of your club?"

I played it off, smirking. "You know my style, Hennessy. I don't get most of their names. And it's not like I asked for her number either."

He rolled his eyes. "Your guy claimed the security cameras haven't worked since you bought the place. That true?"

"Sure is. It's on my list of shit to do." Actually, it was on my list of shit to do last week, but I'd gotten a little distracted.

"Can you at least give me a description of the blonde so I can attempt to track her down for questioning?"

"Come on, Hennessy, don't you have enough information already? Besides, the best description I can give you is *not* of her face." I didn't like talking about Vanessa that way, but, considering it was her reputation I was saving, I got over it.

He slapped his book shut. "Fine. I'll drop the questions about the blonde, but I do need your statement. You want to do it now or come down to the station?"

"You want coffee?"

"Wouldn't turn it down."

"Then come on up."

vanessa

I picked up my cell phone for the eight hundredth time and looked at the screen. It didn't matter that I knew the thing would vibrate if a text came through; I still couldn't stop myself from doing it. It'd become a reflex. A really annoying, totally distracting, absolutely ridiculous reflex.

It also didn't take a genius to figure out whose text I was expecting.

But it never came.

I told myself it was a good thing. And when I stared at the calendar on my monitor, I *knew* it was a good thing. I had to report for duty in three hours at the Botanical Garden for a gala with Lucas Titan.

When I thought logically about my life, I knew that I should be looking forward to the event. It was the kind of thing I was bred for. My closet was full of designer cocktail dresses and evening gowns selected by personal shoppers for such occasions.

Small talk was an art at which I excelled. When it came to people's names, hobbies, children, pets— my mind was a filing cabinet of information. My father was right in some respects. I would have been a damn good politician's wife, but Simon wasn't for me. He never had been. But being seen on his arm had lifted my father's scrutiny for a couple years, and also helped me gain some much-needed confidence to show off my skills. Sometimes it took having a friend at your side to take you from faking it to making it.

But now I was going back to faking it on Lucas Titan's arm. My irritation flared hot and fierce. I was more than arm candy. I was more than a gateway to the inner circle of New Orleans' upper crust. It infuriated me to be used as such. I wanted nothing more than to tell Lucas Titan to go to hell.

I tried to imagine how that scene would play out. Archer's reaction. The disbelief followed by disappointment. It was the disappointment that would hurt the most. I didn't think I could handle seeing that emotion on my last living Bennett relative's face.

So I would go. And I would fake it.

And hate myself for it.

I flipped my phone over again, bringing it to life and swiping the screen.

Still nothing.

Opening my desk drawer, I tossed it inside. I had things to do and wondering why Constantine Leahy hadn't contacted me after last night wasn't helping me accomplish anything.

As soon as I slammed the drawer, my office phone rang. The caller ID showed Archer's assistant's extension.

I grabbed it off the cradle. "Hi, Paulette. Is there something I can help you with?"

"Mr. Bennett would like to see you immediately. He's received some disturbing news."

My stomach dropped. *Shit. He knows.* My heart rate jumped into a gallop, and my palms turned clammy.

"Vanessa? Are you there?"

I pulled myself together. Deep breath in. Deep breath out. "Yes. Certainly. I'm on my way."

"Thank you, dear."

She hung up, but I continued to hold the phone to my ear, listening to nothing but dead air.

Deep breath in. Deep breath out.

I thought about the letter of resignation I'd drafted. The file was saved on my computer. I wondered if I was going to need to print it when I returned to my desk.

My steps were slow and deliberate as I crossed through the cube farm to the opposite corner. Archer's office was directly diagonal from mine and down a short hallway. Although we both had 'corner offices,' neither was anything to write home about. Archer demanded that every penny we could cut from operating expenses went into the foundation's managed funds. Thus the crappy furniture and tiny offices. Even for the executive director.

Our new offices would be much more modern and trendy, but they were being paid for almost completely with newly raised money and long-term, low interest debt.

Except I probably wouldn't get to set foot inside those new offices, because I was about to get fired.

Paulette was already on another call, but she waved me down the hallway. I knocked on his closed door.

"Come in."

I opened the door casually, not letting my apprehension show in my movements.

Archer sat behind the wide executive desk. Dark wood, scarred and marred from years of use, was covered with scattered papers. Stacks of even more papers and files covered almost every inch of the floor. There was a narrow path from the door to the desk. One of his guest chairs was crammed with files, but the other looked as though it'd been newly cleared.

He looked up when I entered. His expression was closed off. And almost...somber.

Oh shit.

Tears burned in the backs of my eyes. Only sheer force of will kept them from materializing and falling. Years of practice smoothed the smile across my face and hid all traces of my inner turmoil.

"Thank you for coming, Vanessa. Please," he gestured to the chair, "sit."

I navigated the paper-lined path and lowered myself into the seat. Smoothing my skirt, I crossed my ankles and laid my hands in my lap. *Ladylike posture until the very end.*

Words that would carry the admission of guilt bubbled up inside me, but I held them back just as effectively as the tears.

I waited for Archer to speak.

He lifted a hand to his face, his fingers starting at his forehead and sliding down around to cover his mouth.

Still waiting...

He dropped his hand to the desk, his fingers clenching into a fist.

"I don't even know how to say this..." he started.

All the breath in my lungs evaporated.

"But Dick Herzog is dead."

I froze. The words—words I hadn't expected to hear—echoed in my head.

"Wha—what?" Dick Herzog was the treasurer of the board.

"Stroke."

"Oh my God." I grasped my forearm with one hand, digging my nails into my skin. It was punishment for the instant relief I'd felt to learn that the news Archer had to deliver had nothing to do with Con and me.

If this were the alternative, I think I would've preferred to hand in my resignation. Dick Herzog had been on the board for as long as I could remember. He'd given me peppermints as a little girl when I'd come to board meetings with my mother.

He'd continued in secret even after she'd made her disapproval about the candy known.

"Yes, well...Melinda's beside herself. As one would expect." Melinda was Dick's wife. *His widow.*

"I'll arrange for flowers to be delivered to her at home. And some low maintenance catered meals."

Archer nodded. "That would be very kind. I'm sure she'd appreciate it. In the meantime, I'm going to send a note to the board sharing the bad news. Melinda wants to have the service on Saturday. She doesn't want to wait."

That seemed rather fast, but I guess...maybe that was normal? Or maybe it was the type of decision you made quickly when faced with this situation.

"Okay. I'll be there."

I stood, legs just as shaky as they had been when I'd entered the room. Except this time for a completely different reason. Death never got easier. It didn't matter who it was, or how minor a role the person played in your life. Death always had the power to rock us by reminding us of our innate human fragility.

My thoughts from last night about being ninety and lying in my bed regretting the things I'd never done came rushing back. Dick had to have been seventy-five if he'd been a day.

"Vanessa." Archer's voice had me pausing at the threshold.

"Yes?"

"Be sure to say a prayer for Herzog, won't you?"

"Of course."

I flinched and turned my head as another camera flashed from just beyond Lucas. It was worse than I'd expected. I wanted to be anywhere but here tonight—and not just because I was dreading what would show up in the papers tomorrow.

"You keep ducking, and I'll arrange for a copy of the society section to be delivered to Con's doorstep in the morning."

I glared at Lucas. "I thought you were worried about ending up dead." *Like Herzog*, I added to myself.

He flashed a practiced smile in my direction, but it didn't reach his eyes. Rarely did any of them reach his eyes. But I honestly didn't care.

"That's only if he found out about our deal. Seeing the pictures will just get him pissed at you." He slid an arm around my back.

I hunched forward, trying to lessen the points of contact between our bodies. "Get your arm off me, or I'll break it myself." I was not in a mood to be messed with.

Lucas tsked. "Play nice or the deal is off."

Forcing back the urge to slap him, I smiled and lifted my hand in a polite wave as a state senator nodded my way. Through gritted teeth I said, "I'm tempted to tell you to go screw yourself and tell whoever you want about Con and me."

"I doubt that, Vanessa. I truly doubt that. You see, I did my research when it came to you. I think

I know exactly what that foundation means to you. And what's more, I think I know what Archer's and your father's respect means to you."

A decidedly unladylike bark of laughter escaped my lips. "And I'm not losing their respect right this minute, standing here with you?"

His expression twisted. "Not as fast as you would if you were standing on a street corner with Leahy."

I loosened the grip on my champagne flute so I didn't shatter it. This conversation was completely pointless. I wanted to be home, chin deep in a bubble bath, a glass of wine resting on the edge of the tub.

The remainder of the night was equally pointless. I smiled. Made my flawless small talk. The only bright spot of the evening was meeting a woman who chaired the board of a kids' sack supper program who had applied for a grant. Hearing about her organization had only reinforced my desire to make certain we allotted funds to as many worthy causes as we were able.

As I climbed into my car, the valet shut the door. I pulled out onto the dark street. It was nearly midnight, and the lack of solid sleep last night and the events of today were catching up with me. Deciding to take the quickest route home, I turned down a side road and slowed at the stoplight.

My head jerked up at a thud against the glass. That crap about time slowing down when something traumatic was happening? It might be true for other people, but it certainly wasn't for me.

Everything happened so. Damn. Fast.

The butt of a gun connected with my passenger window. The glass shattered. The barrel pointed at my head.

"Get the fuck out of the car, bitch."

No, time didn't freeze. But I did.

"Are you fucking deaf? Get the fuck out of the car. Now!"

Not taking my eyes off the gun, I fumbled around, unbuckling my seatbelt and feeling blindly along the door panel for the handle.

Oh shit. Oh shit. Oh shit.

My hand finally connected with the metal, and I yanked on it, flinging the door wide. Instinctively, I reached for my purse, grabbing the strap and dragging it out of the car as I stumbled backward onto the dark street. Wobbling on my heels, I stared as he rounded the hood, the gun still leveled on me. "Throw me the purse."

Reflexively, my fingers wrapped tighter around the strap of my bag, nails digging into the leather. I knew I should listen. Just throw him the damn purse. But I couldn't make myself uncurl my hand.

The gun didn't waver. The traffic signal changed to from green to yellow, and the light glinted off the silver barrel. My entire world shrank to those two impressions: the feel of the leather beneath my fingers, and the changing colors of the traffic light reflecting off the gun.

Yellow flashed to red.

"You stupid, you fucking cunt? I told you to throw the fucking purse here."

I trembled, feeling just as stupid as he accused me of being. Silently I screamed at my muscles. *Lift arm. Throw purse. Just throw the goddamn purse.*

He stepped closer. My heart, already hammering at a frenetic pace, kicked up to double time. I fought against the near-paralysis. Inch by inch, muscle twitch by muscle twitch, I forced myself to relax my death-grip.

Okay. Halfway there. Now just throw it.

And then I remembered my phone tucked into the side pocket.

"Hurry the fuck up, I ain't got all night."

I found my voice. "The keys are in the car. Just take it."

His arm bobbed as he replied, "Did I ask you where the fucking keys are, you stupid bitch? They better be in the fucking car, or your brains are going to be splattered all over the goddamn road."

Fuck the phone. I swung the purse as hard as I could, launching it at his face. He flinched, and I turned and ran.

I vaguely recalled reading once that if someone was shooting at you, you should run and keep your movements erratic because handguns weren't incredibly accurate. A moving target was always harder to hit. I had no idea why I read that or when, but right now, I was running like a drunk person, heading for the brick building to my left.

Two gunshots ripped through the still night, and I dove toward the corner of the building. The movement was instinctive. Like I'd once dove at home plate while playing softball in Phys. Ed.

Curling into the smallest target possible, I lay on the broken and jagged concrete. I waited for more shots, but they didn't come. Yelling did.

"What the fuck, man. You know whose woman that is? He's gonna fucking hunt you down and kill you."

"Not if I fucking kill you first."

The sounds of a scuffle, and fists hitting flesh, came next. I uncurled from my tiny ball and peeked my head around the corner.

A boy dressed in basketball shorts and a T-shirt landed punch after punch on the carjacker until he caught him with a fist to the jaw and sent him stumbling to the ground. I felt a strange glimmer of recognition as I watched the newcomer. How did I know him? My mind whirled, but couldn't latch onto a single coherent thought. My eyes darted, following his every movement.

I needed to run.

The gun clattered against the pavement, catching my attention. Once again I could see the changing colors of the traffic signal reflecting off the metal.

"You think you're hot shit, Trey? You think just cuz you gettin' outta here makes you better than us? You ain't better than no one."

Trey.

The glimmer of recognition solidified. One of Con's boys. The one from the Boys and Girls Club dinner.

Trey crossed his arms and stood over the carjacker. "Least I ain't like you. I'm going somewhere with my life. You're fucking headed to Angola on carjacking charges. Hope your asshole's ready for the reaming that's comin'."

"Fuck you, Trey."

There was a moment of stillness.

And then both of them lunged for the gun.

They struggled, Trey on top and the other guy on the ground. I couldn't tell where the gun was. At least not until the next shot rang out.

Neither of them moved for a beat, not until the carjacker shoved up and flipped Trey off him. Trey landed on his back, and from this distance, I couldn't tell if he was breathing. *Oh my God. Oh my God.*

The carjacker stood for a moment, head jerking from side to side, as though scanning his surroundings, before he turned and ran, leaving my Mercedes quietly idling in the middle of the road.

I scrambled up from my crouch behind the building and stumbled toward the street. My purse lay a few feet from the pool of blood that was growing on the pavement.

I dropped to my knees beside the motionless boy and checked for a pulse. It was there, but faint. His chest barely moved, but he was still breathing. I needed to stop the bleeding. Ripping the cleanest section of the torn skirt of my dress free, I balled it up and pressed it against the wound in his chest. I dragged my purse closer and grabbed my phone.

With one hand, I punched in 9-1-1. The operator's voice was the best sound I'd heard all night.

20
con

I was just finishing up a tat when my phone started buzzing on the counter. I ignored it, but it kept buzzing. And buzzing.

Glancing over, I saw Hennessey's name on the screen.

The fuck?

I rolled away, flipping off the machine, and apologized to my client. Pulling the latex glove off one hand, I swiped across the screen.

"Leahy."

"Need to get your ass down to Tulane Medical Center."

I stilled, the blood rushing through my veins morphing into ice water.

"What the hell happened? Who is it?"

"Just get here. But don't kill yourself on the way. Don't need them bringing you in a bus, too."

"Who the fuck is it?"

"One of your boys. Trey Vincent."

The ice water froze solid.

"How bad?"

"Died once already tonight. They brought him back. Get your ass here."

I looked down at the customer in my chair and the nearly finished red-tailed hawk I'd spent the past four hours working on.

"On my way."

I was lowering my phone, about to hang up, when Hennessey added, "And a blonde came in with him. A hot, rich blonde. So damn rich that I'm standing in a wing of the hospital named after her mama. Says your boy saved her from a carjacking."

What the hell?

"On my fucking way."

I hung up and snapped off my other latex glove.

I turned to say something to my client, but he held up a hand. "Go, man. Do what you gotta do. I'll catch up with you later."

"Thanks," I mumbled and strode out of the room.

"Gotta go, Delilah. Lock up for me? And don't charge the client I'm leaving with an unfinished tat."

"Sure. But what can I do to help?"

"Nothing. Don't worry about it. I'll see you next shift."

I revved my bike and flew out of the alley thirty seconds later. In minutes, I was parking in the 'Reserved for Clergy' spot in front of the ER and hauling ass up to the automatic doors.

"I'm not even going to ask how many traffic laws you broke to get here so fucking fast." Hennessy pushed off the wall he'd been leaning against, and I followed him inside.

"How is he? Where's his ma?"

"Your boy's still in surgery. His ma's up in a private waiting room that Ms. Frost arranged."

I wanted to demand he tell me everything he knew about what had happened to Vanessa, but he was already suspicious. I didn't need to heap fuel on the fire. "Is she okay? You said it was a carjacking?"

Hennessy studied me as he replied, "She's a little scraped and a lot shaken up. Pretty much what you'd expect from someone who was carjacked and witnessed a shooting. Although, I have to say, she's holding it together well. Don't even think she needed stitches."

The thought of someone threatening her... Fuck. My hands balled into white-knuckled fists. When he didn't elaborate further, I tried to make my question sound casually concerned. "Why would she have needed stitches?"

"Cut her knee on some broken glass when she ran from the shooter. Said she dove when he popped off a couple rounds at her. They just butterflied it and called it good."

A haze of red filled my vision. All pretense of casual died a bloody and violent death. "He fucking shot at her?" My roar filled the waiting room, and all heads swiveled in our direction.

The nurse managing triage stood, but Hennessy waved her off.

"What the fuck are you doing standing here? You're the cop. Why the hell aren't you out there," I flung my arm out in the direction of the exit, "tracking the motherfucker down?"

Hennessy crossed both arms over his chest. "Was waiting for you, asshole. Besides, I was keeping an eye on Ms. Frost. Figured I'd offer her a ride home when she was ready to leave."

Fucking white knight complex. Did every cop have one? *Doesn't matter.*

"Where's this private waiting room?"

Hennessy nodded toward the elevator bay about fifteen feet away. "Eighth floor."

Before I registered moving, I was jabbing a finger at the call button and the doors opened. Hennessy followed me inside and pressed '8.'

"If you'd told me Vanessa Frost was the blonde you'd carried out of your club last night, I wouldn't have believed you."

My head jerked up, and I stared at him. "I didn't say jack shit, man. So don't go making things up."

"Whatever you say, Con. But we both know the truth. I'm a fucking detective. This ain't my first rodeo."

The elevator came to a halt. As the doors slid open, I stomped out, swinging my head from side to side, seeing nothing but long, white-walled hallways.

"Which way?"

"Left."

Hennessy shoved past me and led the way to a door about fifteen yards from the elevator. Pushing it open, I found Vanessa and Ms. Vincent inside.

They were seated side by side, hands joined, heads bowed. I caught "pray for us sinners, now and at the hour of our death. Amen."

The *Hail Mary* was never a good sign. Nor were the blue scrubs Vanessa was wearing. *What the fuck happened to her clothes?*

They opened their mouths to start reciting it again, and I realized they must be saying the rosary that Ms. Vincent had dangling from her right hand. The prayer trailed off as they caught sight of Hennessy and me.

Ms. Vincent stood first, releasing Vanessa's hand and hurrying toward me. I caught her wiry body, wrapping my arms around her.

She instantly burst into sobs. "My boy. My baby boy."

"Shhh," I tried to soothe her, but my attempt had no effect. Her sobs grew louder until her whole body was shaking and spasming. "Shhh. You've got to be strong for Trey. He's a tough kid. He's going to pull through."

I knew nothing about his condition, but I had to believe it or I might break down into sobs just as pitiful as hers.

Vanessa stood and crossed the room. She laid a comforting hand on Ms. Vincent's shoulder.

I met her eyes. The normally vivid blue was dull and lifeless. Haunted. She looked hollowed out.

Neither Vanessa's nor my comfort could temper Ms. Vincent's hysterics. A nurse bustled down the hallway and drew her out of my arms. "Let's get you something to help you calm down, ma'am."

She led Ms. Vincent away, leaving me, Vanessa, and Hennessy alone in the small, plush waiting room.

The pale yellow walls were set off by white trim, and it boasted two cream leather sofas, a cream leather recliner, and a cherry coffee table. A flat screen TV was mounted in the corner, and coffee service was set up on a matching cherry sideboard.

Something about the fancy waiting room made Vanessa seem even more vulnerable dressed in those thin, blue hospital scrubs.

"Get the fuck out, Hennessy," I barked.

Vanessa's eyes flashed, as though coming back from the wasteland she'd temporarily retreated to. Her expression said, *Shut up, Con.* But I was beyond caring what Hennessy knew or didn't know. Besides, the smart fuck was already convinced that he knew everything. So what did it matter? He didn't have any reason to share what he knew with anyone, and I'd make certain he didn't develop a reason any time soon.

"I'm not going far," he replied.

"I don't fucking care where you go, so long as it ain't here."

I didn't bother to glance in his direction as he slipped out of the room and shut the door behind him.

Vanessa stood only a few feet away from me. It was a few feet too far, but I stood rooted, needing the temporary distance to see with my own two eyes that she was okay.

"He shot at you." It wasn't a question.

"Yeah." Her beautiful blue eyes glistened, and a tear spilled onto her cheek.

Screw the distance. I reached out and wrapped both arms around her, hauling her against me. "Scared the fuck out of me, baby."

Her tears fell harder and faster, until a patch of my T-shirt was soaked through. When she didn't cling to me, only stood there crying, I whispered, "Hold on to me, princess. I need to know you're with me."

A moment passed before her arms snaked around my waist, squeezing me. This time, it was her body that shook with the force of the sobs.

"It's okay, baby. You're okay."

Against my T-shirt, her words were garbled.

"Slow down, honey. Just slow down." I rubbed a hand up and down her back, trying to soothe her more successfully than I had Ms. Vincent. Finally, her words came out more clearly.

"He shot him. He shot Trey. Trey...he...he was trying to help me. And that guy shot him." Any other words she might have spoken were lost to the sobs once more.

Jesus Christ. I should've gotten the details.

"My fault. It's my fault."

Fuck.

"It ain't your fault, princess. You didn't pull the trigger. So no way in hell is this your fault."

Her lungs heaved, and for the first time, I didn't particularly care that her breasts were crushed against my chest. Not beyond the fact that both of our hearts, which were breaking, were pressed together.

"It's my fault."

I pulled back, looking down into her red-rimmed eyes. "It's not your fault."

"I shouldn't have been there."

"And neither should he."

"But—"

"No." I cupped her cheeks in both hands, tilted her face up to mine. "There's nothing you can do or say now that's going to change what happened. All you can do is what you were doing with Trey's mama—pray."

⚜

We spent hours in that yellow room. The nurse brought Ms. Vincent back after calming her down, and I sat in the middle of a sofa, one arm wrapped around Vanessa and the other wrapped around Ms. Vincent.

Hennessey had stopped back, surveyed the scene, and left. He'd be showing up on my doorstep soon enough to get the scoop—of that I was certain.

When he'd returned to the waiting room, Vanessa had tried to scoot away from me, but I'd pulled her closer to my side. I'd probably catch hell for that later, but for right now, I wasn't letting her out of reach.

A solid knock preceded the door swinging open again, and a man in green scrubs stepped inside. It didn't take a genius to figure out that he was the surgeon.

Ms. Vincent was on her feet before he opened his mouth to say, "I'm Dr. Byron."

She clutched the beads of her rosary until I was certain she'd snap the thing. "How...how is my boy? Is he...please, doctor..."

"He's still critical. I repaired the artery, but he lost a lot of blood. We're going to be monitoring him closely over the next several hours."

His words were guarded, and as much as I tried to find hope and optimism in them, I couldn't.

"Can I see him?" Ms. Vincent asked.

"Just for a little bit, ma'am. He's in the ICU." The doctor looked at us. "Only immediate family, though."

Holding Vanessa against my side, I met Ms. Vincent's eyes. "You go. We'll wait here."

She looked from me to Vanessa. "You take that girl home and stay with her. She's been through hell tonight. I've got Jesus to keep me company."

Vanessa protested. "I'm fine—"

Ms. Vincent stepped closer, and laid a hand on Vanessa's arm. "I see the guilt you're carrying. Don't. No matter what happens, my boy is a hero tonight."

Vanessa stiffened. I squeezed her against me again and answered for her. "Yes, ma'am. I'll be back first thing." I glanced up at the doctor and back to Ms. Vincent. "Anything changes, you call me. I don't care what time."

Ms. Vincent smiled weakly. "You're a good man, Constantine. Now get outta here. I need to see my boy."

Single file, we left the room, Dr. Byron taking Ms. Vincent to one bay of elevators, and Vanessa and I heading toward the ones I came up in with Hennessy.

With both arms wrapped around herself, she seemed to be drawing in and shutting me out. I didn't like it. I didn't question why that was. We stepped into the elevator, the silver doors shutting quietly before she spoke.

"I can call a cab. You don't need to bother yourself with taking me home."

I wasn't about to let her push me away. I slammed a fist against the red 'Stop' button, and she jolted when the elevator stilled.

"What are you doing?"

"You really fucking think I'm going to put your ass in a cab and send you home alone?"

Her hands chafed her arms, as though trying to warm herself.

I stepped closer, backing her into a corner. I wasn't sure how long it would be before the stopped elevator attracted attention, so I knew I had to make my point fast.

"You ain't leaving this building except with me. You ain't leaving the parking lot except with me. You ain't spending the night with anyone but me. You seeing the pattern here, princess?"

My words had the desired effect—they brought some life back to her. She shoved against my chest. "You can't order me around, goddammit. I...I...will not be ordered around."

And then my plan backfired.

She burst into tears and sank to the floor. She'd hit her limit.

Shit.

I reached down and scooped her up into my arms. I jabbed the button with my elbow and readjusted her so I could whisper directly in her ear.

"Baby, you scared the hell out of me tonight. I could've lost you. Right now is not a good time to ask me to let you out of my sight. I can't do it. I need you next to me so I know you're safe."

She hiccupped through her tears, and her nails dug into my shoulders as she held on.

"But Trey—"

I held her tighter against me and pressed a kiss to her temple. "Shhh...It's gonna be okay. Trey's gonna pull through. He's tough. He's a fighter."

The elevator chimed, and the doors opened. Her crying quieted, and she clung to me as I stepped out into the deserted lobby. I'd just crossed the threshold and exited the hospital when I remembered I had my fucking bike. *Shit.* I couldn't put her on the back of it. Not in this state.

I spied a bench and stopped in front of it. "Gotta set you down for a minute, babe. To call a cab."

Her luminous blue eyes darted up to mine, confused. "You changed your mind?"

I lowered her as I replied, "What? No. Just can't put you on my bike. Should've driven the Tahoe. But I didn't think beyond getting here as fast as I could."

Once she was seated, I reached into my pocket, palming my phone. I kept my attention on her even as I scanned through my contacts to find the cab company I normally used. Vanessa swiped at the remains of her tears with the side of her hand and seemed to pull herself together.

"Don't. It's okay. The bike is fine. I'm not going to fall off."

I shook my head. "Don't worry about it. This is easier."

I found the number and was about to initiate the call when she pushed off the bench and stood.

"What—"

I didn't get the rest of my question out before she marched off toward the parking lot.

The fuck?

"Vanessa, wait."

She didn't bother to turn, just kept walking toward my bike—which was still parked in the clergy spot I'd nabbed. I was happy to see they weren't towing people at this hour. Either that or security bought the idea of a clergyman riding a Harley.

I hurried after her, catching up to her just before she grabbed the helmet off the seat. "What are you doing?"

Her lips were compressed, her brow furrowed, and her jaw set. Determined. Mulish, even. "I want to ride the goddamn bike. So let's go."

I wasn't going to argue with the woman. It was damn near four AM, and I wasn't going to win. I wasn't even going to try.

"Fine. Get on. I'll buckle your helmet."

She didn't ask where we were going, and I didn't offer. There was only one place that seemed right. So I pointed the bike back toward the lake house.

vanessa

I wanted to ride the goddamn bike.

Traumatic experiences affect people differently. In the past, I'd always pulled myself inward, shoring up my defenses to create a private, hidden place to let the pain batter me into submission. From the outside, you'd never know the battle raging within.

I'd been building those walls, cementing them even as I said *Hail Mary* after *Hail Mary* with Ms. Vincent. I had a feeling she was doing the same thing. Because without those walls, we'd have no choice but to break. And as women, we didn't have time to break. We were too busy trying to figure out how to cope and fix.

But tonight? Con had screwed up everything. His surprise appearance had derailed my emotional masonry. Instead of standing tall on my own, he'd propped me up, lent me his strength. I didn't know how I felt about that. But now, instead of keeping everything contained, the storm was blowing out of control, and I wanted to do something crazy. Instead of numbing the hurt, I wanted to feel *alive*.

I wrapped my arms around Con as we rode. He was so solid. So steady.

I didn't think when he pulled between the stilts of the lake house. I didn't try to stay his hands as he removed my helmet. I didn't protest when he led me toward the back stairs and then up and inside. I waited for him to pause inside the massive sitting room just beyond the doors.

And then I acted.

I shoved him toward the sofa where he'd given me the most intense orgasm I'd had since...that night he didn't remember and I remembered all too vividly.

"Whoa, princess. What the hell are you doing?"

"Shut up."

Con's head jerked back, and his eyebrows went up as he let me push him down into a seated position.

I reached for the hem of the scrub shirt and...my not-quite-a-plan unraveled when I remembered that I was still gross from crawling around on the ground.

The wave of disappointment hit me so hard, tears burned behind my eyes. I'd already cried too much tonight. I didn't want Con to see me cry again—not when I was just feeling sorry for myself. I spun, turning my back to him, and wrapped my arms around my middle.

"Whoa, princess." The words were the same as those he'd spoken only a few seconds before, but this time his tone was hushed, careful. Like he was worried he was going to watch me lose it again like I had in the elevator.

I fought back the tears and cleared my throat.

"Do you have a shower I can use? I'm disgusting."

I felt the heat of his body against my back before I even realized he'd stood. For a moment I expected a smart-ass comment, and then realized I was operating on my old assumptions. He'd been nothing short of amazing tonight—a stand-up guy beneath all the ink that colored my and society's judgment of him.

"You can use whatever you want. Including me, if that's what you need."

Jesus. I was so transparent. "It's not... I mean... Never mind." I breathed deeply and took a half step forward, but Con's arms wrapped around me from behind and yanked me back against his chest.

He whispered against my hair, "Maybe I need it, too."

I squirmed, and he loosened his arms, as though preparing to drop them. I twisted around to face him. His deep blue eyes lowered to mine. "Then don't make me shower alone," I whispered.

I ran a hand down his rippling bicep, skimmed along the colorful tattoos on his ropey forearm, and laced my fingers with his. I wasn't sure if he was going to take me up on my invitation until he squeezed my hand, trapping my palm against his.

His voice was rough when he said, "Follow me."

I began to second-guess my offer as soon as we hit the bathroom—at the exact moment I realized he was going to see me naked under the bright lights. No dimly lit bedroom. No covers to hide under.

Shit.

He reached for the light switch, and I almost sighed in relief when he slid the dimmer to illuminate the bathroom only halfway.

He'd still see me, but with the distraction of the water and the dim light, I'd be able to hide some of my flaws.

Con tugged his shirt over his head and tossed it to the gray travertine floor and reached inside the glass enclosure to turn on the shower.

All thoughts of my body issues evaporated when I stared at him. My eyes feasted on the tanned and inked skin stretched over ridges of defined muscle. It'd been two years since I'd last seen him shirtless, and he'd definitely made some changes. He was still as ripped as he'd been then, but there were more tattoos. I'd be hard pressed to pick and choose exactly which were new, because unfortunately I didn't have a photographic memory.

Although I did find it hard to believe I'd ever forget what I was seeing right now.

"Your turn, princess."

Uh. What?

He'd turned back to me, and I'd been so caught up in cataloging the ripple of his obliques and flex of his pecs, I'd completely forgotten what I was doing.

I dragged my eyes from his chest up to his smirking lips. He'd clearly taken note of my detailed inspection.

He stepped toward me, and every muscle in my body clenched, including the inner ones.

Moving slowly, as though waiting for me to back away or protest, his huge hands drifted to the hem of my scrub top. When I stayed still, he slipped both hands beneath it, skimming up the curves of my waist and ribs, raising the shirt as he went.

"Arms up."

Inhaling sharply, I complied with his command, and my vision went dark for a moment as he pulled it up and over my head. Wearing only the strapless bra that had been necessary for my cocktail dress, I stood in front of him. This time it was his eyes that strayed—or rather caught on my chest as it lifted with my heaving breaths.

Heaving bosoms.

I don't know where the thought came from, but it was so ridiculous I couldn't help the giggle that escaped.

Con froze, hands hovering just inches from my sides.

"You about to lose your shit, sweetheart? Because we can stop right here, and I'll pretend I'm a gentleman for once in my life, and leave you to shower in peace."

Trying—and failing—to wipe the slight smile off my face, I said, "It's not that. I'm...just ignore me."

This time he chuckled. "Like I've tried to ignore you for years? Hasn't worked yet. Doubt it'll work now." His eyes dropped meaningfully and lingered on my body. "Especially when I've got you almost naked, and I'm fucking sober this time."

All humor fled my brain. There was one thing I had to know; I'd been wondering about it for way too long.

"Would you have taken me home that night if you hadn't been drinking? I always assumed that the only reason you'd forgotten you hated me was because of the booze."

The backs of three fingers skimmed up the bare skin of my arm, leaving goose bumps in their wake.

"I've never hated you. That's the problem."

I jerked my gaze away from his hand and looked up into his blazing blue eyes.

"But in high school—"

"Thought we already covered the fact that the chip on my shoulder is big enough for Evel Knievel to use to jump a dozen school busses."

"So—"

"The way I grew up, it's easier—hell, safer—to pretend you don't want something than it is to admit how you really feel."

"Oh," I whispered. "I always thought..."

"Exactly what I wanted you to think."

"So that night..."

"I've spent more time trying to fill in those memories than I'd ever admit. It kills me that it's nothing but blanks." He flipped his hand, and his palm wrapped around my shoulder. "I've waited long enough. And you better damn well believe I won't forget a second of what happens next."

I shivered, and the heat of his palm skimmed up the column of my throat, until his thumb rested under my chin. He lowered his head, tilted my face, and took my mouth.

Reaching up, I twined both arms around his neck, burying my fingers in his hair. Con's free hand slid down my back until it reached the band of my bra. I barely realized what he was doing before it unclasped, and the pressure against my breasts released.

I let go of his hair and smashed one hand against my bra to hold the cups in place.

Con lifted his head and stared down at me, confusion clear in his expression.

I knew in that moment I had to explain my hesitancy. He'd laid a little piece of his soul bare, and I was going to do the same.

"I have...stretch marks."

His eyes turned sharp. "You had a baby? Who the fuck knocked you up, and how did you keep it quiet?"

My humiliation was complete. I stepped back, squatting to feel around on the floor for my top. I needed to be covered, because now he was studying my midsection.

"No one, you ass. They're from being fat." I squeezed my eyes shut as tears threatened again. "Just...get out."

I wouldn't look at him. I absolutely *would not* look at him.

Until he dropped to his knees in front of me and grabbed my chin.

"Whoa, honey. Calm down."

The tears that had threatened to fall dried. It was official. Con Leahy was just as dumb as every other man on the planet. I jerked my chin from his grip.

"Don't you tell me to *calm down*. I'm freaking calm. You're the one who isn't calm."

Finding the scrubs and using them to cover my chest, I stood and pointed to the door. "So just go."

I expected him to tuck his tail between his legs and skulk out of the room. Why? Because underestimating Con seemed to be a habit I couldn't shake. I'd have to work on that.

His trademark smirk flashed on his lips. "I don't think so, babe."

I glared. "If you think this is still happening, then you're insane."

"I've been called worse."

"The mood—if there was one—is gone. I just want to take a shower and crawl in bed—by myself."

"Too bad." The smirk kicked up a notch, and I had to stifle the urge to smack it off his face.

"You're such an asshole. Get. Out." My voice rose this time, perilously close to a shriek. Didn't care.

Con lunged, wrapped both arms around me, tossed me up and over his shoulder, and stepped into the hot spray of the shower.

"Ah!" This time, there was no question that the sound coming from my mouth was a shriek. It echoed off the glass and tile. The water beat down, plastering my hair to my face. In the manhandling, I'd dropped my bra and the top. My scrub bottoms were already soaked when Con slowly lowered me to my feet. I shoved against his chest as soon as I had my bearings. "What the hell do you think you're doing?"

"I'm not letting you get away again. No matter how bad I fuck up."

Shoving my hair away from my face, I stared up at Con's earnest expression.

"I'm sorry," he started. "I shouldn't have jumped to conclusions. I just—" He jammed his fingers into his wet hair. "I don't give a fuck about stretch marks. I just couldn't stand the thought of someone else...having you." He turned away, facing into the pounding spray. "Fuck. That sounds insane. It *is* insane. Jesus. This can't—"

I didn't wait for him to finish. I slipped between Con and the tiled shower wall and dropped to my knees, soaked scrubs and all. I didn't want to hear him say what this could or couldn't be. I didn't want limits. Didn't want restrictions. For once in my life, I wanted no boundaries. No guidelines. No can'ts. I struggled with the button of his jeans, and his words dropped off.

"What the hell are you doing?"

"Shut up," I told him. It was exactly what I'd told him downstairs, when I'd had my first spur of boldness. It was time to follow through, and I wanted to be the aggressor. I wanted to take what I wanted without thinking.

I yanked at his zipper and tugged his jeans down his legs.

Hello.

The man went commando.

Con's erection bounced as the sodden denim puddled on the floor.

And *hello again*.

My eyes widened. If I were a cartoon, they would have bulged right out of my head.

A silver ball winked from the top of the head of Con's penis, and a matching ball glimmered directly on the other side.

"*That's* new." I wasn't even aware I'd said the words out loud until a burst of Con's laughter echoed in the shower.

"Is that gonna be a prob—"

Con's words cut off, as though he'd been strangled, when I gripped the base of his shaft and licked him from root to tip, tonguing the bottom silver ball when I hit the head.

"Shit, woman."

His thighs flexed, and I imagined that his knees went a little bit weak. I liked that idea.

You just want to be the woman to bring this man to his knees.

I didn't deny the voice in my head, but I did wonder if I'd know what to do once I got him there. The vivid memories of that night played through my mind.

Yeah, I'll know what to do when I get him there... but only because Con had taught me.

I closed my mouth over the head of his cock and played with the piercing before taking him deeper. His girth stretched the limits of my lips, and even with my hand holding the base, there was no way I'd be able to take the rest of him.

Con was...a big man. A really, really big man. Like the largest penis I'd ever seen in person or on internet porn. Not that a lady would ever admit to looking at such things. It wasn't my fault that Elle had instituted a 'dick of the day' texting ritual.

Con's hands found their way to my hair, and he smoothed it back, gripping the makeshift ponytail with his fist. My movements slowed as he cupped my cheek and guided me.

"Just like that, baby. Just like that." He groaned. "Jesus fucking Christ. Yeahhh." His hips surged forward, and his cock hit the back of my throat. Tears sprang to my eyes as I gagged.

Con slid out. "Sorry about that."

I didn't let him apologize any further.

"Shut up."

"You seem to really like telling me that."

"Only because you don't seem to know when to be quiet."

"Bossy."

I tongued the head of his cock. "You have a problem with that?"

"You've got my dick in your mouth, princess. I don't have a problem with any-damn-thing."

Speaking of his dick in my mouth, I swallowed it down again. It became my personal mission: I was going to deep throat this man. My gag reflex would have to submit.

"Whoa, baby." Rubbing his thumb along my cheek, he added, "You don't have anything to prove."

I always have something to prove. My eyes must have telegraphed my thoughts, because he smiled. "Type A. Goal-oriented." He shook his head. "I should know better than to try to slow you down."

He stepped back, pulling his thick cock from my mouth inch by inch. The head slipped through my lips with a *pop*.

"What are you—?"

Con reached down and lifted me to my feet.

Sometime during my drop to my knees and my enthusiastic blowjob, the drawstring of the scrubs had come undone. And as I stood, they slid down my legs and landed in a heap on the floor.

I backed up, the cool tile meeting my shoulder blades. I stood just close enough to the wall to be out of the spray. Con moved closer, his chest pressing against mine. It was like hiding beneath a waterfall. My nipples puckered against his skin.

Con's hands slicked down my arms until they found my fingers. Pulling my wrists above my head, he pinned them against the wall. He reached up and batted the showerhead above me out of the way, and the spray changed directions. Stepping back a foot, he surveyed me.

Except for my thin lace underwear, which revealed more than it covered, I was stripped bare.

And so was he.

Instead of giving in to my insecurities about my body, I got distracted by his.

Jesus. The man was a living, breathing work of art.

If my panties weren't already soaked, they would be now.

I wondered for a moment if he considered my uninked skin boring. But the expression on his face—the way his eyes devoured me—it didn't appear to bore him in the least.

"You're so fucking beautiful. I shouldn't even be allowed to put my hands on you." His chest rose and fell with a rough breath. "Tell me to walk away. Tell me not to touch you. Tell me—"

I tugged at his hold on my wrists, wanting to cover his mouth with my hand. Wanting to silence his words. But his grip was too strong. *He* was too strong. "Don't make me tell you to shut up again."

The intensity in his gaze sharpened. "You shouldn't let me have you."

"Why? Why would you even say that?"

"Because once I have you—and remember every goddamn detail—I can't promise I'll let you go. And you need me to let you go. I need to be able to let you go."

I didn't want to think about what his words might mean—because they didn't matter. All that mattered was right now. And I needed him to touch me.

"Are you really saying you'd rather I tell you to back off and walk away?"

"If I were a better man...that's exactly what I'd do."

"I don't want a better man. I want just you. Right here, right now."

"Then so be it."

Con's dark blue eyes flashed, and his nostrils flared as he released my wrists. I thought he would pounce on me. Pin me to the wall. Fuck me until I couldn't walk.

But he stepped away, exiting the shower.

What the hell?

"Fuck. Need a condom." Con's grunted words were accompanied by slamming drawers. "Shit."

A moment later he was back. Shaking his head, Con said, "You will never know how goddamn sorry I am that I've never brought a woman here." He paused. "Shit. That came out wrong. I mean. Fuck. I just...I don't have any protection. Don't fucking keep it in my wallet anymore. Or in the saddlebags of my bike."

"You've got to be joking."

"Sorry, babe. I'm not."

I covered my face with both hands. *Screw it.* "Are you clean? I mean, have you been..."

"Tested? Yeah. And I'm clean."

"Well, so am I."

"You seriously saying you want to go bare? Because I gotta be honest, I'm not sure I'm okay with that." He crossed his arms over his chest, his expression unreadable.

"Are you kidding me?" The incredulity in my tone could absolutely not be missed.

Con grinned. "Yeah, princess. Of course I'm fucking kidding you. You think I'm going to pass up the opportunity to get my dick inside you with nothing between us?"

I reached down and shoved my panties off my hips. "Then get your ass back in here."

I'm not sure when I forgot to care that I was naked in front of Con. Somewhere in my absolute horror at the thought of ending this night without being with him, I realized that whatever hang-ups I still had with my body—and there were plenty—Con didn't share them. The way he looked at me...the things he said to me...He just wanted *me*.

For the first time in my life, I felt like a seductress. This man was under my power, and I was going to *revel* in it.

Con didn't waste any time. Two long, sure strides, and he had me pinned against the wall again.

"You're nothing like I expected. Not in my wildest dreams."

My confidence faltered. "I—I'm not?"

He shook his head. "No. You're so much fucking better."

Relief rushed through me hotter than the spray of the shower—which was still running and had yet to turn cold.

He continued, "I thought I'd have to warm you up, but you're so fucking hot, you burn me before I can even touch you. It's..." He swallowed. "It's like nothing I've ever experienced."

His hands framed my face, and once again we were all lips and tongues and teeth. I'd never realized that kissing a man could be so...intense.

When he finally pulled away, he spun me around so I faced the tile wall. "As much as I want to look at your gorgeous face, this works better for now."

I could have bristled at his comment because it just reminded me of how much more experience he had than me, but instead I embraced it. Why should I care? I was going to be the beneficiary of everything he'd learned from every one of the women who'd come before me.

He nipped at my ear. "Brace yourself on the wall. It's gonna get a little rowdy in here."

Shivers racked my body as he dragged his teeth down my neck and bit my shoulder lightly before laving the spot with his tongue. My head dropped forward, a ragged sigh escaping my lips.

Strong hands snaked around my body and cupped both breasts. Clever fingers teased and tugged at my puckered nipples.

"Fucking love your tits. Gonna come on them later."

His crass words unleashed a tidal wave of desire inside me. I shouldn't like this. Shouldn't want this. Shouldn't want him.

But I'd never wanted anything more.

"And if you ever try to hide them from me again," he cupped them both in one big hand, "I'm gonna paddle your ass."

I opened my mouth to protest and shut it when a stinging *slap* landed on the side of my left butt cheek.

"Hey!"

"Told you it was gonna get a little rowdy," Con's deep voice rumbled in my ear as his hand covered my tender skin and squeezed. "But you didn't run." He slid his hand around to my front side and cupped me between my legs. "And now this is mine."

I'm not sure what kind of reaction he was expecting to get from his declaration, but it probably wasn't me dropping my hand from the wall to reach back and grab his erection. "Then this is mine." I stroked him, toying with the little balls of his piercing, until he groaned.

"Fuck yeah, it is."

"Then what are you waiting for?"

"If this is my one night with you, I'm not going to rush a damn thing." He pulled my hand away and pressed it back against the tile. "Now wait patiently like the good girl I know you can be."

I ground my ass back into his groin, and another smack landed on the same spot as the first.

"Naughty girl," he murmured darkly. "Guess that's my fault. Haven't given your pussy nearly enough attention tonight." His fingers flexed, and one slid between my lower lips, pressing against my clit.

I moaned and bucked against his hand. I needed more. I needed him inside me. If he didn't get there soon, I was going to start begging.

His hand shifted, and one long, thick finger pressed up and slipped inside me.

"Fuck. Keep forgetting how tight you are."

The combination of him fucking me with his finger and the friction from the heel of his hand on my clit had all of the fibers of my body pulling taut.

A second finger joined the first, and I shivered at the stretch. If I felt like this with only two fingers, how was I possibly going to be able to handle the massive erection I could barely fit in my mouth? His fingers scissored inside me, and my muscles spasmed. I bucked against his palm and an unexpected orgasm burst inside me.

That porn star-worthy moan that filled the shower couldn't be from me, *could it?*

"You wanna come again for me, baby? Before I fuck you?"

I'm not sure how a sane woman would've answered, but I couldn't wait any longer.

My voice was ragged, still coming in heaves and pants when I said, "That depends. How many times are you going to make me come when you fuck me?"

The scruff of Con's jaw scraped my shoulder as he growled into my ear. "Until you beg me to stop, sweetheart." He tugged my earlobe between his teeth, and shivers cascaded through me. "I'll make you come until you fucking beg me to stop."

Shudders racked me again. *Oh my god. I think I just spontaneously orgasmed.*

"Please. Don't make me wait."

"Been waiting two fucking years. Shit, longer than that. No more waiting."

His hand dropped away, and I hated that I felt so bare without him touching me. I didn't have time to consider the thought further because he spun me around and lifted me with one arm under my ass.

"Wrap your legs around me," Con said.

I complied, and he used his other hand to position himself at my entrance. Just feeling the blunt head of his cock against the super-sensitive tissue had the makings of another orgasm shimmering to life inside me.

I could be overstating things, but I was beginning to think the man had a magic penis.

I giggled.

"What the fuck you giggling about, woman?"

"Nothing, I swear."

He didn't move another inch. I dragged my eyes away from the aforementioned magic penis.

"Tell me."

"If you wait too long, this shower is going to get cold."

He shook his head. "Don't change the subject. You want this dick," he swiped the crown across my clit and I shuddered, "then you better spill."

I couldn't take it. Humiliation be damned. "I think you might have a magic penis."

His head jerked back, and the smile that spread across his face was...so beautiful that if I hadn't been on the edge of getting laid for the first time in two years, I might have stopped to appreciate its beauty. But I hadn't. So I couldn't.

"Damn, I like you, princess."

"Good. Then *please* hurry up."

"Whatever the lady wants." And he thrust.

"Holy shit. Holy shit. Holy shit." My body stretched and softened, my slickness easing his way, but not enough so that I didn't feel incredibly, wonderfully, and totally *taken*.

"Jesus. So fucking tight." He shifted his grip so one big hand wrapped around each of my hips and his fingers dug into my butt cheeks. "You good?"

I nodded, almost beyond speech. I managed to get out, "Good. So, so good."

"You ready for me to move?"

"Yes. Yes. Please."

"That's my girl. Now let's see what we can do about those orgasms I promised you."

If I could ever have an out of body experience, I think I'd want to watch Con Leahy as he lifted and lowered me onto his cock, fucking me with sure, swift strokes. His piercing must have been a magnet for my G-spot, because with every thrust, it dragged along the promised land until my inner muscles bore down.

His groan filled my ears. "Ease up, woman. I'm already trying to hold out so I can fuck you proper before I lose my shit."

I fought to relax my muscles, and he kept on with his *proper fucking* as I said, "It isn't my fault...that you have a...magic...cock." As soon as the word 'cock' left my lips, my head dropped back, and another orgasm tore through me.

"Oh my God!"

And still he didn't stop. His thrusts continued, pounding into me, sending me over the edge twice more before he finally slowed and groaned out his own climax.

"Holy. Fucking. Shit."

As if on cue, the water lost its warmth, and we both jerked. Con pulled me out of the stream.

Voice rough, he said, "Fuck. Guess you lost the chance to take a real shower. Sorry about that, babe. I should take better care of you."

I squeezed my eyes shut, as my heart flipped.

How long had it been since someone wanted to take care of me? I couldn't let myself get used to it.

And just that fast, reality intruded.

Con was still inside me, but that didn't keep everything that had happened tonight from crashing down. The blissful haze of orgasm dissipated. I guess his penis wasn't *that* magical after all.

"Put me down, please."

"What? What's wrong?" Con's gaze sharpened.

"Just put me down. Please."

He pulled out of me and wetness gushed from between my legs. Con lowered me to my feet and reached outside the shower to grab a washcloth off a bamboo bench stacked with fluffy white towels. Running it under the spray, he offered it to me. "Sorry, it's cold now."

Given the twinge between my legs, cold was actually welcome. "Don't worry about it."

I cleaned up, and then accepted the towel he offered. Wrapping it around my shoulders, I huddled in the shower, shivering. And not in the mind-blowing orgasm kind of way I had been only minutes earlier.

Yep. Reality sucked.

"Let's get you a robe." Con wrapped a towel around his waist, and my attention dropped to the pile of sopping wet cotton of the scrub bottoms.

They reminded me of the destroyed Alexander McQueen cocktail dress I'd stuffed in the trash in the emergency room. The one I'd worn while I'd crawled across a parking lot and watched a boy get shot trying to protect me. And I'd just had mind-blowing orgasms in a shower while he was lying in the ICU.

Yes, the sex had been life affirming. Maybe even life changing, if I were so inclined. But right now, I couldn't see beyond the giant wall of guilt that slammed down between Con and me.

"Do you have any extra clothes?"

He nodded, slowly, studying me.

"You okay?" he asked.

For the briefest moment, I considered lying, giving the answer I'd given so many times before. *I'm fine.* But right now, I couldn't muster the will to offer up that BS line. Because right now, I wasn't *fine.*

"No." The word came out on a raw, ragged breath.

"Shit." Con tilted my chin up. "Did I hurt you?" His body vibrated with coiled strength. "I know I—"

"No." I shook my head. "It's not you." Tears pooled in my eyes, and I was too tired to hold them back.

"Whoa, honey." He caught a sliding tear on his thumb. "You gotta clue me in here."

I sniffled in a decidedly unladylike manner. "Trey. We just...and he could be dying."

Con stiffened and glanced toward his phone. "Not to say that every minute I was inside you, I wasn't totally focused on you...but if that phone had gone off, I would've been diving for it."

"But—"

With a shake of his head, Con reached out and grabbed another towel off the stack and used it to rub down his chest. "No buts. If you think Trey would've begrudged us what we just did, then you don't know much about kids like him."

Swiping at my tears, my brow furrowed.

Con registered my confusion. "Not how you're thinking. How many buddies do you think he's laid to rest because of drive-bys and other random-ass gang shit? Guaranteed it's a bigger number than you'd think."

I still wasn't following.

He continued, "When you grow up knowing that age eighteen and a high school diploma are no certainty, you take what you can and appreciate the shit out of it while you have it. Because you might not get another chance." Gesturing between the two of us, he added, "A second chance like this? Probably unheard of."

It made a sick and sad sort of sense.

Even so, it didn't completely alleviate the guilt I was feeling. Or the scary idea that it could just as easily be me lying in the ICU tonight.

Con checked his phone. "You going to work today? Because if you are, you better try to grab a few hours of sleep, and then you're going to need to get home to change."

I thought about what was on my calendar for the day. A meeting or two about the building project. Grant application review. Working on next year's budget. Any other day I would've found those things to be critical. But right about now, they were nothing that couldn't wait until tomorrow.

I shook my head. "I'm not going to work, but a couple hours of sleep would be good. Then I want to head back to the hospital and sit with Ms. Vincent."

"Okay." He strode toward the door, but paused on the threshold and turned back to me. "Where do you want to sleep?"

Fatigue was muddling my brain because I didn't really understand the question. "What do you mean?"

"You sleeping with me? Or alone?"

I'm not sure I liked that he was giving me an option. Because that meant I had to make a choice.

A voice whispered in my head, *it doesn't matter what you choose. You can't keep him. Might as well get what you can while you can.*

The logic was a little too much like that which he'd attributed to Trey's upbringing. But it made sense.

So I gave him the truth. "With you."

con

So now I'd had her—and I remembered it. When she'd frozen up after we'd stepped out of the shower, it'd been the perfect opportunity to find her some clothes, call her a cab, and send her on her way. That was what I would've done if this had been any other woman.

Yeah, it would've made me a prick, but at least it would've been simple.

Because lying here, holding a sleeping Vanessa, listening to her breathe, was anything but simple. This shit was getting downright complicated. Because there was no way I was ready to let her go.

When I was sixteen, she'd been the most perfect, unattainable girl I'd ever seen. And despite my current position, she was still just as perfect and just as unattainable.

Maybe if we both turned our backs on this town and started over somewhere new... but that wasn't about to happen.

A soft groan broke through my thoughts and the silence of the morning.

Vanessa's body jerked against the arm I had wrapped beneath her breasts. Loosening it, I propped myself up to look down at her face. Her features were tight and twisted. It was a look I'd seen way too many times before on the faces of my buddies. Hell, they'd probably seen it on my face more times than I'd like to admit. Nightmare.

There was no question in my mind what she was dreaming about. She didn't need to re-live that shit. I tightened my arm around her, giving her a slight shake.

"Baby, wake up."

I'd expected her to stay in the dream for at least another moment or two. I certainly didn't expect her to shoot straight up in bed, trying to knock my arm aside and scramble away from me.

"Whoa, honey. Calm down. You're okay. You're safe."

Her lungs heaved, and I worried for a moment whether she'd hyperventilate. "Shh. Shh. It's okay. No one can hurt you here."

Instead of continuing to struggle, she turned and buried her face in my neck. I wrapped both arms around her and stroked her wild mane of hair. Hot tears spilled onto my bare chest.

For several minutes, I just held her. I let myself get comfortable being her rock, her protection from all the bad things in the world.

The thought was sobering. Because in Vanessa Frost's world, I also qualified as a bad thing.

I pulled her away from my chest and met her vivid blue eyes, shining with the remains of her tears.

This was where a better man would make sure she was okay and then take her home and let her get on with her life. Without him.

And I still wasn't a better man.

She stared up at me, looking lost and scared. Last night, she'd wanted sex to feel alive. That wasn't a tough concept to grasp. I couldn't say how many times I'd hopped off a chopper or rolled back into base after a mission where the bullets had flown too fucking close for comfort and found oblivion by burying myself in a willing woman's pussy. Might've gotten me busted down in rank if we'd ever been found out, but the need was too strong to deny, regardless of the consequences.

And right now, Vanessa's wide blue eyes were too tempting. I opened my mouth to say something—anything—that would win me another hour with her, but she beat me to it. Except she didn't speak, just reached up, dug her fingers into my hair, and yanked my head down.

Her lips collided with mine. She was a woman on a mission, and I wasn't stopping her. The kiss went on for long minutes, until I let my elbows collapse, and we fell back onto the bed, Vanessa sprawled over my chest.

Untangling her hands from my hair and pulling her lips away from mine, she propped herself up. Gone were the shining eyes, and so was the expression I expected to see.

Instead, she looked horrified. The lightning fast change from aggressor to... whatever this was... practically gave me whiplash.

She shoved away from me and scrambled off the bed.

"What the hell am I doing?" she asked the empty room, her back toward me. She ran both hands through her hair and repeated, "What the hell am I doing?"

While I knew the question was rhetorical, it didn't stop me from answering. "Taking something you want."

She spun. Dressed in only one of my T-shirts, her long legs were mostly bare. I couldn't help but remember how they'd been entwined with mine while we'd slept—and how right that had felt.

"Like what I want matters." She scanned the room, most likely for the sweatpants I'd offered her when we'd finally made it to bed early this morning.

"Why shouldn't it matter?" I asked.

"It just doesn't." Spotting the sweatpants on the edge of the tall bureau, she snatched them up and jammed one leg and then the other into them. "I need to call a cab. I have to call my father too."

That last bit gave me pause. "You didn't call him last night? Before I got to the hospital?" I'd just assumed she had. Hadn't even thought to ask.

"No. I was a little... preoccupied."

"Shit. He's going to raise hell. The police. Your car..."

"I know. Which is why I need go. He's going to be furious I didn't call him last night so he could make sure my name stayed out of the paper."

"Might not be too late." I grabbed my phone off the nightstand and found Hennessy's contact. It rang twice before he answered.

"The fuck you want, Leahy? You know what time it is?"

"You already turn your report in?"

"Yeah, after you made it pretty fucking clear I wasn't needed at the hospital any more."

"Shit."

"What's your deal?"

"Is there any way to keep her name out of the press?" I asked, not needing to elaborate on whose name I meant.

"I sure ain't changing my report to keep her name out of it. Then I wouldn't be doing my damn job. And I know you're not asking me to do that."

A dead man couldn't miss the sarcasm in my tone. "Of course not. I'd never dream of asking you to look the other way."

"But I doubt anyone's seen the report yet. I'll call my lieutenant and ask him to see what he can do to keep it quiet. Given your girl's name, I imagine that request will go all the way up to the Superintendent, and he'll be happy to comply. At least as far as I know, he ain't no fool."

I didn't argue his 'your girl' comment, even though I knew I should. "Thanks, man."

"You owe me."

"Always seem to."

I hung up. "Hennessy is going to try to keep your name out of it. No guarantees, but it's the best I can do."

Her eyes assessing, she asked, "Why are you on such close terms with the cop?"

I couldn't help but laugh a little. "Surprised that I actually cooperate with law enforcement?" I stepped closer to her. "It's not like I've spent my entire life on the wrong side of the law. Hell, I was a damn good soldier."

"I know. I remember when you shipped out after graduation. Your dad was proud, but your mom was terrified."

The mention of Joy and Andre hit me in the gut like it always did. The sick feeling dissipated faster than normal when I processed the fact she remembered something like that. "Can't believe you actually paid attention to anything that had to do with me back then. I was beneath your notice."

Crossing her arms over her chest, her face flushed pink. "I don't know why you'd say that."

I lowered myself to the bed and sat with my arms braced behind me. "Because it's true."

Her little huff had my cock jumping in my boxers. Her eyes dropped to my lap, and I knew she hadn't missed it. A grin spread across my face. She was turning out to be more perfect than I could've ever guessed.

Her attention lifted, and her expression was serious. "Did it ever occur to you that I might have noticed you just as much as you noticed me?"

My grin faded.

No. That had never occurred to me. Ever.

"Are you shitting me?"

She rolled her eyes. "No. I'm not. But I don't have time to discuss this right now. I really do need to get home."

Still gobsmacked from the little bomb she'd dropped, I shoved off the bed and grabbed my jeans from the floor. Pulling them on, I jerked my head toward the door.

"Then let's go. But we're continuing this conversation later."

vanessa

I was unsuccessful at making it into the house unnoticed.

"What the hell are you wearing? Where the fuck have you been? I just got a call from the goddamn superintendent of police telling me you got carjacked last night!"

My father's roar echoed off the sixteen foot ceilings of the kitchen. And his outburst explained why he was waiting in the breakfast nook. He never ate at that table. He was lying in wait because I always used this door to come and go from the garage.

I looked down at the giant gray man's sweats and the T-shirt that read ARMY across the chest.

I wasn't a proficient liar on my best day, and the last twenty-four hours certainly didn't qualify as good. I decided to go with part of the truth. Besides, he'd probably already heard some of it.

"There was a boy who tried to stop the carjacker, and he was shot. I went to the hospital to get checked out, and I sat with his mother most of the night. My dress was ruined, and someone was nice enough to find me some clothes."

My vagueness was rewarded because he stood and paced the kitchen. "Your car?"

"The police have it. For evidence."

"And you're okay?"

I cringed when his question about my well-being came after his question about my car. I tried to ignore it as I stared at the Italian marble floor.

"Just some cuts and scrapes and bruises."

"I suppose that should've been the first question I asked when you came in the door. I apologize."

I'd shed more tears in the last dozen or so hours than I had in years, but once again they swelled in my eyes, spilling over onto my cheeks.

At my sniffle, my father studied my face. "You need to take more care. I already lost your mother. I'm not willing to lose you, too."

Then he did something that shocked me—he wiped the tears away like he never had when I was a child. Or a teenager. Or a woman. I honestly had no idea what the hell had brought about this sentimental side of him.

He stepped away and cleared his throat. "I'm late for a meeting. And you're going to be late for work."

"I'm calling in today. I'm going back down to the hospital to sit with Ms. Vincent." At his confused look, I added, "The mother of the boy who stepped between a carjacker with a gun and me."

"That seems unnecessary. We'll pay for the boy's treatment. That should be enough."

I dug in my heels. "Yes, we're paying for his treatment. Every penny. And no, that's not enough. He could still *die* because of me."

My father glanced down at his watch. "Fine. Do what you need to do. I have to go." Without any further discussion, he turned and walked out the door I'd just entered.

I supposed I should be happy he hadn't questioned me further. But I was too tired and wrung out to care.

Before I'd left the house, I'd put a note for my father on the desk in his office. It was the one spot he was guaranteed to visit when he came home. It seemed even at nine o'clock this morning I'd known that I wouldn't be returning to the house tonight. Normally, I wouldn't bother informing him, but after his strange attack of fatherly concern, I'd decided to allay any potential worries.

So the fact that my loaner Mercedes was now parked in the alley behind Voodoo Ink shouldn't be as big of a surprise. But for some strange reason it was. My sweaty hands clenched the steering wheel as I asked myself why I was here. I *shouldn't* be here. I didn't even know if I'd be welcome.

Whatever Con and I were doing, it wasn't defined beyond the boundaries we'd set early on. I was supposed to give him a shot. That didn't mean I had the green light to show up at his place of work and barge in. *Oh wait, I've already done that.*

This is a mistake. I should go home. But by now my father would almost certainly have found my note. I was somewhat surprised that my phone hadn't lit up with calls from him demanding to know where I was. But I supposed he was letting me be. Adhering to my stipulations.

I should be happy about that. But something about it bothered me all the same. One night after my narrow escape from a carjacking and he wasn't concerned that I was out and about.

I shook it off. I was thirty years old, and my thoughts were ridiculous.

Moving on.

I uncurled my grip from the steering wheel and pushed aside any lingering doubts. I was here. And as much as I shouldn't want to, I wanted to see Con. It had nothing to do with a deed and everything to do with needing the strength and protection he'd offered me last night.

Pushing open the back door of Voodoo, I straightened my shoulders—and the lines of my navy jersey wrap dress. My low-heeled gold sandals clicked on the black and white checkered linoleum floor as I made my way to the front counter. I felt odd coming in the back way. Like I was special somehow—when in reality I was probably only a few steps above a trespasser.

I wondered if I'd find Simon's Charlie sitting there, but it was the same woman I'd seen before. Delilah. Tonight her dress was black with silver moustaches printed all over it.

Her eyes widened when she saw me. If I'd come through the front door, it would've been like déjà vu.

She didn't wait for me to speak.

"Con, visitor."

"I'm busy," he called from the direction of his room.

"You might want to get unbusy—" she started, but I lifted a hand.

"It's okay. I can wait."

But the buzzing had already quieted, and he rolled backward out the door of his room. This time, it was Con's eyes widening.

He stood with a quick, "I'll be right back," to whomever was in the room, and came toward me.

He jerked his head toward the break room, and I preceded him inside.

"I'm sorry. I should've called first."

"What are you doing here?"

Well, that wasn't exactly an effusive welcome.

"I...I don't know," I replied. Because honestly, I didn't.

"So why are you here then?" His welcome wasn't getting any warmer.

"I don't know," I said again, before stopping and starting over. "No. That's not true. I know why I'm here, but I'm not sure what I'm actually doing here."

Con frowned and crossed his arms. "That doesn't make any sense."

"I know." My words came out louder and an octave higher than I'd planned. "None of this makes any sense. I shouldn't be here. But there's nowhere else I wanted to be."

His frown slipped away, and his expression turned unreadable. I expected a response. I wasn't sure *what* response. But I expected more than the silence I got.

I could've stamped my foot, but that would've been too humiliating. Instead, I asked, "Don't you have anything to say?" I rubbed my hand down my face. Maybe I was just overwrought. The last twenty-or-so hours had been too much. Maybe I was going to succumb to honest-to-God Southern belle vapors.

Now wouldn't that be embarrassing.

"You good with waiting?" he asked.

That's it? That's all he's going to say?

"I wasn't exactly expecting you to drop everything."

"You drive here?"

"Yeah, but it's a loaner. No one would know it's mine."

"Another flashy Benz?"

"What's your point?"

"You care if it gets stolen?"

"Not particularly." That was the least of my worries tonight.

"Then go upstairs. I think you know the way. I'll be up when I get there."

"That's it. That's all you're going to say?"

He gestured with his latex-clad hands. "I'll have more to say when I get there."

I huffed out an expletive, and a smile ghosted over Con's features. "Got a feeling I'll have a wildcat on my hands if you're this worked up already."

I didn't deign to reply. I spun on my heel and grabbed the handle of the first door to the right and yanked it open. Con's laughter followed me up the stairs even after I slammed it behind me.

Men.

con

I might've expected a wildcat, but what I found when I finally made it up to my place an hour and a half later was closer to a kitten.

Curled up in the center of my bed, Vanessa was dead to the world.

I shook my head at the turn of phrase. After last night, it was too real a possibility—one too narrowly avoided—to consider.

The whisper of her even breathing was the only sound from inside my apartment. Outside, the noises of the city faded away, because my only focus was on her. I'd walked up the stairs expecting to fuck her senseless, but now all I wanted to do was sit and watch her sleep.

And yeah, I knew that was fucking creepy.

The entire rest of my session, one where I'd finished a portrait of a man's dead wife on his arm, I'd thought about her words.

None of this makes any sense. I shouldn't be here. But there's nowhere else I wanted to be.

What the hell did that mean for us?

When she'd stepped back into my life, I'd seized the moment. I'd carpe'd the fucking diem. I'd gone after the opportunity that had slipped away from me and put the mystery to rest. And now? I wasn't sure where to go next.

My life didn't allow for complications. I wasn't going to drag her down into the darkness where I'd spent the last few years.

A darkness that was growing.

Because now I wanted to track down the fucker who'd pulled a gun on my woman and shot at her. What was one more to add to my prospective body count? Hennessy could read me all too well, because when he'd stopped in here today to give me an update on Trey, he'd asked what my plans were. The update, while appreciated, was one I didn't really need because I'd already been to the hospital and gotten one myself just as soon as I'd dropped Vanessa off a couple blocks from home. I'd continued to call the hospital on the hour to see if there was any change in his condition. And Hennessy's question about my plans? I'd punted on that one. Said the right things. Hell, I might've even said, *I'll let the law handle that one.* I'm sure Hennessy knew I was full of shit.

But what could the man really do about it? Not a damn thing.

Back to the sleeping woman in my bed. I tried not to read too much into the fact that she wasn't sleeping on my couch. For some reason, the fact that she was in my bed seemed so much more personal. So much...just *more*.

That is such a chick thought. I shrugged it off and stripped out of my clothes. A quick shower, and I was crawling into bed beside her. Two nights with her in my arms was a bad idea. It was the kind of thing I could get used to, and then once I handed over that deed, she'd be gone, and I'd be back to my one night, hit-it and-quit-it lifestyle.

It sounded so unappetizing when compared to this warm, gorgeous woman in my bed.

But was there really any alternative? Realistically, this was going nowhere. I'd asked her for my shot. And I'd gotten it. I hadn't thought beyond that. Didn't have a plan.

I thought of the deed I'd had my lawyer draft the day after the Boys and Girls Club dinner. It was practically burning a hole in the drawer of my desk in the break room.

A better man would...

"Con?" A sleepy voice cut into my thoughts as Vanessa rolled to face me. "Why didn't you wake me?"

The question was so goddamn domestic, like something a wife would ask her husband when he came home after a late night out and she couldn't quite stay up until he got in. I squeezed my eyes shut for a beat. Just one more thing I liked too much.

"I think I did just wake you, babe."

She snuggled in to my chest, still half asleep. "You smell good."

"That's what happens when you shower."

"Mmmmm." She pressed a kiss between my pecs, and her clever little tongue reached out to flick my nipple.

"Whoa, honey. What're you doin'?"

Her voice husky with sleep, she said, "What does it look like?" Her sharp little teeth caught my nipple and tugged.

"You need to sleep."

A small hand connected with my shoulder, shoving me to my back. "Don't tell me what I need. Too many people tell me what I need. No one ever asks me what I want."

I laced my hands behind my head and nodded down to my body. "Then take what you want. What you need. Only a stupid man would stop you."

She didn't look at me when she asked, "And you're not a stupid man?"

"Not tonight I'm not. Tomorrow could be a different story." And it could be. Because tomorrow I was due to make some decisions. Figure out exactly where this thing was going—and when I was going to end it. But for tonight, I'd take pleasure in being what she needed.

"At least you're honest."

Not hardly.

Vanessa made quick work of peeling off her dress, and the bra and underwear beneath it. Caught up in her creamy, unmarked skin, my fingers ached to reach up and cover her breasts. But I kept them where they were, eager to see how she'd take the reins.

I didn't have to wait long. She dragged the boxers I'd planned to sleep in down my legs and tossed them to the floor. Her hands went directly to my cock, and my groan filled the room.

If I'd thought her hands were clever before, they were fucking genius now. One cupped my balls and the other gripped my shaft.

She lowered her head so her lips hovered directly over my cock. *Just another inch, sweetheart.*

A flick of her tongue across my apadravya dragged a groan from me. "Did this hurt?" The whisper of her breath across the head of my dick stole my thoughts.

"What?"

"The piercing. Did it hurt?"

"Not as bad as you'd think. Why?" I didn't know why I asked the question. I should just want her to move along to the enthusiastic, dick-sucking portion of the entertainment, but this was about her. Not me.

"Just wondering. Because..." Her tongue flicked out again at the piercing.

Fuck. I fought to follow the conversation. "Because what?"

"Because I'm glad you did it. It feels really, really good." She lifted and repositioned herself so she was straddling me.

Apparently the enthusiastic, dick-sucking portion of the entertainment was not to be. But when the hot slickness of her pussy grazed my shaft, I didn't fucking care.

Using my cock and the piercing, she worked herself to the edge of orgasm. My hands, unable to stay still at the sight of this woman using me as her personal sex toy, reached up to cup her tits and tug her nipples.

"You gonna come on my cock, baby?"

A moan and a whimper were the only responses I got.

"You look so fucking beautiful like this, taking what you need."

"Need more." Her words carried an edge of desperation.

"What, baby?"

"Please…"

"Please what?"

"Fuck me."

I released her tits and slid my hands down her sides until I reached her hips. Picking her up, I bit out, "Put me inside you if that's what you want."

One hand shifted down my torso, where she'd been keeping herself balanced, and grasped my slick cock. Angling it upward, Vanessa fit the head against her entrance.

It took everything I had not to slam her body down and impale her with my dick.

Through gritted teeth I asked, "How do you want it? Hard or easy?"

Her hips shifted, as though trying to take me inside her, but my hold kept her from getting what she wanted.

"Please…"

"Hard or easy, princess."

Her eyes flashed on mine. "There's nothing easy about you, Con. I don't want easy."

That was all I needed. I released my grip and let her sink onto my cock.

"Oh my God." Her harsh exhale spurred me on. I clutched her hips and lifted her again before bringing her down and bucking my hips to stimulate her clit with my pubic bone. Her upright posture crumpled against the pleasure, and Vanessa fell forward, catching herself on my shoulders. I released one hip and dragged my hand up her back to pin her to me, chest to chest.

I held her there for a beat before resuming my grip on her hips and the counter-thrusting that would take us both to the edge.

"I'm going to—"

"No you aren't. You're gonna goddamn wait for me, baby."

A moan of frustration and the flutter of her inner muscles clued me in to the fact that whether I wanted her to wait or not, this wasn't lasting much longer.

"Please—"

"Hold on." I increased my pace and the ferocity of my strokes. Vanessa pushed up, riding me like a champ.

The telltale bolts of lightning shot down my spine. "Now, baby. Now." It was probably arrogant to think she'd come on command, so I decided to make it a certainty. Grasping her hip, my thumb slid over to stroke and press down on her clit.

The scream that practically shattered my eardrums along with the clench of her pussy clued me in to the fact that she was rocketing toward orgasm. So I let go.

vanessa

I woke up alone. Con had been gone a while—if the cold sheets were any indication. It took a few seconds before my synapses started firing, but as soon as they did, I bolted up in bed.

Shit.

It was Saturday, and I had a funeral to go to. I was just thanking God that it was for an old man and not a teenage boy. But either way, celebrating a life was on the agenda, and I didn't have time to linger.

Spying my dress and underwear in a semi-folded pile on the chair, I reached for them and hastily dressed. Thank God jersey didn't stay wrinkled for long. I found my shoes and slipped them on. Grabbing my purse, I slung it over my shoulder and tried not to let it bother me that Con had left without waking me. A brief flash of panic hit me as I wondered if his absence had something to do with Trey. I calmed myself with the rationalization that if he'd taken a turn for the worst, Con would have woken me.

Distracted, I made my way down the stairs to an empty Voodoo and out the door into the back alley. I checked the knob to make sure it locked behind me—shutting out the possibility that I could give in to my desire to head back up those stairs and crawl back into Con's bed and wait for him.

But if he'd wanted me to stay, wouldn't he have left some kind of note? I saw no sign of his bike when I climbed into my loaner, which was blessedly still parked in the alley.

I'd just twisted the key in the ignition when a loud rap on the window scared the ever-loving hell out of me.

Even though my glance out the window revealed a disheveled Con standing by my car, the sound was altogether too similar to the one made by the carjacker only a little over a day ago. I squeezed my eyes shut and tried to calm my breathing.

I hadn't gotten myself under control when my door was yanked open.

"What the hell are you doing?"

I held up a finger—the universal sign for *give me a minute before I lose my mind.*

Con was apparently not in the mood to give me a minute.

"You're just fucking leaving? Not a word. Just gone. Guess I shouldn't be surprised."

What the hell?

"What are you talking about?" I asked, pressing a hand to my still-thundering heart.

"You. Running off."

"I have to get to—"

"This should be good, because it can't be work, given that it's Saturday. That's the excuse you used last time."

"Last time? What—" And then his meaning hit me. Yes, I was a little slow on the uptake this morning. But I was also totally confused as to why he was comparing this morning to that one.

"Guess I should've expected it. I mean, what the hell did I really think was going to happen? I got what I wanted; you got what you wanted. Why would you stick around?" Con pitched the coffee carrier he was holding across the alley, and the cups exploded when they collided with the brick wall. "Should've known."

Mouth hanging open, I couldn't even form words. I felt like I'd just been dropped into some kind of alternate reality. This angry Con was the one I'd known *before*.

"What are you waiting for? You got what you wanted. Just go."

I could've gone. The twisted expression, accusing eyes, and bulging muscles covered with ink painted a foreboding picture.

But I didn't. Because I wasn't about to walk away from this encounter with absolutely no idea as to what had caused his behavior. Not even if I was running short on time.

So instead, I climbed out of the car. Hands on my hips, I stood tall and stared him down.

"What in the ever-loving hell are you rambling about, Con? You're the one who left me alone in bed and disappeared."

Con jammed his hands into his hair and shook his head. "Yeah, and it's so fucking convenient that you jetted as soon as you got your hands on the deed."

Now my confusion was complete. "What are you talking about? Seriously. Have you been drinking this morning already? I get that it's five o'clock somewhere, but this is a little extreme... even for you."

"The deed. The one you came in begging for, and the only motherfucking reason you ended up in my bed."

Now that just pissed me off, and I finally was catching on to why he was throwing his little mantrum. "Do you really believe what you're saying right now?"

"You tell me, princess. Why shouldn't I believe it?"

"I don't know, Con. I guess I thought I was in your bed last night because I wanted to be there. But right about now, I don't think there's anything I can say to make you believe that." I looked down at my watch. I didn't want our conversation to end like this, but Con didn't look like he was in the mood for a reasonable discussion.

"You could tell me you didn't take the deed and run."

"I don't think I need to. I'm pretty sure you can march your ass back up to your apartment and figure that out for yourself. Because if there was a deed to be had, it's still there." I got into my car and slammed the door, not waiting for his response.

Before I could buckle my seatbelt, Con ripped the door open again and invaded the cabin. "Oh, no you don't, princess. Changed my mind. You don't get to leave." He snatched the keys from the ignition and shoved them in his pocket before lifting me out of my seat and tossing me over his shoulder.

"Put me down. I'm leaving!"

"You're not going anywhere until I'm good and ready to let you go. I already made that mistake before. Took me two fucking years to recover from it. Not doing it again."

"You're insane!"

"And you're the one making me fucking crazy, so get over it."

I struggled, pounding on his back, probably looking like a cavewoman pissed off at the man dragging her back to his cave.

A heavy palm landed on my ass, momentarily stunning me into stillness.

Did he seriously just spank me?

My shock lasted just long enough for Con to find his keys and unlock the back door of Voodoo and slam it behind us.

"Put me down!"

"All in good time. All in good time." His words came out as grunts as my fists continued to land on his back. If I were a bystander, I'd be laughing myself silly, because we had to look ridiculous. Nothing I did stopped Con. He ran up the stairs, and I bounced on his shoulder with each step. Moments later I was flipping upside down, my skirt flying up toward my eyes, and landing on the bed with a *thump*.

I sprang right back up onto my feet and headed for the door—or at least I tried to. Con's thick forearm caught me around the waist.

"Now why would I let you get away so fast if I just went through all this trouble to get you back up here?"

"Because you don't want another encounter between my knee and your balls?" I snapped.

His chuckle sent my temper flaring even higher. "Come on, princess. Just hear me out. I'm about to apologize, and I'm pretty sure you don't want to miss that."

"All you've spouted is crazy this morning, so I'm not sure I'm equipped to handle whatever you've got to say next."

"Please."

One word. One word spoken in the most sincere tone I'd ever heard come from Constantine Leahy doused my temper. I stilled, and he dropped his arm. My eyes tracked his movements as he crossed the room and grabbed something off the kitchen table. A white envelope. He came back to stand before me and held it out.

I accepted it and stared down at Con's writing on the front.

VAN,

BECAUSE I DON'T WANT TO WONDER IF THIS IS THE ONLY REASON YOU'RE HERE. I'LL BE BACK, AND THEN WE'RE GOING TO TALK.

CON

"Ohhh..." All became clear. "You thought..."

"Yeah." He stuffed his hands in his pockets and watched me.

"I'm glad you didn't let me leave then."

"Why's that?"

"Because we really do need to talk. About this—" My hand shook holding the envelope. "And about what we realistically think is going to happen next."

Con jerked back as though I'd slapped him. And I suppose maybe I should have chosen my words better. "I mean—"

Con's grunt cut me off. "Yeah, I guess we do need to be realistic. Because it'd be a goddamn fucking fairytale if this was anything more than a short-lived affair. You need to go back to your world, and I need to quit stepping outside of mine." He shook his head.

Well, there was a reality check if ever I'd had one. But his words didn't add up with his actions.

"If you're so ready to end... whatever we're doing... then what's with the caveman impression you just pulled off? I would've thought you'd been happy to see the back of me."

His fists clenched and he stepped toward me. "I didn't say that's what I wanted, princess. I just said that's how it's gotta be." Even in my low heels, he towered over me by a good five inches. "We don't always get what we want. At least I don't."

I stared up into his deep blue eyes. This was the moment. He was giving me an out. I could walk away, deed in hand, and get on with my life. A life without Con.

I imagined seeing him on the street again like I had that night two years ago. Except in my imagination, he had his arm around some other woman and was leading her back to this very apartment. Jealousy for that faceless, nameless, *nonexistent* woman pooled in my belly like battery acid.

"I'm not ready." The words were out before I could even consider their impact. I just knew, with a certainty borne of nothing but the feeling in my gut, that I wasn't ready to let go of whatever this was.

Con's eyes blazed.

"Excuse me?"

The words came just as easily the second time. "I'm not ready for this to be over." I held up the deed in my hand. "Even without this between us, I'm not ready to walk away."

He shifted closer, the heat from his body burning through my dress. "Do you know what you're saying?"

I nodded jerkily. Whether I really knew what I was saying was up for debate, but the alternative was utterly unacceptable. "I think so."

"Then God help us both. Because that was your one shot to walk away clean. I don't know if I've got it in me to give you another."

I swallowed. "Guess we'll cross that bridge when we come to it." I looked at the clock on the wall and sighed. "I hate to say this, but I really do need to go. I can't be late for the memorial service."

A predatory smile spread across Con's face, and in that moment I knew I would follow him even if he led me straight to hell. "You ain't leaving until

I get another taste of you." He stalked me until I was pressed against the wall, and memories of the coatroom at the Boys and Girls Club dinner infiltrated my mind. I guess that was fitting, because we were sealing another kind of deal, and there was no telling how this one would end.

"Can you be quick?" I asked, partly joking, partly not.

"Guess we'll find out."

Yep. I'm going to hell.

vanessa

I made it home in time to smooth my hair up into a respectable chignon and slip into a black sleeveless sheath. It was one of my least favorites, which might seem odd because it was the only dress I considered wearing today. My only explanation: once you'd worn something to a funeral, it was impossible to put it on without thinking of death. I'd prefer to taint something I wasn't particularly fond of rather than a favorite. The dress I'd worn to my mother's funeral when I was fourteen years old still hung in my closet. It had hung there for sixteen years—never worn again after that day—and I still couldn't bring myself to give it to charity. It seemed wrong, like I'd be sending away a piece of my mother.

I hurried through my makeup and dashed out the door. Ten minutes later I was slipping into the pew beside my father, one row behind Archer. A form slipped in beside me as we rose for the processional hymn.

I glanced sideways and cringed.

Titan. I guess I shouldn't have been surprised to see him here, but there was no earthly reason why he needed to be sitting in the pew beside me.

I opened my mouth to whisper something to that effect, but the choir quieted and the priest started to speak. Unless I wanted the entire parish to overhear my tirade, it was going to have to wait.

As luck, or something, would have it, my father never seemed to notice the occupant of our pew who sat an arguably-appropriate distance away from me. He was too engrossed in the service. For that I was thankful.

An hour later, when six pallbearers were carrying the casket away, I tried to follow my father out of the pew, but the crowd swallowed him up. Herzog had attracted a full house. I suppose if he were sitting in heaven looking down on this, he'd probably be pleased with the turnout.

I tried to use the number of people to my advantage, but Lucas stayed close on my heels and even grasped me by the elbow to lead me through the throng and out the side door of the church.

Once outside in a deserted alley, I yanked my arm out of his grip.

"Please refrain from manhandling me. I know it seems like a complicated request, but I think you can manage to comply."

"Even a spitfire in church, I see."

"And why are you in church?"

"Figured I should do the upstanding thing and pay my respects to Herzog. After all, he's the outgoing treasurer, and I'm the incoming one."

"What?" His pronouncement caught me off guard. "You? Treasurer? Since when?"

"Since yesterday, at the special meeting of the board Archer called. No staff members were invited to the meeting, but I would've thought Archer would have told you."

Archer probably would have told me if I'd been at work yesterday.

Titan leaned against the railing. "By the way, are you okay?" He looked down at the cracked pavement beneath his shiny black wingtips. "I should've insisted we arrive and leave together for those things. I don't regret much in my life, but I do regret that you ended up in danger because of me."

My eyes widened at his statement. "Then I guess you should back off so I don't have to go to anymore."

His smile was slow and condescending. "Nice try, princess, but I don't think so."

I stiffened. "Don't call me that. Don't you *dare* call me that."

"Hit a nerve?"

I turned to leave the alley and Lucas Titan behind. I needed to follow the procession to the cemetery.

He reached out and grabbed me by the elbow. "I don't like it when you walk away from me, Vanessa. I wouldn't suggest you do it again."

I stilled, and spoke quietly. "I've kneed better men than you in the balls, Titan. Don't think your threat will stop me."

Laughter burst from his lips, and he dropped my arm. I didn't wait for a response before I strode from the alley.

27
con

I yawned and shifted on my stool to get the angle right to finish up the outlining I was doing on yet another tattoo of 'YOLO.' I almost just told the kid to close his eyes while I tattooed 'Dumb Fuck' across his bicep instead. But I'm pretty sure that I'd never hear the end of it. And I'd be footing the bill for the tattoo removal. Just another Saturday night at Voodoo.

Tonight was one of those nights where I definitely felt like I was getting too old for this shit.

I glanced up at the clock. Two more hours to go until I could close up shop and figure out what to do with the rest of my night.

Go over to Tassel and be seen and try to collect some more information, or go upstairs and climb into my empty bed. The empty bed part sucked ass. It'd never bothered me before, because despite what Vanessa seemed to think, I hadn't had a different girl every fucking night of the week. But now... now that I'd had her there, empty bothered me a whole hell of a lot.

"I gotta piss. You mind if we take a break, man?" The kid beneath my tattoo gun grabbed his dick to emphasize his words.

I lifted up my hand and wiped away the excess ink and blood. Outline was done. Thank fuck.

"Sure. Bathroom's around the corner."

"Cool. Mind if I grab a smoke, too?"

I shook my head. "Go for it. Take your time. You can go out to the back alley or out front."

A few moments after he climbed out of my chair and left the room, Delilah poked her head in the doorway.

"You need me to stick around, or you got this?"

I glanced at the clock. It was now two minutes after twelve. "This one will be wrapping up quick. Considering how slow it's been all night, I can't imagine we'll get a slew of walk-ins. No reason for both of us to sit here."

Her thick, blunt cut bangs bounced when she fist pumped. "Good deal. I'm dying to go find some fresh pussy. I've been riding the abstinence train for over a week, and it's starting to make me cranky."

She turned to leave, but my stomach growled.

"You want me to grab you some food before I go?"

"Nah, don't worry about it."

She waited. "You sure?"

"Yeah. Get out of here. Go get yourself some action." If it weren't like imagining my sister, I'd probably fantasize about that shit. What dude wouldn't?

While I waited for YOLO boy to come back in from his smoke, I grabbed my phone and sent a text.

C: I want to see you tonight.

Her response was instant.

V: I want to see you too.

C: Voodoo. I'm wrapping up soon and shutting it down early. Bring food.

V: Did you just order me to bring you food?

C: Woman, your man is hungry. Feed him.

I waited impatiently for her response. I hadn't even thought when I'd typed 'your man.' It just came out. In that moment I hated everything that tied us both to this town. If we could just walk away from it all, go somewhere else, she wouldn't have to come meet me in back alleys and on rooftops.

Although, I had to admit I liked the rooftops.

V: Fine, but I'm choosing.

C: Good, because I don't care as long as you get your ass here.

V: On my way.

I slid my phone onto the counter and headed to the front window. I locked the door and flipped off the open sign. It was stupid to close early on a Saturday night because I'd undoubtedly piss off at least one potential customer, but tonight had been unusually slow. Besides, I'd piss off hundreds of customers if it meant an extra night with Vanessa. Bad business, but what could I do? Even though she seemed into trying to make this work, we both knew it couldn't last forever. And that sucked. Especially because forever wasn't even sounding long enough in my book.

YOLO boy came back in the room and I rewashed my hands and gloved up again to finish his tat. According to his ID, he lived in a rich area of the city, and he'd turned eighteen three days ago. Good money said his mother was going to be dragging his ass to the tattoo removal place when she found out. Not my problem.

There was a knock on the backdoor when I was re-locking the front after letting YOLO boy out.

Perfect timing.

I crossed to the other end of the shop and pulled it open.

It wasn't Vanessa. It was Hennessy.

"What do you want?"

"Got some news for you," he answered.

"Can you make it quick?"

He lifted his chin. "Hot date?"

"None of your damn business."

"Fine. But I don't want to do this in the alley."

I shoved the door open wider and closed it behind him. Hennessy headed into the break room, making himself comfortable on the dog-hair-covered couch. His suit would be furry when he stood, but I didn't particularly care to let him know that. I waited in the doorway, arms crossed over my chest.

"What you got?"

"Your boy, Lord, took a gun in on pawn earlier this week."

"And?" Lord took dozens of guns in on pawn and outright bought even more. We paid top dollar and worked hard to make sure everyone knew that Chains was the place to go to unload your hardware if you needed cash. And we worked with Hennessy to run all of them through the police database. It wasn't something most other pawnshops did, but it was pretty much the entire reason I owned mine. The gun that killed my parents had never been found. It might've been a long shot, but I kept hoping one day it would show up in my shop.

The adrenaline rushing through my veins at his next words gave me hope that it had.

"Lord sent me a spent casing and bullet to run, like he always does. A Smith and Wesson Bodyguard, .38 special." He straightened and met my eyes. "It was a match, Con."

Holy. Fuck.

"Where is it? Who owned it? Registration?"

"Don't know yet. The serial number was filed off, so we're still working on that part. But I thought you'd want to know that we're getting one step closer. I pulled the case files and all the evidence from the warehouse. I'll let you know what I come up with."

I wanted answers. Now. And I remembered the little piece of information Gina Mulvado had shared. About a white guy pulling the strings. I probably should've passed that along to Hennessy, but I wasn't quite ready. It didn't always pay to lay out all your cards.

So instead, I thanked him for coming by. I needed to get him out of here before Vanessa showed. He'd already figured things out at the hospital, but I didn't like the idea of him knowing any more than he already did.

"As soon as you know something, I want it," I added.

"As long as you let the law handle it, I'll keep you in the loop," he countered.

I didn't give him a verbal reply. Just a nod.

He pushed up from the sofa, already brushing the dog hair off his pants. "What the fuck?"

"One of my employees—her dog thinks that's his bed. Sorry about that. I'd offer you a lint roller, but I'm fresh out."

Hennessy shook his head. "You're a prick, Leahy. You know that?"

"Takes one to know one."

I turned and stepped into the hallway. A clear sign that I was ready for him to get the hell out of my shop. Hennessy took the hint.

"I'll let you get on with your night, then."

"Thanks for coming by. I appreciate it."

The knock came on the back door just as Hennessy was reaching for the handle. He pulled it open. I heard Vanessa's sharp intake of breath before I could see her face. I assumed it was a picture of horror.

"Ms. Frost," Hennessy said. "Hope you've recovered from the other night."

I wrapped my palm around the door and pulled it open wider. Vanessa looked as perfect as ever in a pale blue sundress and sandals. A thin white sweater covered her shoulders.

I tried to picture us from Hennessy's point of view. On no planet did we look like we belonged together.

"Detective Hennessy," Vanessa said, clearing her throat. "Thank you for your concern. As you can see, I'm fine."

"Glad to hear it. I'll leave you two alone," he replied.

Vanessa stepped inside, and Hennessy was gone. I locked the door and drank in the woman before me. Her blond hair was loose, and her blue eyes were wide with surprise.

"What was he doing here? Is something wrong?"

Irritation flared within me. "No, princess. I'm not in trouble, if that's what you're worried about."

She glared. "Knock it off, Con. I'm not worried about you being in trouble. I'm worried about someone else. Trey? Your other boys?"

The irritation died as quickly as it rose. My gut reactions were going to get me another knee to the balls one of these days. I almost cupped my testicles protectively at the thought. "Nah. Something else. Don't worry about it."

Her eyes flashed. "I threatened to injure the last man who told me not to worry my pretty little head about something."

The irritation was back. "Who the fuck told you that?"

Her expression cleared, going from angry to unreadable in the space of a second. "No one you need to worry about."

What the hell is she hiding?

I didn't get a chance to push further because she held up two bags. "Brought you dinner. Or whatever a meal is after midnight. A midnight snack? We eating upstairs?"

I'm not sure what prodded me to answer, "How about the roof?"

Confusion creased her features. "The roof?"

"Yeah, got a table and chairs up there. It's… another place I go to chill."

Gesturing with the bags, she said, "Lead the way."

vanessa

I was glad I'd worn flat sandals, because climbing a rickety fire escape in heels would've been treacherous. I wasn't sure what Con's deal was with rooftops, but you'd better believe I was going to get an answer before I climbed back down this deathtrap.

Con helped me over the edge and onto the flat surface. The glow of the pale moon and the city lights revealed a patio set on green outdoor carpet. There were also a couple folding chairs that looked like they'd be fairly comfortable for lounging.

Con, who'd taken the bags from me the moment he'd gestured to the fire escape, set the food down on the table. Producing a lighter from somewhere, he lit a bucket candle on the table and then the tiki torches that edged the roof.

It was very much the rooftop version of a man cave.

"Come up here often?"

It was a stupid question, because he clearly did. But his answer surprised me.

"Yeah, for about twenty years now."

Twenty years?

"That would've made you, what? Eleven?"

Con nodded and began pulling the containers out of bags. It seemed like it was easier for him to talk when he wasn't looking at me.

"This was the place I came when I couldn't handle whatever was going on in my latest foster home. Sometimes it was a longer hike than others, but for the most part, I was always able to get here."

"Why this place?"

Con opened a container and the heavenly smell of lasagna wafted out. His head jerked up, and he stared at me.

"Really? Lasagna?"

I nodded, and looked away, feeling like my choice of food was baring my soul a little too much. It had sounded like a good idea when I'd stopped into a tiny Italian restaurant only a few blocks away just before they'd closed. It had seemed like a way to show him that I trusted him—that I was apologizing for the way things had started.

"I thought we'd give it another try."

Con straightened and crossed the few feet between us. "I need you to make this real clear to me, Vanessa. I don't want to misunderstand whatever it is you're trying to say here. I don't want to read into it and give it my own spin."

I thought carefully for a minute before I spoke. "I guess what I'm trying to say is that I want to figure out a way for this to work. The way you make me feel... I'm not ready to give that up. And the way I feel about you... well, let's just say I've never felt that way about anyone. And I'm afraid if I don't tell you now, somehow it's all going to slip away."

I knew I needed to come clean with him about Titan. It was a huge risk, but I was done hiding it. "There's something I haven't told you." I looked up and met his eyes. "And you have to promise not to overreact."

Con's expression hardened. "What?"

I bit my lip as I worked on finding the right words. "You know that I used to go to functions with Simon, mostly because it was easier to go with a date and my dad laid off the 'let's get Vanessa married' shtick when I was with him."

"Yeah. I'm well aware."

"Well, someone else thought having me on his arm was a good way to get into certain circles he otherwise wouldn't have been given easy access to."

Con's jaw clenched, and his eyes darkened. "Don't stop now, princess. You're just getting to the good part."

"It's not what you think. I didn't want to do it, but he saw us together... and decided that since he knew I wouldn't agree to date him, he'd use what he knew about us to get me to do it anyway."

"Who?" The word came out low and threatening.

"You can't do *anything*, Con. He'll tell Archer about us and portray it in the worst possible light. I need a chance to tell him first. You have to promise you'll let me handle it. I'm already blowing the terms of the deal by telling you. I just don't want to keep any more secrets—"

Con interrupted what was becoming a full-on babble. "Just fucking tell me who, Vanessa."

"Lucas Titan."

"I'm gonna kill him," Con bit out.

And that was exactly what I didn't want to hear.

I laid a hand on his arm. "You aren't going to do anything. I'm going to fix this. I just have to go to one more event with him, and it's done."

"You aren't going anywhere with Titan. He can go fuck himself."

My emotions were split evenly between frustration and something that felt a lot like gratitude for Con's behavior. I squelched that second emotion.

"Stow the possessive routine. I'm telling you because I need you to trust me enough to handle it."

"And you thought lasagna would soften me up enough to make me okay with the fact that some rich fuck is blackmailing my girlfriend, and she's been hiding it from me?" Chest heaving, Con paused. I think we were both internalizing the words he'd just spoken. I'd fixated on one in particular.

"Girlfriend?"

Con's eyes found mine. "You just told me you wanted to keep this going. What the hell else am I supposed to call you?"

The smile flitting around the edges of my mouth spread across my face.

"That works for me." I squeezed his arm. "Now do you want to eat before it gets cold?"

"This subject isn't closed. If you think I'm going to stand down and let Titan threaten you—"

"I know. But you also need to trust me. I have a plan."

Con growled, "I don't like it. But I do trust you."

"Good. Then let's eat."

I'd forgotten to bring wine, but after we'd finished the lasagna, garlic bread, and salad, I was glad for it. Because I had another idea. And since the rest of my ideas had seemed to unfold without blowing up in my face entirely, I was hoping maybe this one would work out okay too.

"What would you say if I told you I wanted a tattoo?"

Con's affectionate smile warmed me.

"I'd say I know a guy."

"Seriously, would you do it? Tonight?"

"What brought this on?" Con asked, one eyebrow quirked.

"Just something I've always wanted."

"A fleur de lis?"

It was what I'd asked for that first time I'd come into Voodoo when Con had laid down the law about the only ways he'd spare me his time. "I'm surprised you remember."

"Don't think I've forgotten anything about you yet, princess."

"So would you do it?"

Con reached over and covered my hand with his. "Yeah. I'm surprised you have to ask twice. Figured you'd realize that I'd do just about anything for you. Even stow my urge to rip Titan to pieces for thinking he could get away with blackmailing you... and especially because he succeeded, because of me." Con shook his head. "That part really pisses me off."

"I don't want to talk about it anymore, and I *certainly* don't want you to feel guilty. I made that choice. I'd probably make the same one again if it got me to this rooftop."

"You're something else, babe. You really want that tat now?"

"Yep."

"Then let's clean up and head down."

29
con

The woman never ceased to surprise me. And I'd found the surprises both good and bad so far—although mostly good.

The bomb she dropped about Titan made me want to dig my old sidearm out of my drawer and hunt the motherfucker down. But I was trying something new: trust. If Vanessa said she was going to take care of it, I was going to trust that she would. I'd gotten over most of my old issues, and the lasagna we'd shared indicated that she was getting over some of hers.

So this was what an adult relationship felt like? With any other woman, I might have missed the variety of my previous lifestyle, but with Vanessa in my bed, I couldn't even remember a single one of those women. She was the ultimate prize. And I would do my damnedest to cherish her.

I helped her down the last rungs of the fire escape, and the ladder squeaked and groaned as it retracted up into its resting position. At eleven, I'd had to climb on a nearby dumpster and jump for it. To this day I didn't know what it was about this building that called to me so strongly. All I knew was, once I had the money, I'd bought it. I'd hired a crazy talented, but retired, tattoo artist to spend a year teaching me both the art and the business. I'd always been able to draw, and it had been therapeutic learning to use my hands to create rather than to kill.

I tossed the trash in the garbage and opened the door, letting Vanessa precede me into the shop. She made her way directly to my room, and I flipped on a few necessary lights. I paused, remembering the drawing I'd been working on a few days ago. It was willful blindness for me to draw it and pretend that I didn't know exactly who I was drawing it for. I ducked into the break room and grabbed it off my desk.

It was a fleur de lis resting in a crown.

Vanessa was waiting in my chair when I entered the room. And she was naked. Buck. Ass. Naked.

I think my heart stopped. But when it resumed, it thudded away in a heavy beat.

"What—"

"Once you told me the only way a woman got time alone with you here was to get a tattoo or get on her knees or back. I decided to go with on my back first and then the tattoo."

Who the hell is this woman?

I dropped the drawing on the counter. Only a stupid man would turn that offer down, and today I was very, very smart.

"Well, aren't you full of surprises tonight."

"I'm going with my gut. It's a new thing for me. Feel free to stop me at any time."

That would be a hell no.

"No, I don't think I will."

I leaned down and pressed a kiss to her forehead, the tip of her nose, her lips, her chin. Her sharply indrawn breath kept me going south. A skim of my lips down her throat. A nip to her collarbone. And then finally my tongue laving the upper slope of her breast. I couldn't keep my hands out of the show. I cupped her tits and lifted her nipples to my mouth.

Vanessa's soft moan and tensing body urged me on.

"I love your tits. Love these nipples. Can't think about them without my cock going rock hard. Can't help but want my mouth on them all the damn time. Someday, I want to fuck these gorgeous tits and come all over them."

Her closed eyes fluttered open. "Don't let me stop you."

I shook my head. "Not tonight. Tonight, you just handed me a fantasy I've had since the last time you sat in this chair."

"Really? You wanted this... then?"

I laughed, and it came out rusty. "Why do you sound surprised?"

"You hated me."

"I never hated you. Just didn't want to want you so damn bad. And now I don't care—because you're mine."

She buried a hand in my hair and pulled my mouth to hers. Her other hand found its way to my belt as she fumbled it open and worked the button and zipper. When her soft hand closed around my cock, I groaned into her mouth and pulled back. Even though I didn't want her to let go of my dick, I had to make her. Otherwise I'd be way too eager when I got inside her.

"Slow down, baby. Gotta get you ready first." I lowered my mouth back to her nipples and let my hand skim down her belly to her landing strip.

"Are you wet for me, princess?"

Her legs shifted slightly as she opened to me. "Find out for yourself."

My fingers slid lower, parting her, desperate to find her heat. And *fuck*. She was soaked. My cock jerked as I groaned.

"So fucking wet."

"Because of you."

I dropped to my knees on the floor, aware that my pants were falling, but not caring. The only thing I wanted in that moment was my mouth on her pussy as she came against my tongue.

Shoving one arm of the chair down, I turned her and pushed her thighs further apart. "What—"

She went silent when my tongue found her pussy, and I plunged two fingers inside her. Fucking her relentlessly, I teased and sucked on her clit until I felt the fluttering pulses of her inner muscles. I crooked my fingers and stroked her G-spot.

She detonated.

"Con!"

I loved hearing my name on her lips almost as much as I loved the taste of her on my tongue.

She was it. The one. I was done for.

When I pulled my face away and took in her dazed look of pleasure, I knew I wanted to see it every day for the rest of my life. I palmed my cock. I wanted nothing between us.

I lifted her chin and asked, "You good with going bare again? Because I can get a condom."

"No. Don't. I want this." Her arms snaked around me, and she pulled me closer. "Just you. Nothing else."

So I obliged, fitting my cock against her entrance and slamming home.

vanessa

"It's beautiful. I... I love it."

I stared down at the tattoo on my hip. It *was* beautiful, and I *did* love it. And not just because the fleur de lis and crown were intricately drawn and amazing. I loved it because Con had been the one to do it. Women everywhere would raise their pitchforks if they knew I considered it a sort of brand. No one could ever look at my naked body again and not see the mark that Con had left on me.

But the black ink on my skin was nothing compared to the mark he'd left on my heart.

Hell, he owned my heart.

I still didn't entirely understand how we'd gotten here, but I was done questioning it. I wanted Con, and I wasn't going to let him go.

My worries about how Archer and my father would each take the news faded away when Con picked me up off the chair—which he'd sanitized after our unorthodox use of it—and carried me up the stairs to his bed.

"You have anywhere to be in the morning?"

I mentally paged through my calendar. "Brunch at eleven with Elle. We try to do it every Sunday."

"Still attached at the hip like you were in school?"

I smiled. "Not attached at the hip, per se. But she's still my best friend. We work together."

"I always liked her. She seemed a little more wild and crazy than the rest of you."

"Are you telling me you had a crush on my best friend?"

Con grinned. "Jealous, princess?"

"What do you think?"

Con slid into bed and pulled me flush against him, so my cheek was resting on his chest. "No reason to be. I always thought she'd be a good friend to have on your side. Can't say I ever stopped thinking about you long enough to think much else about her."

"Oh."

Con's stubbled jaw lowered as he pressed a kiss to my forehead. "I spent way more time being jealous over you and Duchesne. Hated him because of how close you were."

I shifted and wished there was enough light in the room to read his expression. "Even though you know we've never been anything more than friends?"

"I didn't know that then. Not sure I would've believed it."

"But you believe it now?"

"Yeah. And not just because you're in my bed and not his. Besides, I've seen firsthand how hung up he is on Charlie."

"I worry about that." And I did. Simon was head over heels, and I still wondered what he really knew about Con's receptionist. She was almost a female version of him. All tattoos and mystery.

"Don't borrow trouble. No point. They're adults, and they'll fumble their way through it themselves."

Another question occurred to me. "Is that really why you've always hated Simon? Because of me?"

I could feel Con's heart thumping against my palm. He didn't answer for several beats.

"It's not hard to hate someone who has everything you've ever wanted. Just so happened Duchesne was that guy for me. I was a foster kid, a charity case, and he was the son of a fucking congressman. He had parents who thought the sun shined out of his ass, and I had a mom who ran off and a dad who left too many bruises to cover when family services came around."

My heart broke for the boy who'd felt so unloved and unwanted. But it explained a lot about Con.

"But what about the Leahys?" I asked. "I'm pretty sure they thought the sun shined out of your ass, too."

I could hear the affection in his voice when Con said, "Yeah, I guess they did." His tone was more serious when he added, "And look what it got them."

He released me and rolled to his back, reaching his arms above his head to grip the wrought iron bars of the headboard.

"Con?"

"That's exactly why I should tell you to go. Tell you to get the hell away from me. Because now the shit I'm into is even more dangerous. I've spent years in the gutter turning up every filth-covered rock to find justice. And when you do that, you attract all sorts of the wrong kind of attention. If someone thinks I'm getting too close, I don't even want to consider what they might do to stop me. Hit me where it hurts—where I'm weak—and that's you."

The atmosphere surrounding the bed turned cold. I'd never aspired to be someone's weakness. I wasn't certain how to take that.

"So what are you saying?" I asked. "Because I thought we were finally on the same page." *But maybe I'm wrong*, I added silently.

"I'm not saying anything other than I need you to know that if you throw in with me publicly, you need to be careful. A hell of a lot more careful than you have been." He turned and flipped on the bedside lamp before facing me again. "And if you can't handle that, you need to tell me right now. Because I already told you I'm not giving you another easy out."

I may not have understood the risks he was talking about, but I knew one thing for certain—Con wouldn't let anyone hurt me if it was humanly possible to prevent it. I wasn't sure how I could make it any clearer that I wasn't walking away regardless of any out he might offer.

I pressed closer to him. "And I already told you that I want this. We're going to figure out a way to make it work. Now shut up and kiss me."

Con's smile was soft as he flipped off the light and rolled to cover my lips—and my body—with his.

It was a long time before either of us got any sleep.

vanessa

Con wasn't particularly peppy in the morning, which probably came from running businesses that stayed open until well past midnight. Which meant that when he mumbled something the next morning about doing Fourth of July on the roof of Voodoo with some friends, and I had to tell him I wasn't going to be able to be there because I had a prior commitment, he was less than enthusiastic. I'd wanted to invite him to the Fighting for Freedom fundraiser, and it probably would have been the perfect event to bring him to, considering it was supporting the cause of veterans, but I wasn't quite ready to jump into the deep end when it came to public appearances. I wanted to ease into this, not shove it in people's faces and cause a splash.

It may have seemed disingenuous, but I was thinking long term. I wanted Con to be accepted and finally feel like he belonged. I didn't want him to feel like he was on the outside looking in anymore. Because if Archer was still willing to give me a shot at running the foundation, I would want Con by my side at all of the events I attended in the future. I just had to choose our steps carefully.

The only thing that had kept Con from going over the edge was the fact that Lucas Titan was *not* going to be there. This wasn't an event on his list, which was somewhat surprising, but I certainly wasn't offering.

The next week was jam-packed with work for the building project. Demolition was on schedule, and everything was moving smoothly. I managed to see Con a few times, mostly quick breaks for lunch or a stolen afternoon at the gym helping to make peanut butter and jelly sandwiches. I brought all sorts of extras and stuffed those in the bags as well: granola bars, fruit snacks, pudding cups, and all of the other fun stuff I'd always wanted to see when I opened my brown paper lunch bag. One afternoon we'd even taken that shopping trip to get suits for the boys. I couldn't wait to see the pride on their faces when they walked into their next tournament.

Trey had recovered enough to leave the hospital, and I'd arranged to have a nurse visit their home for several hours a day to help out his mother. He'd missed his orientation at West Point, but they'd agreed not to defer him if he could pass his physical before the semester started. Given that Trey was a fighter, I was putting my money on him.

Hennessy's investigation around the carjacking and shooting was successful. The guy responsible was arrested and charged. One of the least pleasant experiences of my life was participating in identifying him during the line up. Con, and a stubborn, but still-weak Trey, had stood on either side of me when I'd said the number aloud. That was at least one instance of justice being served.

I couldn't imagine how it felt for Con to spend years not knowing who had been responsible for killing his parents, especially with the guilt he carried. I hated that it ate away at him, but I didn't know how I could help. I guessed this fell into the category of being a supportive girlfriend.

Archer had been away all week attending a national conference and wouldn't return until Monday. I was surprised he hadn't asked me to attend with him, but I assumed it was because the budget only allowed for one person to go. Ever conscious of how the foundation expended its funds, I didn't protest or complain. But it did mean that I still hadn't had an opportunity to tell him about Con and me yet.

I went back and forth—did I tell Archer first or my father? Neither conversation was going to be easy, but I hoped telling Archer first and having his support might make it less intimidating to tell my father. Because if Archer had no problem with it, I was hoping my father would be influenced to feel similarly. And yes, I was aware that was a whole lot of hope.

❧

I strode up the ramp to the Steamboat Orleans on Fourth of July, my heels and spirits high. I'd come up with a plan. Finally. I would tell Archer before I left work on Monday, and I'd tell my father when he arrived home on Monday night. I'd practiced my speech, over and over, and I was feeling confident that Archer would see things my way.

Con had done so much good in the community without asking for any kind of recognition. We could all learn something from him about giving back without expectations.

Archer would understand. He was a philanthropist to the core. He'd respect that about Con. I truly believed that Archer would want me to be happy. I hoped my father would feel the same way. I didn't want to be estranged from the only parent I had left, but it was certainly a possibility. A very disheartening possibility.

The party was already in full swing when I arrived, and I shook hands and made small talk. I worked the crowd to avoid my father, and occasionally caught glimpses of Simon and Charlie. She looked incredibly poised and almost...accustomed to this type of event.

Now that's interesting.

I didn't have time to dwell on the thought when a warm hand pressed against my lower back.

I glanced over my shoulder...to find Lucas Titan.

"What are you doing here?" I hissed.

"I believe I was invited."

"This wasn't on your list."

"Because I'd already been invited, and I assumed you'd be here anyway."

His arrogant confidence pissed me off. "Well since I didn't agree to meet you here or act as your *date*," I spat the word, "feel free to find others to mingle with."

His jaw clenched, and his green eyes darkened. A frisson of fear rippled through me at his aggressive posture. "I thought we'd already had this discussion *ad nauseam*, Vanessa. The one where I tell you that you've got a lot more to lose in this situation than I do."

I found my backbone and reinforced it with steel. "I'm going to tell Archer. When he gets back on Monday. So your leverage is gone, Titan."

His jaw relaxed into a feral smile. "Oh, Vanessa. Don't try to play games you can't win. All it would take is one phone call."

"You're such an asshole."

"Better play nice." I calmed the urge to slap him by sucking in a slow, deep breath and releasing it. I'd promised Con that I wouldn't go to another event with Lucas. Promised him I was done playing this role. This game. This farce. And now I was breaking that trust. I squeezed my eyes shut for a beat. I just needed to brazen this out.

"I need a drink," I said, turning for the bar. Lucas's hand never left my back as we worked the crowd until we reached our destination.

When Lucas opened his mouth, presumably to order for me, I held up a hand. "I'll have a gin and tonic, please."

Lucas's raised eyebrows cemented my plan to get just tipsy enough to make this bearable, but not so drunk as to make a spectacle of myself.

I thought it was a workable plan.

Three G&Ts in, and I was feeling much better about the state of my life. Lucas had disappeared to discuss business with someone, and I was in desperate need of the ladies' room. Carefully making my way down the stairs to the lower deck, I found the facilities.

After double-checking that I still looked mostly presentable, I exited and headed back up the stairs, staring at my feet to make certain I didn't miss a step.

I reached the top and ran directly into my father.

"I've been wondering when I'd get a moment of your time tonight, my dear. How about another drink with your old man?" he asked, leading me toward the bar.

I followed dutifully, but I was getting sick of being led around this boat like a damn horse. First Titan and now my father. "A club soda with lime for me, please," I told the bartender. It was probably time I lay off the booze.

My father ordered a scotch—over my objections about his health—and paid for our drinks. "Cash bars are so tacky."

"But they help make sure the cost of the event is defrayed so that the donations go toward the cause they're supposed to be supporting." I thought the words came out coherent, but my father eyed me suspiciously.

"You've had a few."

I was doubly glad I hadn't ordered another.

"It's the Fourth of July. I guess I was in the celebratory mood," I replied.

A knowing look spread over his face. "And here I was hoping you were celebrating your new man."

I froze.

He couldn't know. I looked down at my club soda and sipped, trying to hold it together and come up with something to say.

But my father kept going, "Although Lucas Titan isn't the one I would've picked. He's an arrogant bastard. Doesn't understand how things work around here. But if he's your choice, I suppose he and I can have a come to Jesus talk and settle our differences."

My head jerked back, and my glass almost slipped out of my hand. *Lucas. He's talking about Lucas. Not Con.* I should have been happy that my secret hadn't been discovered, but with the initial shock of his words had come a sense of relief—relief that I could finally stop hiding it.

But no. And now I had to dig my way out of this.

I cleared my throat and fumbled for an answer. "It's not what you're thinking. Lucas and I aren't—"

My father's expression hardened, and he steered me toward a break in the crowd and an unoccupied corner of the deck. "I said I wouldn't have picked Titan, but I can find my way to approve of him. If it's not what it seems, then maybe you should work a little harder to make it what it seems, Vanessa. You're not getting any younger, and your mother would be rolling in her grave to know that you still haven't settled down. So unless you're going to steal Simon Duchesne off the arm of that tattooed trollop he's here with, you better go find Lucas Titan and get to work."

I gritted my teeth, and fought to hold back the angry words bubbling up inside me. I'd had *enough* tonight. Somehow I managed to regain my composure and force a smile. *Monday*, I thought. *Monday*.

"I'll take your suggestion under advisement, sir." I turned my back on my father and strode to the bar.

So much for not needing another drink.

I thought I heard him say my name, but I didn't slow. Fourth G&T in hand, I crossed the deck, smiling my fake smile and laughing the fakest laugh to ever leave my lips.

I made my way to the railing on the complete opposite side of the boat from where my father stood. I still didn't see Lucas, which was a relief.

I did, however, see Simon and his Charlie. My father might have called her a tattooed trollop, but it seemed that every man's eyes were on her tonight. She looked *stunning*. And what's more—Simon looked happy.

When I got close, Simon reached out an arm to steady me. I hadn't realized I was wobbling on my heels. So much for pretending I was sober.

Charlie held out a hand and said, "I'm Charlie. It's nice to finally meet you."

I loved the swirling colors of ink running up her arms, and I thought about the tattoo on my hip. My hidden secret.

"I've heard so much about you, Charlie." And I had—from Simon himself and a little from Con. "I'm so glad to finally meet you too." I shook her hand and added, "You've found yourself a good man. Don't let him get away."

Both Simon and Charlie eyed me carefully, and I wondered if I was slurring my words. I straightened, attempting to look decidedly *not drunk*, but caught my heel on a gap in the planks of the decking and stumbled. My drink sloshed onto the floor, narrowly avoiding Charlie's shoes.

Neither Simon nor Charlie missed my stumble and resulting beverage foul.

Simon asked, "What's going on? You seem a little..."

My face burned with mortification. I was officially *that girl*. Might as well own it.

"Drunk? Then mission accomplished."

Simon and Charlie maneuvered me into a corner, presumably to keep me from making an even bigger fool of myself in public. Lovely.

"What the hell is going on, Vanessa?" Simon demanded.

I lifted my glass and sucked back the last of my drink. *Fuck it.* I tossed it over the railing and smiled as it hit the water of the Mississippi. And then I realized I'd just littered. *Crap.*

I looked up to see Simon waiting for an answer. He was a good man. She really did need to hold on to him.

"Nothing you need to worry about, Simon." Movement over his shoulder snagged my attention. Lucas Titan. Heading toward my father.

I had to get out of here. And I surely didn't need my father to see me with Simon either. God only knew what conclusions he'd draw.

"I think I've had enough festivities for the evening. It's time for me to go. Especially if you don't want my father to think you're still potential husband material."

My words caught them both off guard, but I was more worried about getting off the boat.

Simon came to the rescue once again—because he was a genuinely good guy. "Let's get you a cab then. Unless you want us to see you home."

I didn't need to ruin their night because I couldn't get control over my own.

"No, a cab is fine." I turned to Charlie and whispered, "Treat him right; he's one of the good ones." I thought about threatening to harm her if she hurt him, but restrained myself.

Simon took my arm, and he and Charlie led me down the ramp, across the dock, and through the crowd to a cab. Simon gave the driver my address and paid him. I waved lamely as the cab pulled away and began to inch through the traffic.

One thing was for sure though: I wasn't going home.

I gave the cabbie a different address.

con

I wasn't sure what happened last night on that fucking steamboat, but the after effects on two of the most important women in my life made me wish I could have been there to throw some punches.

Vanessa had hammered on the door, and when I'd opened it, she'd practically fallen into my arms. The scent of gin coming off her had been intense. When I'd tried to get answers she'd just mumbled gibberish. The woman could not hold her liquor.

After she'd puked her ass off in my bathroom while I'd held her hair back, I'd forced her to down a glass of water. She'd already been passed out by the time I'd tucked her into my bed.

And then Lee had shown up. She'd let herself in, dead calm and determined. Her requests had been simple, and there was no way I could refuse her. I'd pulled my Tahoe out of the alley garage behind Voodoo, and we'd gone back to her place. She'd packed one bag, and we'd loaded up her mutt. I'd watched her drive off, and Huck, her giant of a dog, was left sleeping in his crate in the break room.

And then Simon had shown up. It was like a fucking revolving door. The only upside was that Vanessa had slept through it all. I wasn't sure that she was ready to tell Duchesne about us, and I wasn't going to do it for her. Besides, the man had already had a hell of a night.

One thing I knew for sure: Vanessa was going to be answering my questions this morning.

Which was why I was sitting on the edge of the bed, waiting like a schmuck for her to wake up.

It was almost eleven, and she was going to miss her standing Sunday brunch with Elle. Although I didn't expect she'd be interested in eating when she woke. She was going to have a hangover to rival all hangovers.

She rolled, and a groan escaped her parted lips. Her eyes fluttered open, and I reached for the glass of water and ibuprofen on the nightstand. This wasn't my first rodeo.

Vision focusing on me, Vanessa lifted a hand to her face and rubbed. "When did I get hit by a truck?"

"It wasn't a truck so much as a truckload of gin." I offered her the pills and water. She took them and swallowed dutifully.

She collapsed back onto the pillow. "Oh my God. I feel...this sucks." She rolled onto her side to face me. "Why did I drink so much?"

"That's what I've been wondering since you showed up last night." I thought for a moment about telling her about Charlie and Simon and decided that now probably wasn't the best time. I reached for her phone instead. "You might want to text Elle and let her know you're not going to make it to brunch." I paused. "Unless you are planning on going. It's already ten forty-five."

She groaned again. "No. Definitely not going. I'm never eating or drinking again. Ever. Never. Ever."

I smiled. I wished I could take away the hangover, but even I didn't have a miracle cure. "You'll change your mind eventually." I held out her phone, my thumb bringing it to life.

I couldn't help but read the text message on the screen.

"Who's Chief Fuckwit?" I asked. "Because he wants to know what the hell happened to you last night."

She sat up quickly at those words. Too quickly, because she grabbed her head with both hands.

"Shouldn't move so fast, babe," I reminded her.

She reached out blindly for her phone, and her reaction had my curiosity spiking.

"Chief Fuckwit?" I prompted.

"Can we talk about that later?" she asked.

Now I really wanted to know. But I took pity on her condition. "Fine."

She tapped out a text to Elle, who replied immediately to say she had a raging hangover as well.

"Was Elle there last night?" I asked as Vanessa cuddled back under the covers.

"No. But Simon and Charlie were. She seems really nice. From what I can remember through my drunken haze."

"You'd be right about that. Lee is a good woman."

"You're the only one who calls her that, aren't you?"

"Told you, I like nicknames."

"Don't I know it." Then she started to ask, "So how long were you and her—?"

"It's ancient history, babe," I replied before she could finish the question.

But it was the perfect opening to fill her in on what had gone down last night with Lee and Simon. I laid it all out for her. "Holy shit" was her only response.

"Yeah."

We both sat in silence for a few minutes, but there wasn't much we could do about the giant shitstorm that was about to rain down on those two.

"What are your plans for the day?" I asked.

She shrugged. "Sleep and tell myself repeatedly that I'm never drinking again."

I chuckled, softly, so as not to hurt her head more. "You sleeping in my bed?"

"Do you mind?"

"Not at all. I'll bring you some lunch later."

She threw a pillow at me as I stood and crossed toward the door. "Don't talk about food. It's just mean."

I couldn't wipe the smile off my face as I made my way downstairs to work on the books and take Huck for another walk. I liked this. A lot. These regular moments that anyone else would take for granted? They meant everything. Even with wild bedhead and grumpy with a hangover, she was the most beautiful woman I'd ever seen.

That was when I realized I was in love with Vanessa Frost.

vanessa

Your weekend slips by quickly when you spend an entire day in bed. But given the state of my hangover, there was absolutely nowhere else I would've rather been—because I was in Con's bed.

Monday was long, and I spent it gathering my courage and reinforcing my confidence. Archer would be on my side. There was no other acceptable outcome.

I waited for the building to empty out before I strode from my office to Archer's. I lifted a hand to knock on the closed door, but two voices stopped me.

Archer's, which wasn't surprising.

And Lucas Titan's.

That asshole. I hadn't responded to Chief Fuckwit's text, and I'd also forgotten to tell Con after he'd let the question drop. I'd tell him tonight. But first...

I moved closer, trying to catch their words.

But the words I caught were not at all what I expected to hear.

"I finally pried the accounting records out of the hands of the CFO on Friday. I wanted to make sure we were on target for budget, and if we weren't, how much more we'd need to raise to hit it. And you know what I found when I finally dug into them yesterday? Your CFO had already booked a bequest from a Mrs. Iris Mayes for the month of June."

My brain stumbled over Lucas's statement. Iris Mayes? I'd read this morning that she'd died in a car accident on the Fourth of July. She'd been the chairwoman of the Junior League, and her death had been big society news. Her funeral wasn't being held until Saturday because her huge family had to travel from all over to get back to New Orleans.

Either way, I wasn't following where Lucas was going with this.

"What's your point?" Archer's words were clipped, impatient.

"My point is she died on the Fourth of July, Archer. Not in June when the entry was booked."

I blinked. That didn't make any sense. It must have been an accounting error.

Archer's response supported my thought. "An accounting error, that's all. Probably got dropped into the wrong month. It's nothing to get excited over."

Lucas's words turned sharper. "Nothing to get excited over? Did you know that her bequest put the foundation just over the mark to hit our fundraising goals for this fiscal year? And cemented our place on your Top Fifty Most Influential Foundations list? I did the math—that's something I'm good at—and without that bequest, we might have still made our budget, but there was a good chance the Bennett Foundation might have gotten knocked off the list."

"I neglect to see your point, Titan."

"Well, *Archer*, let me see if I can make it a little more clear: I went back to the CFO this morning with another request for your historical accounting records. I've spent my day digging through the last few years, and I noticed a really strange pattern. So I went back farther, about ten years. And you know what I found? A lot of conveniently timed deaths and accompanying bequests in the fourth quarter of the fiscal year. I compared those years to the threshold to hit your precious list. The evidence is pretty damning."

"What exactly are you saying, Titan?"

"I'm saying that I think once is a windfall, twice is quite a stroke of luck, but six times is impossible. And probably criminal."

The words *impossible* and *criminal* ricocheted through my brain. There was no way in hell Lucas's accusations could have any merit. No. Way. It didn't make any sense. It had to be a coincidence. Didn't it? My hopes were crushed when Archer spoke again.

"What do you want, Titan? How much to forget everything you saw." The words were like a fist to the gut. An admission of guilt, if I'd ever heard one. I covered my mouth to stifle a gasp and staggered to lean against the wall.

"What makes you think I have a price?" Lucas asked.

"Everyone does."

"You're a piece of work, old man."

"It's nothing anyone else in my position wouldn't do. Sacrifice one for the good of thousands.

"I think they call that a God complex."

"Call it whatever you want, but I'd do it again. All of those people had already chosen to leave a portion of their estates to the foundation. I did nothing more than ensure that gift was received at a time when it would be the most beneficial," Archer said.

Tears welled in my eyes, but in my shock, they didn't fall. I heaved in breath after breath, but still felt like my lungs had been completely robbed of oxygen. My stomach revolted and bile rose in my throat.

Oh. My. God.

I was going to hyperventilate.

I fought to listen over the harsh sounds of my own breathing.

"So," Archer continued. "Name your price. And if it's Vanessa you want, I think we can make that happen. After all, that's the whole damn reason I let you on the board to begin with. Your motives were obvious. Your execution has been... less than impressive. I'd expected a man like you could dissuade her from wanting to run this place and find a happy existence at home as your wife."

My heart twisted and clenched. *That's why Archer has been so supportive in allowing him on the board? To get me out of the way?* Which meant... he'd never wanted me to run the foundation to begin with.

I let the realization sink in. *I don't know him at all.*

He'd arranged for people to be *murdered* to benefit the foundation. My stomach roiled, my late lunch churning and rising. I turned to run for the bathroom, but Lucas's words froze me mid-step.

"I don't think Vanessa is going to be taking directions from you when you're behind bars. And what's more, she's in love with someone else. A man whose parents I'm pretty sure you had killed. She'll never forgive you for that."

I gagged as vomit rose. I bolted from the hallway and ran around the corner, slamming through the bathroom door and banging open a stall. I dropped to my knees and heaved until I had nothing left.

I didn't even hear the sound of the bathroom door opening or recognize the presence of another person until my hair was lifted off the back of my neck. I jerked my head out of the toilet to see Lucas Titan holding out a piece of paper towel.

"You're lucky Archer didn't hear you," he said.

Stomach still twisting into knots, tears streaming down my face, I took the paper towel with a shaky hand and tried to stifle my sobs.

I found myself ensconced in Lucas's Aston Martin, and I didn't know what to do. What to think. What to feel... beyond betrayal, outrage, and utter disbelief.

"What now? Is Archer packing his bags? Is he going to run for the border?"

Lucas shook his head as he changed lanes. "No. He told me to do whatever I felt I must, and that I should know that if I breathed a word of what I knew, the entire foundation would crumble, and I'd be hurting thousands of people."

"*You'd* be hurting thousands of people? He's the one who did this." *The sick bastard*, I added silently. In the space of a few moments, he'd gone from mentor to monster.

Lucas glanced over at me. "I hate to say it, but your uncle is severely disturbed. He needs help. And he needs to be stopped. So what we do from here on out is up to you."

"Me?"

"This is your heritage, your legacy. Ergo, your decision."

The burden was a heavy one, but I would find the strength to bear it. Testing Titan, I asked, "And if I said I wanted you to keep it quiet?"

His jaw tightened. "I'd think you were a heartless bitch who deserved a cell alongside your doting uncle. But I wouldn't put you there."

That worked. "Good. Just wanted to make sure we're on the same page. Because there's no way I can let this stand." I took a deep breath and asked the question I was terrified to confirm. "Did Archer have Con's parents killed?"

Titan's attention stayed on the road as he replied, "It fits the M.O. and the timeline. They left almost ten million in a bequest. Archer needed a particularly big bump that year to stay on the list. And there was one other donor who was also murdered during a home invasion. About two years before Con's parents. Cases were damn near identical. Both unsolved. Similar evidence." His eyes shifted to me for a beat. "So yeah, I think he did."

"How do you know all that? The evidence? The other case?"

"I called in a favor today from a mutual friend of ours: Detective Hennessy."

Does everyone know that man?

"What did you tell him? Does he know?"

Lucas shook his head. "He knows not to ask questions. But he'll put together the similarities. He just won't have the means to figure out who the money man was behind the trigger."

I was still processing everything I'd learned. It was absolute insanity. Even if Hennessy did put it together, what Lucas had figured out was so crazy, there was no way logic could get you to that answer. It was the work of a madman.

"Archer has to pay for what he did." And when he paid, so would I. Because Con would walk away—no, *run* away—from me. And the foundation would be no more. My fingernails cut into my palms as I balled my hands into rigid fists. I was going to lose everything just when I thought I could have it all.

I squeezed my eyes shut. "I have to tell him."

"Yeah, you do," Lucas agreed.

Somehow, at this moment, Titan's company and support weren't completely unwelcome. "You're not as big of an asshole as I thought you were, you know that?"

He smiled. His hands gripped the steering wheel tighter when he said, "No matter what happens, my offer is still good."

My brow furrowed as I looked at him. "What offer?"

"This one: If Con can't get over this... I'll be here. Waiting."

I turned my head to stare out the window, shocked to see we were pulling up in front of Voodoo.

I grabbed the door handle, steeling myself for what I was about to do. I hesitated for a moment, needing to make sure Titan was clear on one thing first. "If Con can't get over this... I'm pretty sure you'd be waiting a lifetime. Because I don't think I'll be able to get over him."

"You love him?"

"You're smart, Titan. I'm pretty sure you can answer that question for yourself."

My nerves were jumping as I pushed through the door to Voodoo. The female tattoo artist, Delilah, shook her head when she saw me. "He's not here."

"Where's he at?"

"The gym."

My heart fell. How could I tell him in front of his boys? I couldn't. But I also couldn't put this off.

Titan was still parked at the curb, so I climbed back inside the Aston and gave him directions to the gym.

"You sure about this?" he asked as he pulled into the back parking lot.

I saw Con's Harley and decided that I was absolutely not sure about this. The apprehension thrumming through my veins was kicking up my nerves to new heights.

I got out of the car anyway.

I knocked on the door and waited.

Reggie opened it. "Ms. Frost, didn't know we were expecting you."

"Impromptu visit," I said, attempting a smile. Reggie gave me a strange look—which led me to believe that my attempt had failed. He held open the door, and I stepped inside.

I knew the way to the gym and didn't wait for Reggie to lead. I stepped into the open space and saw Con with another man. They were in the ring and appeared to be demonstrating for the boys. Or maybe it had started as a demonstration and turned into a full-on boxing match.

I waited, my heart hammering harder with every strike either man landed, until one of the boys whacked an old school boxing bell with a mallet.

Con and the man separated. They were about the same height, same build, with same hair color, although the other man's was buzzed short. And then there were the tattoos. The resemblance was... uncanny. They could've been brothers. I froze. *Are they brothers?* Con had never mentioned a sibling, but he'd also never said he *didn't* have one.

But if they were brothers, why would Joy and Andre Leahy have adopted only Con?

Con saw me and grinned.

The knots in my stomach twisted even tighter, and my guilt at what I had to tell him multiplied.

"What're you doing here, babe? Should've called first."

I stalled, wanting to see him smile for just a few moments longer before I ripped his heart out.

He slipped between the ropes and hopped out of the ring.

"You look like you've been cloned." I nodded toward the other man, who'd turned to talk to the boys.

"That's Lord," he said.

"And he is...?"

"The manager of Chains. Helps out here sometimes too."

"And?"

Con stripped off his boxing gloves and lifted my chin. "And I think you've figured out what else."

My eyes widened at his confirmation. I wasn't sure how many more surprises I could handle today.

"You have a brother?"

"Yeah."

"And I didn't know this because?"

"We don't really tell people. But I was going to introduce you on the Fourth. He was one of the buddies who was coming over."

"Oh." I stumbled backward until I felt the bench behind me and sat

"Whoa, princess. You don't look so good. I guess I should've told you—"

"It's not that. I have to tell you something." Lord walked up just as I finished speaking.

"So this is the famous Vanessa Frost, in the flesh? I can see why Con wouldn't let me meet you until he had you locked down. He was afraid you'd leave his ass for me."

At any other time, I would've found the words funny and even charming, but right then I couldn't process them. Con had sobered.

"Lord, take over with the boys. I need to talk to Vanessa."

Lord's joking demeanor evaporated. He was like a chameleon, taking on Con's same expression. I couldn't handle it.

"Whatever you need, man."

Con reached down and wrapped a hand around my upper arm, helping me to my feet. "Let's get you some air."

I followed him down the back hall and out into the parking lot—where Lucas Titan was waiting, leaning against his car.

Con stilled mid-stride. "What the fuck?" He looked to me and then to Lucas. "What. The. Fuck?" he growled again.

Lucas didn't flinch at Con's tone. But I did.

"I gave her a ride. She wasn't really in a condition to drive, Leahy. You might want to hear her out."

I wanted to put a muzzle on Lucas. I wanted to find a corner, curl up into the fetal position, and not think about everything I'd learned today. I felt like my entire life—my sanity—was unraveling. Only Con's strength held me up.

I didn't know how to tell him. I should've fought Lucas when he'd taken me to Voodoo. I should never have given him directions to get here. I should've come up with a plan first. Should've come up with the right words to explain. Maybe if I'd given myself more time, I could've found words that would soften the blow.

Except there weren't any.

So I just laid it out baldly. "I think I know who killed your parents."

Con dropped his hold on my arm, and then immediately snatched it back up again and turned me to face him.

It was like looking at a stranger. "Who?" he bit out. "And how?"

I sank my teeth into my lip until I tasted the coppery tang of blood. "I don't know who pulled the trigger, but I'm pretty sure I know who ordered it."

He shook me, as if trying to rattle the information out of me quicker.

"Who, goddammit?"

His chest was rising and falling, his anger building and ready to burst like a thunderhead.

"Archer," I whispered. "We think it was Archer." I gestured to Lucas, taking the coward's way out. "Tell him what you found."

Con dropped my arm like I was diseased and turned on Lucas. My knees gave way and when Lucas lunged to grab me, Con blocked him, letting me fall to the pavement.

The back door of the warehouse flew open, and Lord stalked out.

Con barked, "Take her inside."

Lord scooped me up, and I fought against his hold.

"Calm down. I don't know what the hell is going on, but Con looks like he's about to fucking detonate. You're better off outside the blast radius."

"No. I have to—"

Lord stopped trying to convince me, and his hold became unmovable. "Don't matter what you want."

The last thing I saw before the door slammed shut was Con pacing, hands jammed into his hair, as Lucas talked.

When the back door opened and footsteps echoed in the hallway, I expected to see Con in the doorway to the kitchen. But it was Lucas.

"Where is he?" I asked, shooting to my feet, my chair toppling over behind me.

"Gone."

I looked to Lord, who was leaning against the wall and rubbing a hand over his face. "He say where?"

Lucas's attention was on me when he answered, "I think it's safe to say he went after Archer. That's where I'd go if I'd just learned who was responsible for killing my folks."

My stomach sank to my toes.

Lord turned and punched the wall. "That's what you just told him? Who killed Joy and Andre? *Fuck.*"

What would Con do? What he'd sworn that night at the lake house? Vigilante justice? An eye for an eye?

Jesus help us all.

"We have to stop him," I whispered.

Lord's gaze snapped to mine, and I realized that his eyes were lighter blue than Con's. And they showed that he was *pissed*.

"This is all your fault," he told me. "He never should've gotten involved with you. Told him it wasn't worth the risk."

So Lord seemed to know who Archer was. At least that was one thing I didn't have to explain. But I did have to explain something else: "It's not Archer I'm worried about protecting. It's Con. If he... kills him... then he's going to go to prison. I can't let that happen."

Lord's anger cooled a few degrees. "Then we stop him. I'll go to Chains. You go to Archer."

"Chains?"

"He's going to get the gun," Lord replied matter-of-factly.

"What gun?"

"One that someone pawned. He was supposed to turn it back over to Hennessy. The casing matched the murder scene."

"And if he uses it to kill Archer..."

"Then you're right; he's definitely going to prison."

I wanted to sink back into the chair, but instead I strode toward Lucas. "Let's go."

34

I spun the lock on the safe until it clicked and threw the handle. The door swung open. Reaching inside, I pulled out the gun. The one someone had used to killed Joy and Andre.

My phone buzzed, and I ignored it. It was either Lord or Vanessa, neither of whom I wanted to talk to right about now. I was mapping out my plan for the evening.

Archer Bennett was going to confess all. And then I'd decide what to do with him.

A deadly calm had settled over me. A killing calm. One I hadn't felt since my last mission in Afghanistan.

I grabbed a box of .38 special ammo off the shelf and slid a round into each chamber of the revolver. I'd only need one bullet, but I'd be a shit soldier if I went out with an almost empty gun.

I was back on my bike and roaring toward the foundation when I felt my phone vibrate over and over. A beat up 1970s Mercedes was still parked in the small lot. I only had one guess as to whose car it was.

vanessa

Con's bike was already in the parking lot when the Aston Martin screeched to a halt beside it.

Oh my God. What the hell were we going to walk in to? I wasn't sure I wanted to know. If we went inside and saw Archer with a bullet hole anywhere in his body, I'd never be able to look at Con the same way again. Never.

Lord and Lucas might think Con's actions were perfectly understandable, but that didn't mean they wouldn't change *everything*.

Archer was sick. Quite possibly insane. But I couldn't let Con kill him. Not because Archer deserved to live, but because it wasn't up to Con to end his life.

I didn't want his blood on Con's hands. And I really didn't want to face the moral dilemma of what you were supposed to do when your boyfriend killed your great uncle because your great uncle arranged to have your boyfriend's parents murdered before he was your boyfriend.

I'd thought Archer's approval was all I needed for Con and I to be together, but now Archer was going to be the reason Con and I were torn apart—but for a whole different reason.

I hurried into the building, Lucas on my heels.

"You need to stay back, Vanessa. This isn't going to be—"

The sound of raised voices cut off his words, and I ran toward them.

"Vanessa!" Lucas yelled.

I slammed to a stop when I hit the threshold of Archer's office. He was on his knees, and Con was standing over him. The barrel of the shiny, black revolver in Con's hand was pressed against Archer's temple.

If you'd expected Archer to be begging for mercy, you would've bet wrong.

He was *irate*.

And every insult that came out of his mouth was pushing Con closer to the edge. For a brief moment I wondered if this was the equivalent of suicide by cop. I wondered if Archer *wanted* Con to kill him.

If that was true, it was the coward's way out.

"Don't. Don't do it. Please, Con. Don't." I was the only one in the room begging, it seemed.

"You shouldn't be here." Con's words were calm and even—completely at odds with the fact that he was holding a gun to a man's head.

He was someone else entirely right now. Con the soldier. Con the avenger. And I didn't know him at all.

I had to try to talk him down; no one else was attempting to. "You shouldn't be here either. But you are. So I am. Let's both leave now, and we'll figure this out. We'll call your buddy Hennessy, and we'll let him handle it."

"And you'll kiss this foundation goodbye if you get the cops involved." Archer laughed maniacally. "You're not as smart as I thought you were, Vanessa."

Con dug the barrel into his temple. "Don't talk to her. You'll just piss me off."

"Figures that trash like you would be reaching for something so far above yourself. You'll never be good enough for her."

"Shut up," Con bit out, and a measure of his calm slid away.

"Leahy, drop the gun," Lucas said from behind me. "It's over. I called Hennessy. He's coming to take Archer in."

I was surprised by Lucas's statement, but Con didn't seem to care. "Then I guess I better hurry this up."

The blood froze in my veins, and my knees gave way as Con's finger squeezed the trigger.

I screamed as I dropped to the floor.

But there was no explosion of gunpowder and lead from the barrel. Just a single, metallic click.

Con tossed the gun to the ground next to Archer, where a puddle of acrid smelling liquid was soaking into the carpet.

Urine.

Con didn't even look at me as he stalked out of the room.

con

I should've killed him. Should've left the chambers loaded. But I knew I couldn't do it.

I sat in an Adirondack chair under the pavilion at the lake house, listening to the waves lap against the dock.

Any time now I expected Hennessy to show up with handcuffs. I didn't come here to hide. I came here to mourn.

Regardless of what happened to me, I believed that Joy and Andre would now get their justice. Rich pricks like Archer Bennett might get away with murder on a regular basis, but from what Lucas Titan had told me, Joy and Andre weren't the only ones he'd put a hit out on. There was no way he'd continue to walk the streets a free man once his crimes became known.

Titan had also said he would let Vanessa choose how they told the police what they'd found, but at the end of the day, he'd make sure it happened.

So as much as I wanted to hate that son of a bitch, Titan—the one I presumed was Vanessa's Chief Fuckwit—I had to respect him.

What I did hate, though, besides knowing that Joy and Andre had lost their lives for fucking *money*, was knowing that Vanessa was losing her chance at her dream. There was no way the Bennett Foundation would survive this. And that wasn't fair to her.

The dock creaked with the weight of a person. I leaned back in my chair and swigged my whiskey. I wouldn't resist. I would cooperate.

But the person who sat down beside me wasn't Hennessy. It was Lord. My brother. The one I never told anyone about because he didn't want people to know unless they figured it out themselves. He was a weird motherfucker, but considering the shit he'd been through after we'd been separated as kids, I didn't push him on it. That was his story to tell. Once I'd finally opened up to Joy and Andre about Lord, they'd started trying to track him down. He'd been a runaway, so finding him wasn't easy. Andre's private eye didn't get a lock on him until just before I graduated from high school. Lord had popped up in the system because he'd enlisted in the Army. So I did the same.

"I was expecting the cops," I said.

"I figured. You got me instead. Thought you'd want to know that your girl's at the hospital."

My hold on the whiskey bottle slipped, and I grabbed it just before it hit the wood. "What the fuck? Is she okay?" I demanded, fighting the urge to bolt out of my seat and go to her.

"The old man collapsed after you walked out the door. I called an ER nurse I've been fucking, and she filled me in. EMTs worked on him all the way to the hospital, but he didn't make it. Probably a heart attack."

My tensed muscles didn't relax at his explanation. *Fuck.*

"So I killed him anyway." My grip on the glass tightened, and I made myself lift my arm and take another drink. "Now I'm even more surprised the cops aren't out here to take me in."

Lord lowered himself into the chair beside me and sat something on the table between us.

The gun.

My eyes cut from the revolver to Lord. "What the hell?"

"Your girl gave it to me. Told me to take it. She covered for you. Said they were all working late and she found him collapsed on the floor."

"What about Hennessy? Titan said he'd called him. Said he was on his way."

"A bluff."

"Fuck." I dropped my glass onto the table next to the gun and swigged the whiskey straight from the bottle, welcoming the burn as it slid down my throat. "Taking it to his grave, then."

"I doubt it. Your girl doesn't seem like the type to let something like this lie."

"I think after tonight, it's safe to say she might take issue with being called my girl." I hated to say the words, but they were undoubtedly true.

"You might be surprised."

"After I killed her great uncle? I doubt it." I stared at the horizon, lifting the bottle to my lips once more.

"So you're just going to walk away from her? Let that Titan prick have her?"

The thought gutted me.

For once in my life I should be the better man. Let her go. Or at least not chase her down when she walked away.

Lord snagged the bottle from my hand, interrupting my thoughts, and took a long pull.

We passed the rest of the night like that, only moving to get another fifth. We drank in silence, both lost in our own thoughts, until the sun rose over the lake.

vanessa

I would be pulling a funeral dress out of the closet yet again. My emotions were all over the map. I was still trying to reconcile the facts that Lucas had uncovered with the Archer I had known until yesterday.

Not to mention trying to process what Con had—and *hadn't*—done. And the aftermath.

If I'd wanted to run away and hide from the world before, I *desperately* wanted to do it today.

But I couldn't. I had to sit in my office, white knuckling the arms of my chair while the board of directors held an emergency meeting. In that meeting, Lucas would lay out all of the information he'd discovered. We'd discussed it, and I'd agreed. It would be up to the board to decide what to do with the foundation. Even though it was my heritage, I was just an employee without a say. Hell, I didn't even get to attend—not unless the new chairman invited me. Which he hadn't.

So instead, I sat and wondered what Con was doing. If he'd washed his hands of me. If I should be washing my hands of him.

I was having a difficult time holding what he'd done against him.

The need for vengeance had been driving him for so long, I wasn't sure he knew how to operate without it. And the fact that his vengeance intersected with my relative's nefarious activities... that was something I couldn't see him ever getting over.

I honestly didn't know what to do.

One thing I was certain of: I needed to hear what the board decided before I'd be able to face him. I needed to be able to tell him that steps would be taken to make things right. Or if not right—because things could never really be *right* again—at least... better. Somehow.

I stacked all of my project folders and notes about the new headquarters and nonprofit incubator in a box. It would never happen now. I thought of the deed in one of those folders. How Con had given it to me because he didn't want to wonder if that was the reason I was with him. How pissed he'd been when he'd thought I'd taken it and walked away.

What should I do with it now? Tear it up? Give it back? I was supposed to go to the parish clerk to have the deed recorded and made part of the legal chain of title for the property, but I'd kept forgetting to take it there.

Maybe that was fate.

Because now it seemed abhorrently wrong that Con had donated it when he'd already lost so much because of the foundation.

Regardless of what the board decided today, I would give it back. It would at least give me a flimsy excuse to go see him.

And God, did I ever want to see him.

The wildcard was whether he could look at me and not think about what had happened to his parents.

At least Con no longer had to carry the guilt of thinking he was responsible for their deaths. It was a tarnished silver lining.

A knock sounded on my office door.

I tensed, glancing at the clock on my wall. It had only been an hour and a half since the meeting started. How could they be done already?

"Come in," I called.

Elle poked her head in, and I relaxed in my seat.

"Hey, babe. How are you holding up?"

I waved her in, and she shut the door behind her before sliding into one of my guest chairs.

"Okay, I guess. Don't have much of a choice. Are rumors flying yet?" Lucas had given me the go ahead to tell Elle, surmising accurately that I'd be unable to keep it from her.

She shook her head. "No. None that I've heard anyway. Everyone is just shocked by Archer's death and very sad. That bastard." She looked up at me. "Sorry. I probably shouldn't say that around you."

"It's fine. It's nothing worse than what I've already called him in my own head. And you didn't even hear him. There was absolutely no remorse. He was so confident that he'd done the right thing. He was... sick. But that doesn't excuse his actions. I mean, I want to believe that he'd just gotten old and senile, but he'd been doing this for at least a *decade*, Elle. That's insane." I met her eyes as she slouched in her seat.

"I know. And now we're all going to be out of a job. Which sucks, because I like being underemployed. Now I'm going to have to go back to being a trust fund kid while I look for another job I'm overqualified for."

I was shocked her words could pull a halfhearted smile from me.

"So," she continued. "Enough about Archer. What are you going to do about your man?"

I shrugged. "I'm not sure yet. I'm waiting for the board's decision. I need all the facts before I can go to him."

She narrowed her gaze on me. "You sure you're not just procrastinating?"

I'd considered that already. "I'm sure." I leaned over and pulled a folder from the box at my feet. "And I'm going to give him back this." I flipped it open to reveal the deed.

Elle chewed on her bottom lip before saying, "Yeah. I can see why you'd want to do that. It's not like we need it now. So then what?"

"What do you mean?" I asked.

"Are you going to try to get him back? Or are you going to let him walk away?"

"You make it sound like I have a real choice."

"You always have a choice, Vanessa." The words were so similar to some Con had once spoken to me.

We sat in silence while I considered them. "I don't know what to do," I admitted.

Elle opened her mouth to say something more, but another knock stopped her.

"Come in," I called.

This time it was Lucas.

"Vanessa. Ms. Snyder."

"What did they decide?" I asked without preamble.

Elle rose. "I'll leave you two alone then." To me, she added, "Let me know if you need *anything*."

"I will." Elle closed the door as she left my office.

I couldn't stand the anticipation. "So? What's the verdict?"

Lucas didn't sit. He just crossed his arms and leaned against the wall. "We've decided to turn the entire matter over to the Attorney General."

It was what I expected. It was the right way to handle it. Anything less would be highly unethical and illegal. After all, the charity division of the Attorney General's Office was the ultimate authority the foundation was accountable to as a nonprofit in the State of Louisiana. I considered what that meant. Likely a very public exposure of the scandal and a complete dismantling of the entire organization. All of the funds would probably be doled out to other charities in the state, and maybe some even given back to the families of the victims. Which would also make sense.

"That's the choice I would have made."

"Anything less would make the whole organization as guilty as Archer." Lucas paused. "And the CFO. He admitted to being complicit in Archer's plans and has been living above his nonprofit salary for years.

Says Archer used his personal money to pay him off. He'll face criminal charges. Herzog knew as well."

A chilling thought struck me. "Archer didn't kill Herzog, did he? That was natural causes, right?"

Lucas nodded. "Herzog was getting regular kickbacks from Archer, too. It was unlikely he'd been hit with a fit of conscience at this stage in the game. I think it's safe to say his death was unconnected."

"Okay. Then I guess it's time I handed in this." I slid my resignation across the desk. I hadn't had to change much more than the date from the last time I'd printed it.

Lucas picked it up. "And what if the board wants you to stay on during the investigation?"

"How could they? I'm family. It wouldn't be right. There'd have to be a conflict of interest there."

"So you're saying you wouldn't, even if they asked?"

I bit the inside of my cheek. I wanted so badly to agree, to say that I would stay for every single minute they would let me, but I knew it would be that much harder to walk away when it was time to leave.

And there was one other giant reason I couldn't stay.

"I can't. I just can't," I replied.

Lucas stared at the paper for a few moments before changing the subject to one I didn't want to discuss with him. "What are you going to do about Leahy?"

I didn't answer.

"Come on, Vanessa. I think we've gotten to know each other well enough that you can talk to me about it."

"I'd rather not."

A muscle twitched in his jaw, but he smoothed his irritation away. "You realize he might not want you after this."

The words—thoughtless words—hit me like spikes to the heart. I sat straighter. "Thank you, Mr. Titan, for that little slice of insight. I can't believe I hadn't considered the possibility myself." I bit out the words, over-emphasizing them in my sarcasm.

He tilted his head to one side. "I'm not trying to be a dick—"

"Then you're failing."

"I just..." he trailed off, took a breath and released it. "I just want you to know you've got options. And one of those options is to let Leahy walk away and still not be alone."

I stared at him intently. "What exactly are you saying, Titan?"

"That regardless of the fact that you think I'm a dick, I'm a dick who likes you a hell of a lot. I respect you. I think we'd be good together. You want to make a difference? You want to run a foundation? I'll fucking start one. I've got an extra billion to throw at it right now. Just say the word, and it's yours."

Everything I've ever wanted. On a silver platter.

"For the low, low bargain price of marrying a man I don't love?"

He huffed out a humorless chuckle. "Did I mention one of the things I like most about you is your honesty? This whole time, the only thing you've ever tried to hide was what was going on between you and Leahy. I've never had to guess where I stood with you. That's not something I get from most people."

"Yeah, well, I guess I've never been worried about impressing you."

"Which is why I think we could make this work."

I opened my mouth to decline, but Lucas held up a hand. "Don't. Don't answer yet. Just think about it, Vanessa. This doesn't have an expiration date on it. Like I said before, if you go to him and find you don't get the reception you're hoping for, my offer will still be waiting."

He stood and turned to leave. Pausing at the threshold, he looked back at me. "I know you'll go. So please, just be careful. A lot of people care about what happens to you."

I didn't like what he was insinuating. "He's not going to hurt me." Of that I was absolutely certain.

"Maybe not physically. But don't be surprised when he lashes out."

I gave a curt nod, and Titan was gone.

I stared down at my desk and the deed that lay upon it.

Could I do this?

38

I pressed rep after rep, the burn in my chest and biceps fueling my intensity. I was supposed to be at work, at Voodoo, but I couldn't force myself to go in. I was liable to maim someone in my current state.

My muscles shook as I pushed the bar up and in to the holder above my head. I was lucky that I wasn't going to be pumping iron in prison.

Hennessy had been by. He'd filled me in on everything he knew. Not a word about me being present. When he'd asked for the gun, I'd told him that it was still at Chains, in the safe. Given that Lord had taken it with him when he'd left the lake house, I assumed it was actually there.

Speaking of Chains, I'd signed it over to Lord this morning. I didn't need it anymore. Didn't want anything to do with it. Tassel was going up for sale tomorrow. Voodoo was the only one I was keeping. Because it had been my first, and the only one I'd actually enjoyed. I might take a break from there too, though. I'd had Delilah cancel all of my appointments for the next couple weeks. I'd have to see about getting someone to take my spot. Delilah's brother was a badass artist at another place in town. I'd seen his work all over her. I wondered if I could steal him away.

I sat up on the bench and flexed my hands. I busied my brain thinking about all of this little shit so I didn't have to think about the important things.

Because Jesus fucking Christ—what was I supposed to think? About Archer? About Vanessa? About the fact that because of what Archer had done to my parents, her dream—fuck, *her life*—was probably unrecognizable today.

There was no way the foundation would stay intact. Hennessy had been pretty sure about that. Apparently there'd been some fancy meeting of the board, and Lucas Titan hadn't wasted any time filling in Hennessy.

I thought about what Titan had said to me outside the gym after Lord had taken Vanessa inside.

"Whatever you do, remember this isn't her fault. She had nothing to do with it. If you don't see that, then you don't deserve her. And if you do something stupid, you're going to lose her. And what's more, you're going to lose her to me. Because I can give her what she wants. I can make her dreams come true. I can give her a fucking foundation to run. And I will. If you walk away, you better believe I'll make it happen."

The prick didn't have to state the obvious. Of course it wasn't her fucking fault.

But that hadn't stopped me from doing something stupid.

I'd never forget the sound of her scream when I'd pulled that trigger.

Fuck.

My need to scare the literal piss out of an old man had changed the way she'd see me for the rest of her life.

Titan was right.

I didn't deserve her.

I'd known it last night sitting on the dock with Lord.

I knew it today.

I scrubbed both hands through my hair.

It was still too long.

"You need a haircut." The words were practically stolen out of my brain. I looked up. Vanessa stood beside the ring, only thirty feet away. She was covering her mouth with a hand. "Sorry. I guess that's not an appropriate opening line in this situation."

I barked out a laugh. I hadn't thought I'd find a reason to be laughing any time soon. Leave it to Vanessa.

"I think we're beyond what's appropriate, princess." The nickname slipped out, and the reason for calling her that had never been truer. She was fucking regal standing there. To this day, the most beautiful woman I'd ever known. That was a fact that wasn't changing.

Part of that regal look was because her posture was so stiff. I hated that she looked so uncertain of her welcome. I hated that what I'd done had thrown up this wall between us. I hated that she had every right to hate me right now. My gut twisted with the thought. Titan's words echoed in my brain. *Fuck that asshole.* If there was a chance in hell Vanessa could get past what I had done, I wasn't walking away. I wasn't good enough for her before, and I wasn't good enough for her now. I didn't have it in me to be the better man—but I sure as fuck could be her man.

I opened my mouth to speak, but shut it again. I wasn't good with fancy words and didn't know how to ask what I needed to know.

Her heels clicked across the floor as she came closer. Almost close enough to touch. My hands tensed with the need to drag her against me and muss up her perfect hair and tear down the wall between us. But I didn't reach for her because she was holding out a folder.

"This belongs to you."

I found my voice. "What is it?"

"The deed you gave me. I never took it to the parish clerk to make the transfer official. It didn't seem right for the foundation to take more from you than it already has."

I stared at the folder but didn't touch it. That deed had started this whole thing, and she was giving it back. *Fuck.* Disappointment, swift and sharp, rushed through me.

My eyes snapped up to hers. "You trying to say you're done with me, princess?"

Vanessa's fingers dug into the folder and the edges bent, but she didn't answer my question. She continued, "I also came to tell you that the foundation is going to be investigated by the Attorney General's Office, at the board of directors' request. It's likely going to be dissolved, and all the funds dispersed to other organizations. There's a chance you might even get your parents' money back, although I really can't say for sure." She paused. "Everyone will know what Archer did. I know it's not the justice you wanted, but it's something anyway."

"I don't give a fuck about the money or even the foundation—except I'm sorry as hell you're not getting your shot at running it."

She blinked, head jerking back at my response, but I didn't let her speak. I grabbed the folder out of her hands and tossed it on the ground.

"You didn't answer my question, Vanessa."

Her teeth sank into her lower lip for a beat before answering. "I think the question is whether you're done with me. I mean... what Archer did..."

I shook my head. "Didn't have shit to do with you. So don't take that on. You've got nothing to apologize for. I, on the other hand..." I let my words trail off, not wanting to highlight once again why I was a total fucking prick. But I manned up and finished, "I killed him. Doesn't matter that I didn't put a bullet in him. It was my doing."

Vanessa took a step forward, closing the space between us. Laying a hand on my chest, she said, "You've carried guilt for something that wasn't your fault for too long. Don't make that mistake again here. This wasn't the first heart attack Archer's had.

He's been in congestive heart failure for almost a decade. After Titan confronted him, he knew this was all going to come toppling down. He baited you. The things he said... I think he wanted you to pull that trigger so he didn't have to face up to what he did. If you ask me, he'd already given up on living, and his body reacted accordingly." She paused. "It's not a medically sound opinion, by any means, but that's how I see it."

Her brilliant blue eyes shined up at me, and in them I saw absolution.

If she had it in her to offer me forgiveness for what I'd done, then I'd be a stupid man not to grab it—and her—with both hands and never look back. And for the record, today, at least, I wasn't a stupid man.

We stood in silence for several seconds while I gathered my words. They might not be fancy, but they were the truth.

"I haven't loved many people in my life, because there's always been a constant: I've never been able to hold on to any of them. Lord and I were ripped apart when we were just little kids. Joy and Andre were gone too soon. I walked into this expecting that I'd never be able to hold on to you. I didn't want to love you, because not only would it be a certainty that I'd lose you, but when I did, it'd wreck me. But it was fucking impossible not to fall in love with you." I hesitated for only a moment, taking in the tears shimmering in her eyes, and framed her face with my hands. "So if you're waiting for my answer: I ain't done with you. I'll *never* be done with you. If you'd hated me for what I'd done, I would've found a way to change your mind. Because you're *mine*, and I'm *yours*—and I'm never letting you go."

Her tears spilled over, and I caught them on my thumbs. "Don't cry, princess. You know that shit kills me."

The smile that spread across her face clued me in to the fact that these were happy tears.

"It's a good thing you're not done with me, because it would've been really awkward when I handcuffed myself to your bed and told you I wasn't going anywhere."

My chest shook with laughter, and I dropped my hands from her face to her ass and hauled her up against me. Vanessa clutched my shoulders as I lowered my mouth to her lips.

vanessa

The initial rush of relief I felt at Con's words was burned away by the white-hot need streaking through my veins. He devoured me with his kiss, but I wanted more. Needed more. I pulled my head away.

"I want you. Here. Now." My words were desperate, hungry.

I needed to feel his claim all the way to my bones. I needed him inside me to reinforce the fact that he wasn't going anywhere. That what we had was real. Solid. Forever.

Con's eyes darkened to a deep blue, and in them I saw hunger that matched my own. He broke our stare, taking in the interior of the gym with new purpose. When his gaze landed on the weight bench, I grinned inwardly. He turned, saying nothing, as he carried me to it. Lowering me carefully until I was seated, Con dropped to his knees in front of me, pulling off my shoes and shoving up my skirt. He dragged my panties down my legs, and I was bared to him. Con's eyes darted up to mine again before he cupped me between my legs.

"This is mine. And so is every other fucking part of you."

I reached forward and buried my hands in his hair. "Just like every part of you belongs to me."

"Always. Forever."

"I love you, Con." I lowered my mouth to his, wanting his taste on my tongue again.

Against my lips, he whispered, "Love you more, princess."

When our kiss finally broke, Con laid me back, dropped his shorts, and growled, "Better hold on, baby. This might get a little rowdy."

I grinned, because when he straddled the bench and thrust inside me, it did.

40
con

When you've had the kind of reunion I did with the woman you were crazy in love with, you didn't question her when she told you to 'follow her.' You got on your bike and you followed that woman anywhere she led you. And when those twists and turns took you into the heart of the Garden District and behind the fence of her father's house, you grabbed hold of yourself by the metaphorical balls and you manned up, regardless of the fact that you once passed out drunk against that very fence. Old insecurities fought their way to the surface, but I crushed them as I lowered the kickstand and swung my leg over the bike. I opened Vanessa's door and helped her out of the car.

"Princess, we storming the castle for some reason?" Because this was pretty much the last place I wanted to be right about now. Or ever.

She smiled and replied, "Sort of. I think it's long past time I introduced my father to my boyfriend. Or reintroduce, as it were."

A fist of uncertainty grabbed hold of my gut and clamped it tight while I fought for some semblance of nonchalance.

"You really think that's a good idea? From where I'm standing, it ain't necessary."

Vanessa grabbed my hand and laced my fingers with hers. Her blue eyes shined up at me with love and sincerity. There was nothing I wouldn't do for her when she looked at me like that. Hell, it really didn't matter how she looked at me, I'd do anything for her.

"It's very necessary. How else would I ever convince you to pick me up at the front door for a date?"

My eyebrows hit my hairline. "Now you're fucking with me."

She shook her head. "No. I'm serious. It's time we bring this out of the shadows and into the light where we both deserve it to be." She squeezed my hand before she added, "I'm not hiding anything anymore, especially not how I feel about you."

Well, fuck. When she put it like that, what could I say?

I leaned down and pressed a kiss to her temple. Eyes squeezed shut, I whispered, "You humble me. And that's just one more reason I fucking love you."

I pulled back, and we walked hand in hand up to the front of the elegant, antebellum mansion. Vanessa pulled her keys out of her purse and let us inside. Her father's booming voice echoed in the house. "Vanessa, is that you? What did the board decide? That fucking Archer. If he wasn't dead, I'd kill him myself."

I couldn't help but nod my head absently in approval. Maybe Vanessa's father and I weren't as different as I'd always thought. But as she led me deeper into the house and across the threshold into his study, that sliver of confidence was snuffed out.

"What the hell is he doing here?" Royce Frost was seated behind a desk as large as a '57 Chevy. It probably cost more than one, if my limited knowledge of antiques was accurate.

"Dad, you remember Constantine Leahy."

Frost's gaze zeroed in on our clasped hands.

"And I repeat, what the hell is he doing here?"

I had to give Vanessa credit, she didn't falter in the slightest.

"You wanted to know if I was ever going to settle on a man, and I wanted to introduce you to the one I've settled on."

"Is this some kind of joke?"

I straightened, refusing to shrink under his stare. "No, sir. And there's no joke about the fact that I'm in love with your daughter, and she's in love with me. I know I don't deserve her—"

"Damn right, you don't."

"Daddy, if I were you, I'd watch what you say right about now. I've made my choice, and if you can't be happy about it, then I'd prefer you say nothing at all." Vanessa's words were quiet, but firm.

Frost eyed me with all of the ice his name implied. "You willing to cause a rift between a father and his only child just to get a piece of ass, boy?"

I dropped Vanessa's hand and stalked forward, slapping both palms down on the surface of the desk. "Don't you fucking talk about her like that, old man. I don't give a damn what you say about me, but you will fucking respect her. I don't care how old you are, I'll teach you some goddamn manners myself."

I expected him to rise, which he did. He laid both hands on the desk and leaned forward, mirroring my posture.

"What did you say to me, boy?"

"You heard me, old man."

His blue eyes were an aged and paler version of Vanessa's, but they speared me all the same.

"You going to threaten to beat every man who disrespects her?"

"Without a fucking doubt," I vowed.

I expected him to reach across the desk and plant a fist in my face, or maybe reach under the desk and pull out a shotgun, but this time my expectations were off. Instead, he nodded, straightened, and held out a hand.

"It's nice to see you again, Mr. Leahy."

I stared down at his outstretched palm, shocked that he was offering it to me.

"Excuse me?"

"You may not have been my choice, but any man who'd threaten to kick my ass in my own house for disrespecting my daughter is a man I can respect, even if I don't particularly like him."

His words floored me. I was still processing them as we shook.

"Better treat her right, though. If I hear even a whisper otherwise, I'll hunt you down like a dog."

I wasn't going to argue with that. "Fair enough, sir."

"Then it really is good to see you again, Constantine."

The handshake may have only spanned a few seconds, but its impact on me was monumental. It might have been grudgingly given, and provisional, but Royce Frost was showing me his respect. Like I was an equal. My shoulders straightened of their own accord, and I stood taller. The chip Vanessa had accused me of carrying seemed to shrink.

When I stepped away from the desk, Vanessa moved to my side and tucked her arm into mine.

"Con will be staying for dinner."

"Damn right he will be," Royce said, studying me. "Going to take me three courses of grilling him to make sure he really passes. Heard you were a military man."

I nodded. "That's right. Army. Special Forces."

He lifted his chin. "Impressive."

"And that'll be the end of the grilling," Vanessa interrupted. "You'll make him feel welcome or we won't be coming back for dinner any time soon."

"You live here; I think not coming back for dinner would be difficult, Vanessa," her father pointed out.

"Not for long. I'm moving in with Con."

I jerked my head to the side to look down at her. "You are?"

Vanessa gave me a playful smile. "Yes. You were just getting around to asking me."

"I was?" This was not something she should have dropped on me in front of her father. If he didn't want to kill me before, now he'd want to for sure.

"Sounds like we've got more to talk about over dinner than I thought," Royce drawled.

We left Vanessa's father's house four hours later. There'd been no bloodshed at dinner, and I was surprised to find I'd actually enjoyed myself, aside from the discussion about Archer and the havoc he'd wreaked. I was done thinking about it, done dredging up the ghosts of my past. For the first time in my life, I had a future I couldn't wait to experience.

When I'd opened the door of Vanessa's car for her to get in, she'd shaken her head and said, "Nope. I'm riding with you."

And she had, waving to her father from the back of my bike as we'd driven away. I think my pipes had rattled the windows of the neighborhood, but I didn't care about anything but Vanessa's arms wrapped around me.

I parked beneath the lake house and led her out to the pavilion.

"So we're moving in together, huh?"

Vanessa's eyes danced. "Yes, we are."

"And if I said we'd be living above Voodoo?"

She laid her hand on my chest and looked up at me. "I don't think you get it yet, Con. I'd live anywhere with you."

"How do you feel about the apartment during the week and here on the weekends?"

"I told you, anywhere you are is where I want to be."

I pressed a kiss to her forehead. "I still can't believe you took me to your dad's house."

"It was long overdue."

I glanced around and surveyed the houses on both sides of us. Dark.

I reached for the hem of my T-shirt and yanked it up and over my head.

"What are you doing?" Vanessa asked. "Not that I'm complaining about you shirtless."

"Something else that's long overdue."

I spun her around and unzipped her dress. She didn't protest, just craned her head to watch me unzip my jeans and tug them off.

"We're going skinny dipping," I elaborated.

Vanessa grinned and let her dress fall to the dock.

"I take it you're game?" I asked, holding out my hand.

She reached around her back and unclasped her bra before tossing it onto the growing pile of clothes. Her underwear followed.

She took my hand.

"Hell yes, I'm game."

We sprinted toward the end of the dock and jumped off the edge into a future neither of us could've predicted.

Not only did I get my second chance, I finally got the girl.

EPILOGUE
vanessa

Shit. I went overboard again. I blew out a puff of air toward my forehead to push the stray hair off my face. It didn't work. I jammed the knife in the strawberry jam and used the back of my wrist to smooth it away.

I surveyed the stainless steel surface in front of me. Well, you'd be able to tell it was stainless if it wasn't completely covered with paper lunch bags filled with peanut butter and jelly sandwiches, applesauce, granola bars, pudding cups, fruit, and homemade chocolate chip cookies.

The kitchen timer unleashed a series of beeps.

Crap. I spun, but felt a presence behind me as I reached for the oven mitts.

"Sit down, princess. Let me get those for you."

Con pressed a kiss to my neck and snagged the oven mitts from the counter.

"I'm pregnant, not helpless, Con."

But even with my protest, I stepped aside and took a seat at one of the giant dining tables. Con pulled open the massive oven and lifted two cookie sheets out and placed them on top of the stove.

He chuckled. "I can tell you're not helpless. The hundred or so bags on that prep table clued me in to that. You were supposed to make—"

"I know. I know. And then I was supposed to come sit and watch. But I got—"

"Carried away. I know, baby. You always get carried away." He slipped off the oven mitts and left them on the counter before moving to where I sat. Crouching in front of me, he reached up and smoothed his thumb across my temple. "How the hell did you manage to get jam on your face *and* in your hair?"

I shrugged. I could pretty much get jam *anywhere*. It was a talent of mine. "You didn't complain when I put jam on your—"

Con crushed his lips to mine, silencing my next words.

"All right, all right. Enough with that shit, you two." I pulled away from the kiss at the familiar voice. I jumped to my feet, knocking Con back on his ass.

He grumbled, but didn't stop me as I waddled across the room. "Trey!" I looked back at Con, who was pushing up to his feet. "You didn't tell me he was home!"

Trey reached out to hug me, but I held up my sticky hands. "I don't want to get your uniform all messy. It looks so perfect." He hauled me against his chest anyway.

"None of that, now, little mama. I'll have it all back to rights in no time. And that sure won't stop me from hugging you."

Trey was devastating in his uniform—the gray-blue jacket with all those shiny brass buttons and black braid. In his final year at West Point, he rarely made it back to New Orleans. I loved that he hadn't even bothered to change before coming to see us.

"You just travel in that uniform to get perks on the plane," Con laughed.

"And how is that a bad thing?" Trey asked. "Plus, the ladies go wild for a man in uniform."

Trey finally released me, and I stepped back to study him. Con stopped behind me and wrapped an arm around my belly.

We both said the same thing to him, "You look good."

Trey grinned at me. "So do you." He glanced at Con. "You did good, man. Real good."

I rested a hand on my belly, atop Con's, and the diamond on my ring finger sparkled in the light.

It was Joy's ring. The one that Andre had given her when he pledged to love her for the rest of his life. The one that had been stolen off her finger the night they'd been killed. Someone had pawned it at Chains about a year after Archer died and the foundation was dissolved. Lord had recognized it from the list of stolen items and returned it to Con.

According to Con, it was an undisputable sign that it was time for him to make an honest woman out of me. I hadn't argued with him—I'd just said yes. Just like I hadn't argued with him when he'd leased out the apartment above Voodoo and moved us into Joy and Andre's house in the Garden District shortly after he'd proposed. The house had sat empty for years, because Con had felt it was the kind of home that deserved a family. And now we were finally giving it one.

Trey grinned when he saw the multitude of brown paper sacks on the prep table. "You expand the program more than I'd heard?"

I could feel Con shaking his head behind me. "Not quite that big. Vanessa just gets—"

"Carried away," Trey finished for him.

I beamed, not caring that everyone knew about my penchant for going overboard.

"But we have expanded more," I said. "We're doing mixed martial arts in addition to boxing. We're up to forty boys and twelve girls." I was proud of what we were doing here. I'd taken over the administrative side of the gym and turned it into a real nonprofit organization, and applied for grants from several agencies. The gym had been expanded and now operated in an official partnership with the Boys and Girls Club. We put on joint summer camps for underprivileged kids and continued to run after-school and weekend programs. We had a staff of three, in addition to Con, Lord, Reggie, and me. We'd also expanded the sack supper program to provide for all of the kids at the Boys and Girls Club and their siblings at home. Finally, over the last four years, we'd helped obtain scholarships for more than twenty-five kids to go to college. These might not have been accomplishments on the scale of what I could have achieved by being at the helm of the L.R. Bennett Foundation, but they were immensely satisfying accomplishments all the same. I knew, without a doubt, we were making a difference. Just seeing Trey in his uniform hammered that point home.

"Go get changed, man. We can use your help in the gym," Con said and then paused, adding, "Unless you need to get home to your ma."

"Nah, she's at work for a few more hours. I came to help."

"Good deal."

Trey flashed another brilliant smile and left the room.

Con turned me in his arms. "Damn women are all the same."

"What?" I asked, confused.

"Dazzled by a man in uniform," he said.

"Never got to see you in yours." I ran my hand up Con's chest. "Does it still fit?"

Con rolled his eyes and leaned down. "Of course it still fits. But the only way I'm wearing it is if we get to play conquering soldier, innocent maiden."

This time, I rolled my eyes. I looked down at my belly. "Some innocent maiden I'd be."

Con's lips brushed mine. "Just roll with it, princess. Tonight."

"It's a deal." And like all of the deals I'd made with this beautiful, tattooed, and complicated man over the years, it turned out to be a whole lot more than I'd bargained for—in all the best ways possible.

the end

which book do you want next?

Lucas and Lord both have secrets to hide and stories to tell. If you have a few minutes to leave a review for Beneath This Ink, also tell me whose story you want to read next! To help me tally the votes, send a link to your review to meghanmarchbooks@gmail.com, and I'll thank you with a personal note.

To stay up to date on the latest Meghan March happenings, including new releases, sales, special announcements, exclusive excerpts, and giveaways, subscribe to my newsletter: http://bit.ly/MeghanMarchNewsletter.

Read on for an excerpt from Beneath This Mask, Simon and Charlie's story.

charlotte

I stepped off the witness stand feeling like I'd been skinned and gutted, my insides laid out for public viewing. I refused to meet my father's piercing aqua stare—the same one I saw every time I looked in the mirror. Instead, I focused on the sleeves of his navy pinstripe Armani suit jacket and his gaudy diamond cufflinks winking in the buzzing fluorescent light of the courtroom. My father was a general, flanked by his army of thousand dollar an hour defense attorneys. Not that they could save him. The disgust on the jurors' faces spoke louder than any convoluted defense they could mount. I slipped through the swinging wooden gate and glanced at my mother, sitting primly, ankles crossed and hands folded, in her favorite Chanel suit and tasteful gold jewelry. Lisette Agoston was the quintessential picture of a woman standing by her man. She expected me to take the seat next to her. The seat I'd vacated hours before, hands sweating and stomach churning, to give my testimony and endure the brutal cross-examination. But I couldn't do it. I couldn't sit down and be the supportive, naïve daughter anymore. So I kept walking. I didn't look at the gawking members of the press or the scornful sneers of the victims. I pushed open the heavy, carved wooden door and took my first deep breath of air that wasn't laced with lies.

I was done.

With them.

With this life.

With all of it.

It had all been a meticulously constructed fairy tale, and I'd been too blind and trusting to see through the façade. *I was done.* Burning shame swamped me. The Assistant U.S. Attorney's words rang in my ears:

How does it feel to realize your privileged life has been paid for with other people's dreams?

The objection came too late to prevent the cutting words. But no objection could erase the fact that he was right. My life had been paid for with money diverted from the hard-earned savings of tens of thousands of innocent victims. Move over Bernie Madoff. Alistair Agoston figured out a better way. Exponentially more complex and devastating, because the moment the scheme started to topple, $125 billion disappeared into thin air. Or hundreds of offshore accounts. No one was really sure. My father refused to admit anything, but the dozens of charges leveled by the Securities and Exchange Commission and the Department of Justice would ensure he spent the rest of his life in federal prison.

And after the cross I'd just been subjected to, it was clear the Assistant U.S. Attorney thought I should be joining him in an orange jumpsuit. If trusting your father was a crime, he'd be right about that, too.

I exited the courthouse, running down the marble stairs through the gauntlet of shouting reporters, dodging the microphones and cameras they shoved in my face.

"Charlotte, did you know—"

"Charlotte, where's the money?"

"Charlotte, are you being charged? Did you cut a deal?"

They battered me with questions until I dove into a waiting cab and slammed the door.

"East 60th and 3rd, please." My plan was simple: have the cabbie drop me off a couple blocks away from home and sneak into the service entrance of our building without being seen or recognized. My strawberry blonde hair—heavy on the strawberry—was too distinctive. That would be the first thing to go as soon as I got out of this town. I clutched my purse to my chest. My future, a one-way ticket to Atlanta, where I could disappear to my final destination, was tucked inside. I was flying coach for the first time in my life—a fact I wasn't proud of. I bundled my hair into a low bun and fished a giant pair of sunglasses and a scarf out of my purse. Somewhat disguised, I kept my head down until the car slowed to a stop. Tossing some bills at the cabbie, I slid out of the taxi.

The service elevator trundled its way up fifty-one floors, stopping at the penthouse. My hand shook as I typed in the code required to enter. Pushing the door open, I stepped into the cavernous, ultramodern space that was my family's Manhattan home. After the inevitable guilty verdict came down, it'd become the property of the federal government along with the rest of the meager assets that the FBI had managed to find and freeze. To finance my escape, I'd cashed in $20,000 worth of savings bonds I'd found tucked into my First Communion bible. I tried not to dwell on the irony of my salvation being found in the good book.

My one bag was already packed, but a casual observer would never know I had taken anything from my walk-in closet. The racks of designer suits and couture my mother insisted I wear were untouched. The shelves of Manolos and Louboutins were intact. They had no place in my future. I'd never put on another suit and walk into Agoston Investments, or any other reputable company. Never apply to Wharton and get my MBA. I'd naively thought I could somehow atone for the sins of my father by throwing myself into charity work. Put my newly earned finance degree to work for a good cause. I'd been laughed out of every organization I'd visited over the last two months. No one wanted me. And I couldn't blame them. I wouldn't trust anyone with my last name either.

After the last rejection, I'd come to a decision: I would never use my degree for my own benefit. Ever. I didn't deserve it. I might have earned it myself, but how could I profit from it with good conscience? Along with that decision came a stark realization: I had no future in this city, where I'd forever be watched under a cloud of suspicion. So I started planning my escape.

I stripped out of my black Saint Laurent wool blazer and V-neck dress and hung them up in their appropriate places. I pulled on a pair of black skinny jeans, an American Apparel tank and hoody, and the contraband pair of black Chucks I'd kept hidden in the bottom of my closet. This was the new me. This was the me who would never set foot in this penthouse again. After I dressed, I left my cell phone on the dresser, hefted a black duffle bag over my shoulder, and headed through the kitchen to the staff entrance. It seemed fitting. Come in the front door one way and leave out the back a different person.

acknowledgments

This book wouldn't exist if I didn't have the best cheerleaders on the entire planet. They all deserve more thanks than I could ever convey. I'm so fortunate to have the most incredible people taking this journey with me. My family—your love and support humbles me on a daily basis. Thank you for encouraging me to chase my dreams. Angela Smith—my amazing friend and first reader, I love you so hard. You're the best friend a girl could wish for, and I can't count the number of times you've held me up when otherwise I would have fallen. I'm so thankful you're part of my life. Kendall Ryan—I honestly can't thank you enough for your encouragement, your friendship, and your insight. You give me the confidence to believe I can really do this. Chasity Jenkins-Patrick—you talked me off the ledge when I thought I'd never finish. I'm so glad I found you and the team at Rock Star PR! Serena Knautz—you're one of the kindest, most genuine people I've ever met, and I feel blessed to call you a friend. I'll gladly sit between your kids' car seats any day. Madison Seidler—I'm not sure why you didn't strangle me when I pushed my editing deadline back a dozen times because I couldn't get the book to come together, and then made you work over Christmas. You deserve hazard pay. Thank you for your patience, and as always, your fantastic work. I'm ever grateful. Rachel Brookes—you are a constant source of positivity and uplifting energy, and I cannot wait for all of our dreams to come true! 2015 is going to be epic. Sarah Hansen at Okay Creations—thank you for once again creating a mind-blowingly beautiful cover. The number of people who want to lick it is a credit to you. To my Runaway Readers—thank you for loving my books and chatting about them and sharing them with others. You have no idea what your support means to me. I've met so many incredible people since I've started this writing journey, and I'd love to thank them all individually, but this part might be longer than the damn book. So, last, but certainly not least—a huge thank you to all of the book bloggers who take the time to read and review my books. Not only do you make the indie book world turn, you do it graciously, with excitement, and for the love of books.